THREE IMMORTALS

THREE IMMORTALS

Galacticide Book 1

Bert-Oliver Boehmer

SpringwaldWeller, New York

For Sonja

1—FRIENDS

Kel Chaada, disgraced hero and immortal, had survived wars across the galaxy against fearsome foes, only to be killed by his best friend. He felt the cold metal of the handgun pressed against his forehead. The wound was going to be deadly; even his rapidly regenerating tissues were unable to compensate for severe brain damage. His skull would resemble the torn-apart ruins around him, ravaged by the forces who had destroyed his life and his nation, just to get one step closer to power on a galactic level.

The quest for ruling humanity had begun nearly 900 orbits ago with receiving the gift of immortality, but it was not shared among the decimated humans. Instead, it was kept for a small elite. Another legendary technology, the Human-AI interface, had been left on a desolate world in hidden ruins. The attacking forces sought the multi-awareness the interface granted, and they had known it was on this ruined planet long before Kel did. They had threatened his home world and forced his hand to either serve an eternal prison sentence or leave humanity behind.

His "friend" must have implicated him. Pretending to help Kel escape, he had put him on a transport vessel for delivery directly to the enemy. Had the aliens not boarded the transport and dragged him to their spiral arm of the galaxy, the plan might have worked. But Kel had disappeared from their reach. Now, 20 orbits later, they were still looking for the interface. His former friend needed to deliver it to a person in charge. His scheming was intricate, and his betrayal of Kel shocking, but Kel knew he was not the driving force and reported to someone else.

In all the outcomes Kel had seen, he would die—except in this one. "You will not make the same mistake twice, will you?" he asked.

The gun muzzle pressed harder against his skin. "What are you talking about?"

"About the technology you were supposed to recover. When you were right here, in these ruins, as a young commando soldier, you shot the man who carried the interface. His brain had absorbed the nano replicons forming the interface, and you shot him. In the head. You could have had the Human-AI interface back then, but you blew it straight out of that scientist's skull."

"This is some nreedz, Kel! Why would he have had it?"

"Because he discovered the nano replicons, and had inhaled them the same way I did when we stood over his body. Remember?"

"Kel, you wore a helmet with visor, like all of us."

"Yes, but mine got damaged and no longer sealed."

His friend's triumphant expression turned into a steely stare. He remembered, and now he was questioning his next steps.

Kel needed to keep pushing the blade of doubt into this opening, his only chance to survive. "If you shoot me now, you will lose the interface again—by the same method, even."

"Who says we need you?" His friend took the handgun off Kel's forehead, then pointed at the AI core next to him. "We could just take the Krrut, and get the information from him."

"Well, my friend, maybe he has the data for the interface, maybe he does not. Seems like a huge risk. Even if he does, you would need to replicate it, construct it first. Ancient supertech from before the galacticide. How long is that going to take? Another 20 orbits? I am right here, the interface attached to my brain and the replicons swimming in my bloodstream."

His friend's face was hard to read, but Kel knew him

well enough to understand that he was weighing the risk of disappointing his masters against his urge to shoot Kel. When the wrinkles on his forehead disappeared, Kel knew he had decided.

"We take both of them! Back to the surface! Prepare the ship! Kel, take your AI core and walk right in front of me."

Kel knew the way. Any path back to the planet's surface would lead through access tunnels. Long, narrow access tunnels, forcing the commando soldiers behind Kel to walk in single file. The AI core, Me-Ruu, hovered ahead of him, leading the procession. His friend, weapon trained on his two prisoners, followed Kel.

"Kel, one thing is still not clear to me. When your transport got destroyed 20 orbits ago, how did you survive?"

"The Traaz saved me."

"The Traaz? Who are they?"

Screams, interrupted by the chilling sound of broken battle armor and bones alike, echoed along the tunnel from the rear of the line. Kel looked at his former friend, a hint of pity in his eyes. "You are about to find out."

2—ANCESTOR QUEEN

22 orbits earlier...

Sya Omga had one regret: being able to kill her father only once.

Prepared for the daily audiences, she looked down from the balcony of her dressing chambers and saw where she had laid the trap, seen him die: the palace gardens, filled with the rarest specimens of flora from over 6,000 worlds, a living, growing testament to the vastness of her realm. Her father and her grandfather had conquered most of these worlds. Sya did not remember Grandfather, who had died when she was only one orbit old. Cautious courtiers and anxious chambermaids only whispered his name, as if not to reawaken the man who had built the largest star fleet and annexed more star systems than anyone else in known human history. Mnazkash "the Subjugator" had been a military leader, an expansionist, a man with a vision—uniting all of struggling humanity under one protective leadership. Sya's father had been none of these things. He had not expanded the fleet, but he had used it—against many systems. Some were targets of conquest, but most campaigns were expeditions of punishment, planetary-scale devastation in response to uprisings and dissent. Father had enjoyed these spectacles of death and spent much time away with the fleet, providing a reprieve for her mother and herself. Vnaas, her father, had earned the moniker "the Cruel," and he had not reserved his torturous ways only for his enemies.

The palace gardens. He would chase her along the intricate web of walkways and through the thickets of the plant life. As a child, she could not outrun him. The chase always ended the same way. He would catch her, followed by corporal punishment, severe physical abuse—or worse. She never escaped but once, when the hulking mass of her father's body had collapsed mid-chase, and the automated sentinels had to call the court physicians. Her mother had explained that Father had trouble breathing caused by an allergic shock. She would not reveal any more, always fearing she was saying too much, until she hardly spoke at all before the orbit of her death.

During Father's next campaign, Sya questioned the head court physician, out of concern for her father's well-being as she lied to him. He explained that certain species of garden plants caused the allergic reaction. Some of their pollen, when inhaled in larger quantities, caused a severe reaction, including allergic shock, which—he added—could be life threatening. The physician never realized that from a certain perspective, it was he who had doomed Vnaas the Cruel. Sya had developed a keen interest in xenobotany and started helping in the gardens, learning as much as possible about the different species present, adding new plants to the collection. When Father had caught her planting a Drredian brush, he had laughed, dismissing it as a clumsy attempt to please him, but he let her proceed. He loved this garden. Sya had loved the garden, too, as it was going to kill him. Drredian brush rarely produced any pollen, except during a peak bloom every three orbits. The pollen was invisible, but would siphon out of the plant in enormous quantities. She planted handpicked specimens, all having the same level of maturity as her studies confirmed, and which would pollinate around the same time.

She waited, spin after spin, campaign after campaign, abuse after abuse. Finally Father had returned from a short punitive expedition, blood-rushed from the deaths he had caused and lusting for a chase. It was going to be his last. Sya was 14 orbits old then, and the chase took longer, leading through memorized sections of the wide planted areas, passing by or through the innocent-looking Drredian brushes, all of them at the peak of their pollen output. He must have inhaled billions of particles, mildly annoying to most but toxic for him. By the time he slowed down, he was having difficulties taking a full breath, not feeling he could get enough air in his lungs, exhausted from chasing his own daughter like a prize animal. His immune system, fighting off the tiny invaders like any other pathogen but being overwhelmed by the massive onslaught, went into overdrive trying to rid his body of the pollen by washing it out of his lungs, filling them with watery discharge, too much to be coughed out, drowning the man in his own bodily fluids. Unaware of this battle raging inside him, Vnaas the Cruel had looked up from where he fell to see Sya standing over him. She remembered his eyes fixated on her, his hand reaching out for help, his mouth forming inaudible words. She stood still, returning his stare. He knew it was she who had caused his death; maybe he did not understood how, but he knew she had killed him. She stood there watching him die, listening to the last few animalic sounds he produced before he lost consciousness. By the time the physicians arrived, he had died.

ΔΔΔ

The court physicians had been executed a few spins after Vnaas the Cruel's death, along with the palace gardeners.

Sya did not leave any loose ends as she ascended to the throne of Aloo Dash. She became the Shaajis, the Ancestor queen, absolute monarch of the largest nation in the galaxy, suspected of regicide, yes, but feared for the example set by the swift elimination of potential witnesses. Anyone who spoke up could be next, so nobody dared. Sya had learned one thing from her forefathers: how to instill fear. Being feared continued to be her strongest weapon, the only protector she had. How much longer would that protection last?

Two generations of constant warfare had left the Ancestrate of Aloo Dash on the brink of economic collapse. The fleet her grandfather had built was formidable, but expensive to maintain. Even successful space campaigns yielding rich loots barely covered the costs. The captains of the Ancestrate's industry bemoaned the missing influx of cheap labor and resources. Glory-seeking admirals reminisced about the days of constant conquest. Her secret service had taken on a paranoia-driven life of its own. The representatives of her delegation to the galactic government were the worst. After joining the elitist circle of Assembly Members, some forgot where true allegiance had to be.

At 23 orbits of age, the Shaajis needed to reconsolidate all influence and all authority that had trickled its way through the palace portals to all those pretenders and refocus that shining light of absolute power on her, and on her alone. She was to become more than her fathers had been. Mere men they had been: driven, ruthless, supported by a large military, like thousands of rulers before them throughout human history, but mere men regardless. She would live up to her title, the Ancestor queen, and wield the ancestral powers, the Shaaj Jetsem, revered by the religion of Aloo Dash, passed down from the first people. There were famous powers, like the ones wielded by the Assembly Members of the Galactic Government. Other powers were more mythological, dismissed by most as tales from the wild times during the reemergence of humankind after the galacticide.

Few believed they were real. Powers turning an ordinary human into something more. Even fewer had searched. Nobody had found them.

△△△

Rroovu Ogbaa was a believer.

He had searched for the ancestral powers his entire life.

Now he was waiting for the Shaajis Sya in the Hall of Artifacts. The ceremonial clerk had informed her of his arrival over a shift ago, but she left him waiting as she left all audience-seekers waiting. Also to give him an opportunity to look around the exhibits of rare items from so many worlds. The Shaajis appreciated Rroovu, one of the leading scholars in Aloo Dash, and his brilliant mind. Expanding his knowledge obsessed him. Unlike so many, he was not a threat to her, but a kindred spirit.

She turned away from the balcony, leaving to see her only ally.

"Revered Shaajis, I came here to bow!" said Rroovu Ogbaa in perfect Old Galactic, the ancient language of the Honored, who had rebuilt humanity after the galacticide. The Shaajis saw him walking around the collection in the Hall of Artifacts, which served both as a private museum for galactic history and a war trophy room. Rroovu was one of the few people who knew what the hundreds of objects were and appreciated their significance. No doubt he had enjoyed his time while waiting for her to arrive. He offered his formal greeting with a deep bow as soon as he saw her approaching. The Shaajis waited for her retinal implant to show that the three sentinels hovering over her, silent, invisible to the untrained eye, had created a private shield sphere around her and Rroovu, making their conversation impossible to eavesdrop upon.

"You may stand," said the Shaajis, responding in Old Galactic, acknowledging his perfect Aloo Dash etiquette, then continuing in Jeesh Per, the contemporary New Galactic tongue: "What have you brought? Good news?"

"Exciting news, revered Shaajis! One of your secret service liaison officers you so generously assigned to my mission informed me about an intercepted communication from a ground war across the Korrats Ridge, specifically a message from a combat unit discovering an extensive ruin—they called it a temple complex in the communication."

"A temple?" asked the Shaajis.

"I do not believe it is a temple," said Rroovu. "Even from

their vague description I am convinced it is the location we have been looking for!"

"Where across the Ridge is this?"

"Revered Shaajis, the location is in the borderlands of the Wel Edge, a contested region claimed by several smaller nations. It lies where our arm of the galaxy veers off into the Aloo Spur, toward the outer ring, a very likely flight path of refugees during the galacticide."

"Do you believe this is the location of the meeting between the three?"

"I have very little doubt, revered Shaajis, but I would like to confirm my conclusions in person and at the location. With your permission, I humbly propose to prepare an expedition to the ruin complex, authenticate the time period, and…" Rroovu's voice began to tremble. "Retrieve the artifact, if the ancestors will it."

"You shall have what you require, but we need to keep the team as small as possible. We will hire private security instead of Aloo Dash agents, and you will travel in an unmarked ship of foreign design. Note that you will be traveling into a war zone."

"Revered Shaajis, do not concern yourself with my safety. The expedition shall be small and unassuming, as you decree. All that matters is the artifact!"

The Shaajis cared about his safety, but he was right —all that mattered was the artifact indeed. "Walk with the ancestors," she said, while she turned and walked away, leaving a bowing Rroovu behind.

3—TEMPLE

"The elite walks!" was a saying in the Nominate's armed forces, poking fun at the fact that their special forces were the only units who performed spin-long marches through all kinds of terrain, while other soldiers rode in hover transports. Vyoz Vyooma's mission on the contested planet Prral could not afford for them to be seen or heard, showing up on scanners of any kind while they were approaching their target. He and his three commandos had to walk all the way from the orbital drop point to what HQ assumed to be an enemy forward base.

A scout craft on a low orbital flight had spotted the building, but it did not register on any scanner. They had concluded that some stealth technology was present, making it a likely active site. They were walking toward it, one heavy step at a time, 57 percent higher gravity than on their home planet pulling on their heavy limbs, slowing down even the best trained of the Nominate. Vyoz had seen some strange worlds during his career as a professional soldier, but Prral had to be one of the weirdest.

Prral was tidally locked to its star, with hot rocky wastelands on the perpetual day side, and glaciers on the eternal night side. His team had been dropped into the thin twilight ring band between the extremes, where temperatures were tolerable. It was a cold environment, compared to his home planet, but he welcomed the lower temperatures as they had to wear the life-sign-suppressing layer below their combat armor at all times during the march, and he had learned to hate its insulating properties when deployed on scorching desert worlds. The arid landscape they were marching through was a desert, too, but at least it was not a hot one. There was no liquid water anywhere, but the slot canyons they navigated, concealing their presence, looked like glacial runoff water had carved them into the surface.

Vyoz hoped HQ was right with their assurances that there was no surface water left on Prral. Water could fill these canyons while they were stomping through the maze it had formed. They had needed to veer off a somewhat straight path to the target several times and then backtrack when reaching a canyon dead end. Their scanners proved unreliable in giving clear readings on these surface formations, something he would have dismissed as a malfunction caused by the orbital drop insertion, but all scanners from his team showed the same, occasionally incorrect, landscape model.

Vyoz heard his call sign over the team's helmet comms: "Starrise, Twilight reports life signs ahead, three dots, stationary," said the leading trooper, crouched down 50 steps ahead of Vyoz, hand signaling an approximate direction of the contacts her scanner had picked up.

"Possible patrol in side canyon to the left," radioed Vyoz to everyone in the team. "Night and Day, go right and circle around to contact. Twilight, with me!"

Twilight moved back and then followed Vyoz into the narrow side canyon. Not much of the reddish starlight illuminated the stretch ahead, but their full-face visors switched to improved vision, allowing them to see clearly.

"Contacts on the move, fast!" said Twilight, eyes on the life scanner, trusting Vyoz's visual scan of their surroundings.

"Can't see anything," said Vyoz. "Coming to you, Night and Day, you should have contact in a few ticks!"

"Copy that," said Night. After a brief moment, she added, "Contact!"

Vyoz and Twilight rushed forward, their automatics at

the ready to support their teammates, but came to a dead end of the canyon, with no one in sight, neither friend nor foe.

"Report?" asked Vyoz. He heard Day laughing thorough the comms: "Animals. Negative on enemy contact. Some local critters."

They lowered their weapons. Twilight pointed at some holes in the canyon wall. "Recently dug, some sort of burrow, I bet they went through that before they scared Night and Day on the other side." She held up the life scanner. "But where did they go? You guys didn't shoot them, right?"

"Negative," said Night. "No fire."

Vyoz looked at the scanner screen. No dots present, as Twilight had said.

"I know where they went," said Day. "You guys should come around to this side and take a look!"

Vyoz and Twilight caught up with the others, standing in front of a door-sized opening in a half-buried stone wall. "They ran in here, little scaly critters, half the size of a head, lots of legs." Day pointed inside the opening.

"Still no readings," said Twilight, life scanner pointed toward the stone wall. "Exactly what the orbital patrol described, visible structures, but could not scan the interior! This must be it."

"The target? But we should not be there yet, not even close, based on the coordinates from orbital," said Night.

Vyoz peeked inside, his visor compensating for the low light conditions, showing a long stone-walled corridor ahead, clear of dirt or debris, with an intact ceiling as far as he could see.

"Ever gotten good coordinates from orbital?" asked Vyoz.

Day grinned. "Good point!"

"I guess our friends missed how large this complex might be. We are entering here. Twilight, switch to mapping mode! I take point."

Twilight nodded and entered the corridor, following Vyoz, with Day and Night forming the rear. They moved ahead at a walking pace for two passes, with Vyoz sliding his hand along the corridor wall. "Perfectly cut and smoothed."

"Not bad for primitives!" said Day.

"This was not built by primitives," said Twilight, looking at the mapping data. "Everything is straight and level."

"But nobody builds with natural stone, except the Aloo Dashaad," said Day.

Vyoz moved his hand back and gripped his weapon tighter: "Nobody we know."

ΔΔΔ

The projectile hit Rroovu Ogbaa's forehead, penetrating his frontal bone and lobe and expanding while piercing through the parietal lobe, destroying most of it, shattering the rear of his skull, ejecting the cerebrum parts and skull fragments as a white-red mist, irreversibly destroying one of the galaxy's most brilliant scientific brains. While his head whiplashed back, Rroovu's remaining cognitive functions gave him a last, brief view of the attackers, exchanging fiery bullet bursts from their automatic weapons with his security detail: the men and women who had failed to protect him.

His body collapsed backward, the injured remains of his brain still creating thoughts, free of pain but full of regret. His work here would remain uncompleted, his findings misunderstood, and the enormous potential of the nano replicons untapped. Unlike the cybernetic nanobots of Rroovu's own design, these ancient artificial cell-like structures he discovered in the temple could reproduce at near unlimited speed. He could not recall the applications for the technology anymore, but he remembered the list to be long. "In the temple"—these words echoed in his fading consciousness. This was not a temple, but a battleground.

Falling onto the same stone floor where eons ago many of the brilliant inventors of the nano replicons had died before him gave him an absurd comfort. The impact remained unfelt by his dimming sentience. He could not complete a thought about his family. Rroovu reached for a personal memory, but the intricate neural network, sustaining images and sounds of his wife, his children, or his mother, was gone—reduced to droplets sprayed over the adjacent wall.

In death, Rroovu felt alone. He thought he closed his eyes. No motoric signals reached the muscles to do so. It got dark nevertheless.

∆∆∆

Inside the ruins, Vyoz's team mapped a complex labyrinth of corridors and smaller rooms, all on the same level underground, all walled by the same laser-cut stones. They had reached a point from where several ramps led down to larger chambers, ceilings twice or thrice as high as the corridors they had followed so far, branching off into different directions. They sneaked toward the far end of a chamber, toward a noise the ambient acoustic filter had picked up. Twilight quickly confirmed their suspicion about not being alone, reporting, "Life scanning!" Someone else down here had a life scanner active. "Countermeasures!" said Vyoz. "Give them something!"

Twilight fed the scanner data from earlier, when the three life forms had scurried away from them, into the counter scanner, simulating the presence of local wildlife. The life sign suppressor they wore would not mask them 100 percent from someone scanning nearby. But better to provide them with a plausible result than having them check out an unidentified, weak dot on their instruments. The team broke formation and spread out, to match their faint life signs with the fake critter signs. Then they waited. Nobody came.

They worked their way lower into the bowels of the ruins, moving toward the source of the noise. Climbing down a ledge, they noticed holes with the remains of corroded metal in them, first signs that whoever had built this place knew metalworking. Besides these remains in the wall, the chambers and rooms of varying sizes were empty in a picked-clean kind of way. Maybe looters had ransacked the place.

A bright muzzle flash from one of the left corridors broke the darkness, a spray of ricocheting projectiles, and Twilight's armored body collapsing on the stone floor broke the silence. Vyoz, Day, and Night fired into the general direction of the surprise attacker to suppress whoever had gotten the jump on them. Twilight had carried the life scanner and not alerted the team, so the attacker likely wore similar equipment, blinding out their life signs.

Voices came from ahead, left and right. Some were alarmed, some determined, different dialects, hard to understand. Whoever they were, they seemed surprised by the massive fire the commando team had laid down, their belt-fed automatics connected to ammo backpacks having no need for reloads. Day and Night moved along the walls left and right while Vyoz crouched behind a stone column. A muffled cry. An enemy hit. "Day, Night, forward one!" said Vyoz, and the team moved forward to the next suitable cover position while he kept laying down suppressing fire. Once in position, they resumed fire and he sprinted over to Twilight, lying still on the floor. He turned her around, feeling the lack of tension of a lifeless human body.

Two holes in her chest armor had sealed from the inside to stop major bleeding, but the location showed one had hit her heart. Vyoz's mind snapped back to the fight. His visor briefly showed two enemies shifting positions in a corridor ahead. Without hesitation, his hands following well-established muscle memory, he pulled a grenade from his belt and clipped it onto the muzzle of his automatic. The weapon switched to launcher mode. He took aim, fired. The grenade took out both targets.

"Left clear!" said Day.

"Front clear," said Vyoz.

"Right, two targets, maybe three! How's Twilight?" asked Night.

"Down," said Vyoz.

"Nreedz," cursed Day. "Let's get them!"

The three remaining commandos moved into the two corridors leading to the right, helmet visors on maximum contrast. Only clear line-of-sight enemy body parts highlighted, like hands holding a weapon blind-firing around a corner, or an occasional head peeking into the corridor. *The stones must suppress almost all scanning*, Vyoz thought. Nothing had shown on Twilight's life scanner just before she got hit. She would have reported it otherwise. What was it that scanned them, though?

No time to think. Enemy blind fire was not precise, but they were generous with their ammunition. His team moved forward, firing at anything sticking out from the stone walls. Someone yelled profanities, likely a hit in the arm. In the following brief fire break, Day and Night stormed forward to the end of the corridor and surprised both enemies, one holding his wound, the other reloading, with quick shots to their heads. It was quiet now. One heat signature lay flat at the far end, no signs of resistance. Day scanned the room twice, then said, "Clear!"

They entered a small chamber with high ceilings and looked around. "Permission to verify Twilight's status?" asked Night. Vyoz was certain she was dead but granted Night's wish regardless: "Go. And bring her scanning equipment!"

The dead enemies—men and women—looked like a strange mix of contracted security—no markings, no official uniforms—and technical personnel. Snippets of commands and yells Vyoz had overheard could place them into many regions of the galaxy. At the far end of the room lay someone dressed like a civilian engineer. "I'm no expert," said Vyoz, "but their equipment looks like they were on some archaeological dig."

"A dig?" asked Day. "In a war zone?"

Vyoz shrugged and gestured toward the only other exit of the chamber. "Check where this leads to!"

Night returned stone-faced, having confirmed for himself that their comrade of many missions was dead. "Are we going to leave her here?"

"We won't," said Vyoz, "but we will press on until we have

all major parts of this complex covered and can bring full recon data back. We will pass back through here and bring Twilight with us to the extraction point."

The ruins were extensive, and it took them several shifts to map all major chambers they could find. The same soil that covered some of the stone floors blocked the ramps leading further down. It looked solid, like the lower levels had been closed off a long time ago. Maybe surface water, when it existed, had washed the soil in. Only the dig site around the area of the firefight had any equipment lying around, and those items almost certainly had been brought in by the group they had fought earlier. On their way back to the surface, they collected Twilight's body, carefully placing her in a sturdy collection bag, ungracefully dragging her back to the canyon entrance. Using a levitation generator could give away their position to enemy scanners, so the team did not bring one.

Life scanners showed some of the critters they had encountered before, so they stepped outside carefully. Even the dim natural light felt less claustrophobic than the helmet-cam-augmented darkness of the ruins. They stopped to plan their way back along canyons with a smoother surface, making it easier to drag a body in the higher gravity, at least a little.

"Halt! Drop your weapons!" The command came in broken New Galactic, then repeated the same words in Keel Zhaja, the language of the enemy. Day, Night, and Vyoz pressed against the canyon walls, weapons high at the ready. Aiming at the canyon ridge, Vyoz saw at least 20 upper torsos and helmet-clad heads, with an equal amount of weapons trained on his team.

"Hold fire!" said Vyoz. "Drop weapons—slowly," he ordered, knowing that this command was likely the last he would give in this war, or maybe forever.

4—GROUND WAR

Kel Chaada stood up from his kneeling prayer position and overlooked the site for the prisoner exchange. Something felt wrong about this mission, but he could not pinpoint the source of his unease.

He covered his face with his hands, but the fine dust of Prral's desert, carried by gentle yet persistent winds, found its way into his nose and mouth, cutting his prayer to Mnagwa Zmaam short. She was a cruel and demanding goddess, but popular on Kel's home planet, EsChiip. She demanded uninterrupted attention of her followers, so her devotees covered their faces with both hands, symbolizing shame in asking for Mnagwa Zmaam's help with any challenge lying ahead of them, only sparing a few moments to worship her.

Kel did not believe in Zmaam, but he made the prescribed gestures and said the ritual words. Most soldiers under his command were strict devotees and would blame any misfortune befalling their unit on anyone skipping a brief prayer. As the commanding officer, Kel knew it was bad for morale not to lead the impromptu ceremony. Troop morale had been low for the entire campaign on Prral. Many units deployed here came from EsChiip, and they were used to an atmosphere richer in oxygen and less gravity. Just being on this planet, let alone fighting a war on it, was tiring, and every activity demanded willpower and focus, even for the mechanized troops.

The war the Nominate of EsChii waged against the Electorate of Keelaak had dragged on much longer than anyone expected. At first, the space fleet made good progress and started controlling solar systems and interstellar space in the region, but the following ground war was slow and bloody. The planetary campaign on Prral was the worst, because it seemed not to make sense to fight here at all. Both factions claimed Prral, but it was an unincorporated world with no colonization or resource mining and only partially habitable around the twilight ring band.

Military Command insisted on the strategic importance of the world—being close to the border region with the Ancestrate of Aloo Dash—acting as a staging ground for a defense against the aggressive and powerful neighbor. While this made some sense, Kel was not convinced if it was the true reason for fighting a ground campaign here. It would have been easier to secure the space in and around the Prral system with the fleet and then occupy the planet after winning the conflict.

Exchanges of prisoners of war were common between the belligerents of this and other interstellar conflicts. A dry, near-straight riverbed ran from their position through the open, arid plains and created a natural path which the Keelaakaad had announced they would take to arrive with their group of EsChii prisoners. Kel had been instructed to receive three or four of their own in exchange for the woman standing close to him. He looked at her once again. Besides her unveiled disapproval of the religious ceremony she had just witnessed, there was nothing he could read from her face, neither now nor at any earlier time he had tried to glean anything from their prisoner. She had been quiet during the transport to the exchange site. Her uniform looked like some sort of senior technician rank, as far as Kel could tell, but her demeanor and grim determination hinted more toward a combat-experienced veteran, someone who had seen—and brought—death.

Turning around, he saw more stoic, determined faces—his own unit. He knew these faces well, knew their names, many of their life stories, occupations before their military service, favorite foods, images of their children or partners. This was less because of Kel's memory being great than to the fact that this unit had comprised exactly the same men and women since the war began. As a combat leader, Kel had yet to lose a single soldier under his command. "Natural tactical aptitude" is what the command officer's board had cited as the reason for his recent field promotion. He knew that among the soldiers his reputation was that of a "lucky" officer, one to stay close to during combat, one they would follow willingly, trusting him to keep them alive. Kel did not mind praying with them, even if it was to a sociopathic egomaniac of a deity like Zmaam. He was certain to have put their minds at ease, but his mind was not.

"Contacts?" he asked, and one of his specialists checked his handheld screen again. "Just the one, sir. Approaching our position like before with unchanged speed. Should be in visual range any moment."

Kel pulled his breathing mask up and slid his helmet visor down. Several button pushes on his field armor's left bracer brought the magnification on the inside visor projection up to maximum level. Half of his view was filled with a somewhat blurry image of the distant vehicle approaching. The small Keelaakaad hover transport was a familiar sight, enough capacity for a small fire team, but one of the least threatening vehicles in the enemy's arsenal, appropriate for the planned exchange. Kel turned off the magnified view and addressed his team using the helmet comms: "One light transport incoming. Get ready, people! When they stop and disembark with our guys, we confirm identities and if everything checks out, I will walk the prisoner to the exchange point."

The hover transport closed in fast and came to a halt just out of earshot. Kel saw several figures emerging from the rear door. "Facial recognition checks out," said one of his specialists. "Three of our boys awaiting exchange, sir!"

Kel saw an Electorate soldier waving a gesture of readiness. Kel waved back, signaling the exchange was about to begin. The prisoner had her arms shackled in front of her; he slightly pulled her right arm and said, "Let's go!" Both of them started walking toward the other group, the three EsChii prisoners moving in front of the same number of Keelaakaad guards. Military custom dictated each exchanged prisoner be handed over by one guard.

Until a few passes ago, Kel had not worried about this protocol, but now he realized that he was going to face three guards when they all reached the exchange point if something should go wrong. They had cleared half the distance to meeting the other group when the projection of an unknown male face appeared in his visor. The rank and clearance code showed he was with military intelligence. Kel pushed the comm button on his bracer to open the channel.

"Subsection Officer Chaada here," he reported dutifully. The prisoner had noticed the operation of his comm gear and turned her head to look at his face. She could not hear the conversation through the closed visor, but Kel gestured for her to keep looking and walking ahead.

"Division Officer Kyokp speaking. I am with military intelligence. Time is of the essence, Subsection Officer—are you still in control of prisoner B12-145?"

Military intelligence contacting a field unit was unusual, Kel thought, then double-checked the ID number on the prisoner's shackles and confirmed the match: "Yes, sir! I am about to complete the exchange, as ordered."

"Do not proceed with the exchange! You are now ordered to abort the exchange and transport the prisoner back to base immediately!"

"Sir, we have started the exchange protocol already, and the Keelaakaad are here with our men..."

"I order you to abort the exchange and return the prisoner to base!" repeated the division officer, raising his voice.

"Sir, I have orders to proceed from my commanding officer —"

"I outrank your commanding officer just as I outrank you, and I am giving you a direct order to abort the prisoner exchange!" insisted Division Officer Kyokp.

"Sir, if I abort now, the enemy will see this as a betrayal of the protocols, and our men will suffer the consequences of their anger!"

"I understand your concern, but you cannot hand this prisoner back to the enemy!"

Kel knew he was scraping the borderlines of insubordination, but he felt compelled to ask anyway: "Who is she?"

"Come again, Subsection Officer?"

"Who is prisoner B12-145?"

Prisoner B12-145 turned her head once more, sensing that the conversation behind his visor and the slowing of his walking pace, pulling her arm backward to slow her down as well, his focused gaze becoming nervous, had something to do with her and her exchange for the three soldiers marching steadily toward them, guards following closely. She, however, did not look nervous, or change her expression in any way Kel could discern.

"Eyes front!" he shouted through the helmet speaker, and she complied. He could hear the intelligence officer's angry voice on the external comm channel and rushed his mind through the options he had. "Who is she?" he repeated, adding, "You have to give me something, I will not abort and leave our men in enemy hands without a reason!"

The comm went silent for a moment, and just when he thought the division officer had closed the channel, his voice came back, calmer, resigned: "She is the head of Electorate intelligence. This was just discovered when her intercepted call sign was correlated with known Keelaakaad operations and intelligence ranks. You are about to hand back the spymaster of the Electorate."

△△△

Three enemy guards would outnumber Kel at the exchange point and he neither wanted to hand over this high-value prisoner nor abandon his fellow soldiers. He kept walking forward, maintaining a tight grip on the prisoner's right arm to control her pace. They drew close enough for him to take a proper first look: three men, dressed in dirty bodysuits, worn as a layer underneath the typical EsChii battle armor. Their faces showed light injuries, maybe from combat, maybe from interrogation. They were all of similar height and build, muscular, looking like they had walked straight out of a recruitment holo. Most remarkable, their dirty, bruised faces did not show a hint of fear, in contrast to the Keelaakaad soldiers walking behind them, who looked just as tense as Kel felt himself.

Kel released the grip from his prisoner's arm and switched to his team comm: "Jam all communications, all channels!"

The team's e-warfare specialist's voice came on, confused. "Sir? We won't be able to talk to you. I—"

"Do it now!" said Kel.

"Jamming all channels now!" said the specialist.

The comms went silent and a brief static confirmed the specialist had executed the order. Kel saw one of the Keelaakaad tapping his helmet—no doubt he heard the static jammer discharge, too—followed by a sweeping hand gesture across his torso.

It was too late to realize he meant this signal for the prisoner when she whirled around, slamming her shackles into Kel's visor. The speed and force of the attack made him step back. The prisoner's foot was right there to make him stumble, falling rearward on his back. She leaped on his abdomen, knee-first, pushing her kneecap with all her body weight behind it into the opening between his torso armor and his equipment belt. It felt like a stun hammer hit, pushing the air out of his lungs without a scream, followed by a piercing pain that could not have been worse had she stabbed him clean through his lower body.

Not waiting for him to recover from the attack, she started slamming her shackles into his helmet visor. Once more. And again. Kel made a halfhearted effort to raise his arms, protecting his deteriorating, cracked visor, when he heard loud popping noises and the familiar hiss of projectiles overhead. His attacker rolled off his throbbing body, searching for cover. Kel had no doubt his unit had started firing, likely not for effect, but in the air above the exchange point to break off the melee. EsChii military embraced a strict "high initiative" doctrine, and when in doubt, troops were instructed to lay down fire or make other aggressive moves, always maintaining said initiative and keeping the enemy in a reactive mode.

Still on his back, lifting his head, Kel saw a mirror image of his own situation between the EsChii prisoners and their guards: All three had overwhelmed their captors, dragging them, arms around their necks, using them as bullet shields, moving backward toward his position. A movement on the edge of his peripheral vision, limited by the helmet frame, turned out to be his prisoner, rolling back next to him, trying to pull his sidearm from his equipment belt. He pushed her hands down, trying to get control of the weapon himself, while his abdominal muscles clouded his consciousness with more pain. The prisoner was about to get the upper hand in the struggle for his gun when a voice barked something sounding like a threat in the enemy's language. The helmet translator, broken by the onslaught of his prisoner, no longer operated, and Kel understood only a few words of Keel Zhaja.

A projectile smashed into the coarse, dry flakes of soil between the legs of his assailant. Both she and Kel looked with the same astonishment at one of the EsChii soldiers, who had not only overwhelmed his guard but pulled away his handgun, aiming and shooting with speed and precision, leaving no doubt he could have hit her torso or head if he had aimed for it, while speaking what sounded like very authentic Keel Zhaja. Who were these people?

The soldier repeated his command. Clenching her teeth in frustration, the first emotion she had shown, the prisoner released her grip from Kel's gun and rolled to the right, away from him.

He saw the Keelaakaad unit kneeling in the distance, weapons aimed at the exchange point, but holding their fire, likely fearing to hit their comrades, and maybe even more so harming their high-value intelligence chief. Were they aware of who she was or kept in the dark like his unit? No time to think this through—dismissing his curiosity, Kel struggled to his feet, still feeling numb in the abdomen. He slid the remains of his visor up and pulled his breathing mask down, yelling, "Get back to my unit!" at the three EsChii soldiers, drawing his gun, stepping over to his yet-again prisoner, resting the weapon's muzzle against her temple and pulling her backward, imitating the grasp his more capable fellow soldiers used to keep their former guards under control. "Everybody back!"

During the way back to Kel's unit, which felt like a long march through the riverbed, walking backward, prisoners in tow, the Keelaakaad did not use the time for any obvious change of their position. The small group remained close to their transport. Kel looked back and saw several of his own unit's members gesturing. A specialist noticed Kel's open helmet visor, unlocked his own, and said, "Multiple contacts incoming, closing in fast!"

The soldier who had fired the shot which ended the wrestling match between Kel and his prisoner also turned around, speaking Kel's native language, Jeesh Gep, for the first time: "This is a trap! Sorry to say this is not much of a rescue, Subsection Officer! See those dust columns on the horizon? Those are enemy transports or light combat speeders coming in. We are sitting here in the flat, there is no cover, and your only transport is unarmed!"

Kel shouted orders back to his unit. "Ready to move to combat positions! One to add!" Then, addressing the exchange soldier: "Release your guards!"

"What? Subsection Officer, this is all we got, to maybe, just maybe, come out alive. We can trade them back, or at least hold off or slow their incoming attack!"

"Send them back, soldier!" Kel commanded. "We cannot

transport any additional prisoners! Do it!"

It was clear the man staring back at him was not used to receiving orders from a subsection officer, let alone from one whom he probably saw as incompetent, not able to control his single, unarmed prisoner and then leaving them exposed in a wide-open place with a larger enemy force closing in fast. Almost against his will, Kel added a weak-sounding "Trust me." Much to his surprise, the man with the steely stare let go of his prisoner and ordered his two companions to do the same. A few words in unintelligible Keel Zhaja seemed to inform the enemy guards of their changed fortune, and they, first hesitating, then picking up pace, moved back toward their own unit.

Still pulling the female prisoner along, he gave the three-man team instructions to run over to his unit and split up, one of them per group formed in small circles. The steely-eyed man followed him. The other two ran toward different circles each. "All right, Subsection Officer, I trusted you, what's our move?"

"Get in the hole!" Kel nodded toward the center of the closest circle his unit formed. Just then noticing the small, circular opening in the riverbed, the steely-eyed man glanced back at Kel, then climbed into the opening without further hesitation. Kel released his grip on the prisoner and gestured her to follow his example, gun aimed at her head. She struggled to climb down the short metal ladder with her shackled hands, but the steely-eyed man grabbed her, speeding up the process and clearing the way for Kel's men and women to climb down in quick succession. Kel looked around at the dust columns, their lower ends having turned into visible enemy vehicles.

A quick count showed at least 12 to 15 incoming transports and light combat speeders, a full Electorate mobile combat outfit, too large and significant a force for securing a regular prisoner exchange but befitting the importance of prisoner B12-145. Kel climbed down last and pushed a button to close the opening overhead. His crew had taken their combat positions as ordered, and the steely-eyed man had made himself useful by securing the prisoner in a spare jump seat, the seat belt knotted around her shackles. He looked around and back at Kel. "This is a hover tank, isn't it?"

Kel grinned. The room they descended into was the rear interior of an EsChii main battle tank indeed.

When the Keelaakaad suggested the exchange point in the desert plains, he had known it was an indefensible position, putting his unit at risk of an enemy trap or even full-scale attack. He had accepted anyway, certain about having put the Electorate commanders in a perceived position of strength. They could overrun and outgun his small group with ease, the lonely transport they had brought not being fast enough to offer escape. It looked like those commanders wanted to make certain this was the outcome, as they had thrown the entire mobile force of the front sector at the exchange point.

"I had wondered what kind of unit you guys were," continued the man. "I guess the missing shoulder pads on your armor would have shown that you are tankers, right?"

"Yes, wearing them could have ruined the surprise," said Kel, still grinning. "Come with me."

He climbed forward through a hatch into the command module of the tank, gesturing toward another jump seat for the man to use. "I am Division officer Vyoz Vyooma," said the man, sitting down, operating the foldout seat and seatbelt harness like a veteran.

"An honor to have special forces with us, Division officer!" replied Kel, the man's rank confirming what he suspected: This was not just any group of prisoners of war, but an elite commando team. Vyoz Vyooma outranked him by several ranks, so he asked, "Are you taking command, sir?"

"No," said Vyoz. "This is your show, Subsection Officer!"

EsChii hover tanks were the heaviest weapon in the ground forces' arsenal. The armored vehicles had not been easy to hide in the desert flats, but the dried-out riverbed had offered a soft enough soil for the combat builders to excavate three large holes with their heavy machinery, and to refill a thin layer of the topsoil over the tanks. They had been put in place several spins ago, giving the tanker unit time to redraw the chipped soil patterns of the riverbed. On Kel's command, the three heavy war machines spun up their engines and the powerful hover boosters pushed them through the loose soil that had covered their presence.

The main guns moved out of their protective encasing, with a subdued hydraulic whir betraying the enormous weight of the weapons, now freely swiveling around, aligned by the target computer with the predicted flight paths of the incoming enemy vehicles. A formidable force just moments ago, the Electorate mobile outfit broke off their attack run, first into controlled evasive maneuvers, then into panicked scatter, as the heavy tank guns took out one combat speeder per shot in short succession, the reload belt refilling the long barrels with fresh rounds, each capable of destroying an enemy speeder or transport.

After three passes, the engagement was over, the desert landscape littered with Keelaakaad wrecks and metallic debris.

5—FIRST COUNCILOR

Sitting in front of the EsChii military inquiry board, Kel thought about Prral, swearing he could still feel its dust between his teeth. The world where Vyoz Vyooma and he had met. Where they had become comrades-in-arms, friends. The world that had made them heroes. On that planet, the fighting had been brutal, yet clear and simple. The struggle ahead, through the legal aftermath of their action, would be convoluted and treacherous. Kel needed to tread carefully if he wanted to stay a free man.

The prisoner exchange had turned into a pitched battle between Keelaak and EsChii forces. His tank group routed the enemy and left the Keelaakaad without protection or reserves at that part of the front line. The commando soldiers, led by Vyoz, who joined his unit after the exchange went bust, knew about an enemy point of interest: an old temple just at the edge of the desert flats where they destroyed the Electorate mobile forces. Vyoz had explained that his team had infiltrated the temple. It blended in with its surroundings and was—most remarkably—shielded against all scanning technologies. This piqued command's interest, and they had ordered Vyoz's team to recon potential enemy activity and strength. It had surprised Vyoz when his team did not find a stealthy forward base or operations center, but an archaeological dig site. The site had nonmilitary security forces, who engaged the commandos in a brief and bloody firefight when they spotted them, resulting in the death of one of Vyoz's commandos and the entire dig team.

Based on Vyoz's report, Kel had concluded that the Keelaakaad front line had a vast gap, and that there was not a single enemy soldier between his tanks and their planetary command post. Instead of delivering the commandos back to base, returning the Keelaakaad prisoner, and regrouping with the rest of the tank forces, he moved his tanks to the temple at full speed, searched and secured the old buildings, and then made a push toward the enemy's command center.

They had hovered through the difficult terrain edging the perpetual night side of the planet but reached their target unchallenged. The command post was lightly defended with some infantry and gun emplacements, but its location in a depressed flat made it ideal for a quick moving tank assault. Kel's tanks circled around the post, taking out any source of enemy fire. Vyoz's team advanced to the main building on foot, taking the few guards by surprise and securing the control room within a few passes. Stunned by the fast, unexpected attack, the control room occupants surrendered to Vyoz's three-man team, including the highest-ranking planetary officer in charge of all Electorate ground troops on Prral.

Assuming a large-scale breakthrough, the planetary officer had called his troops to stand down for a cease-fire arrangement to follow. Kel did not know what happened to this officer when he and his superiors on Keelaak—much later—realized that the unstoppable breakthrough force comprised 12 tanks and 3 commandos, still wearing only their helmets and underwear, as none of the tank crew's body armor fitted their impressive physiques. The "tanks and tights" attack became legendary among EsChii military forces.

The cease-fire had cascaded into incoming Keelaakaad reinforcements and supply transports staying in orbit, not wanting to land in a cease-fire zone, or wrongly assuming the ground war was near lost. With no communication from their planetary command and no incoming supplies, many Keelaakaad units felt they had been cut off, feeding more credibility to the "major breakthrough" rumors spreading in the ranks. Advancing EsChii forces met no resistance; some enemy commanders engaged in local cease-fire talks, other units surrendered. With their Prral ground campaign collapsing, Electorate command concluded that they had been beaten in space and were about to lose on the ground. They advised the Electorate's president to seek peace while they still had many active units and could negotiate reasonable terms. Both sides' politicians could settle quickly when it became apparent that Prral was considered lost by the Electorate.

Kel's and Vyoz's bold actions at the exchange and the following attack had won the war. At least, this was the simplified version popular with soldiers at first but catching on with the EsChii civilians as well. It was a delightful story of two Nominate soldiers rising to the occasion. However, there had been problems with military command's view of the events. While Kel had brought the commandos home, kept the enemy's intelligence chief from being exchanged back, and won a great victory, he had also defied direct orders from his commanding officer, and launched an unplanned and unsanctioned assault deep into enemy territory without support or anyone even knowing about this impromptu operation.

The success was undeniable, but many of the officers in Kel's direct chain of command felt snubbed. They thought the success of the Prral ground campaign, and its victorious conclusion, should not be looked at as the heroic actions of two soldiers only. Vyoz drew less ire than Kel did, as most officers respected Vyoz for being a lifelong professional soldier. They saw Kel as an upstart citizen-soldier who got lucky being in the right place at the right time after ignoring chain of command.

A reprimand issued by military command was not seen as sufficient by his superiors, and they summoned an inquiry board to prepare a court-martial.

ΔΔΔ

"In summary: Subsection Officer Kel Chaada's actions on

Prral were nothing short of exemplary military leadership," said Vriifaach Deegb, addressing the inquiry board, standing next to his client.

Vyoz had vocally supported Kel's decision to make an aggressive push for the enemy's command center. Despite their different upbringings, both men had developed mutual respect, and their short, yet intense, common war experience forged that respect into trust. Vyoz had been a commando soldier for almost five orbits and had taken part in several covert operations, blurring the borderline between determined aggressiveness and unethical war crimes. He knew and valued Vriifaach Deegb, a soft-spoken yet brilliantly effective military lawyer, who had defended both Vyoz's team members and Vyoz himself in hearings like the one Kel had to expect. Unlike a court-martial, where all proceedings and their content were confidential, the initial hearing was public and drew enormous attention by the E EsChii, the people of the Nominate.

It was video streamed to most Nominate worlds and introduced as an attempt of jealous generals to discredit a war hero, who had delivered swift victory where military leadership failed to do so. The Nominate of EsChii's recent history had seen several military coups overthrowing governments of appointed or elected representatives. High-ranking military members were unpopular and always eyed as the next potential group of tyrants. The current civilian government had brought economic stability and civil peace, and reinstated trust in a unifying leadership for the Wel Edge region. The video streams of unpopular generals trying to criminalize a citizen hero's deeds threatened to unbalance this fragile political equilibrium. Kel's defending lawyer, Vriifaach, was well aware of this and amplified the effects of this public perception during the inquiry meetings: Kel was a lead engineer in a spaceship shielding company, an educated but otherwise ordinary EsChii citizen, who answered the call of his nation when war broke out and quickly rose to the rank of subsection officer based on merit only, without personal connections to use as influence.

Vriifaach had read out loud Kel's performance records, commendation entries, and promotion justifications, some of them authored by officers now sitting on the inquiry board. He pointed to Kel receiving conflicting orders in the middle of an ongoing prisoner exchange and how his choice had proven to provide the best possible outcome. When board members cited regulations requiring approval for direct action against enemy forces behind established front lines, he countered with the central argument of his defense: the inability to communicate with command. Kel had given orders to jam all radio communications, which affected the enemy's comms as much as his own, so the board saw this as a willful act of severing an effective chain of command and would not allow it to justify all following actions.

Kel remembered Vriifaach turning to him with a smile when the board made this argument, the smile of someone knowing he had caught his opponents in their own web. Vriifaach challenged the board to show the regulations that defined what unit leaders should do when communications broke down. No part of the military code described how the breakdown had to occur, but they were specific on what had to happen next—the main EsChii military doctrine of "high initiative" advised combat leaders to exert as much pressure on enemy forces as possible to retain battlefield dominance. Kel —so Vriifaach argued—had followed this doctrine in the most exemplary way, exerting pressure to a degree that won the entire campaign. This legal punch was followed by the final statement of the accused, Kel himself. He felt no need to further dwell on the technicalities of the events and did not justify his actions; instead, he opted for lauding his unit's bravery and determination, mentioning many by rank and name, and gave ample praise to Vyoz's commandos, even granting a nod to the Electorate officers describing the civility of their cease-fire negotiations. His speech ended the inquiry proceedings and was the last video stream a growing public audience witnessed. The civilian government was well aware of growing unrest in the population centers of the Nominate, with protesters in many cities demanding an immediate halt to the inquiry and court-martial. Leading military officers outside of the panel also saw how public opinion mounted against the military once more and feared to lose the brief boost of popularity they had enjoyed after victory in the war. Kel never learned the details of the backroom meetings between government and military command, but those talks must have happened quickly, as the inquiry board announced dropping all potential charges just two spins after the proceedings ended. Kel was to be granted an honorable discharge, with all his commendations and promotions intact.

The public video streams had done more than help with getting absolved of all accusations. They were an effective campaign to make Kel Chaada one of the most recognized and well-known EsChii alive. His home city of Thuuny appointed him to the city council as a gesture of honoring their famous son, and from there, the Nominate's appointment system propelled him to higher and higher-ranking positions, riding on a wave of unbroken popularity and emerging as the first true citizen candidate for the high office of the First Councilor. While Vyoz, the leader of the commandos storming the enemy's HQ, enjoyed near equal public admiration, his professional soldiery reminded too many in the Nominate of the days when all their leaders came out of the military caste, without exception. Kel was seen as a fresh start, a common man of "integrity and determination." It became the slogan the current civilian government used in supporting Kel for high office.

△△△

Kel Chaada had led people before—soldiers. What was it going to feel like to lead everybody?

Although the inauguration was video streamed nationwide across all EsChii worlds, an enormous crowd had gathered at the Nominate Plaza and around it for what looked like several city blocks in every direction. EsChiip's climate was mild, and the lack of a planetary axis tilt resulted in no noticeable seasonal changes, as were commonplace on other habitable worlds. It would be dark soon, and the inauguration, which was going to be accompanied by grand holographic displays in the evening sky, was the last step to becoming the First Councilor.

E EsChii frequently held large gatherings outside for athletic or cultural events, but nothing could prepare Kel Chaada for the sea of human heads he could make out in the bright inner-city lights when he was escorted out onto the main balcony of the Plaza building. His escort, including Vyoz Vyooma and several other dignitaries, stood several steps behind him when he reached the railing and waved to his audience. The roar of the crowd was deafening, the air tangibly vibrating with the interlacing shouts and cheers of the 300,000 voices below, putting him into a trance-like flurry of feelings ranging from fear to pride to joy. Official rites, performed by appointees from the main EsChii worlds and a Mnagwa Zmaam priest, were short, and Kel's part in them was easy. The question was if he accepted his appointment. When he answered with a hoarse "Yes," the crowd drowned the Plaza in a wave of audible approval and excitement.

Kel would never forget this feeling for as long as he lived, an all-encompassing, almost palpable manifestation of being granted power.

△△△

The pressure of not screwing up the ceremony in front of billions watching was gone, but the weight of responsibility pushed Kel deep into the speeder's seats. What was he going to do first?

The dimmed windows allowed Kel a view of the two escort vehicles ahead, the walls of the subterranean ring road flying by at high speed on both sides. The ring road was the main speeder transport way of Yuutma, EsChiip's capital city and seat of the Nominate's government, and it was very busy at this time of the rotation. For special occasions or important guests, the general traffic was cleared from the wide tunnels to allow VIPs a fast and unobstructed journey to and from the Nominate Plaza. Today, Kel was that VIP. First Councilor Kel Chaada, on his way from the inauguration ceremony at the Plaza building. The First Councilor was the executive leader of the Nominate of EsChii government and the ceremonial head of state.

As of a few moments ago, he was the leader of the Nominate, this young and somewhat troubled nation of six solar systems with ten incorporated worlds. What started as a loose alliance of mining companies had become a joint-security venture of colonies and eventually a nation of planets with a united government of appointed representatives from each colony. This group appointed the First Councilor. Nominate's worlds held rich resources and some of the most lucrative mines along the Wel Edge region.

The Wel Edge had one main reason for being sparsely populated and prospected: It was the border region of the Ancestrate of Aloo Dash, the galaxy's most powerful and aggressive nation. The last two Shaajrrurrhes, who ruled as absolute monarchs, had pursued expansionist policies and expanded their empire through relentless conquest. Many saw the Wel Edge as unsafe, with a constant threat of the Ancestrate's next expansion looming. Several prospectors braved into these borderlands and returned with rich mining claims, many of which became the primordial cells for the large EsChii cities of the current day. The recent victory in the war against the Electorate of Keelaak had cemented the local dominance of the Nominate of EsChii in the region and added the Prral system to their list of governed worlds.

Vyoz Vyooma sat across from Kel as the speeder left the ring tunnel system and gave the passengers a parting view of the outer Nominate Plaza. Vyoz looked at Kel and smiled. "We can still stop the speeder, and I can smuggle you out of the city through the sewer system—if you have second thoughts!"

Kel grinned. "No such luck! I am afraid you will have to continue to serve, Maz Tiikiip!"

Vyoz was to be appointed the Maz Tiikiip in the EsChii Armed Forces, the highest officer rank and de facto position of a commander-in-chief. "Still a subsection officer and still giving me orders. Nothing has changed since Prral."

Kel laughed, then turned more serious. "Do you still think about Prral? Sometimes?"

"Sometimes," said Vyoz. "You still think about the scientist?"

"Yes. I never understood what he was doing there and why the Keelaakaad refused to admit having an archaeological dig site on Prral."

After the battle following the attempted prisoner exchange, Kel's hover tank group had stopped at the temple site, which the three commandos had raided just two spins before. The recon operation turning into a brief shootout once they were discovered had cost the apparent head scientist of the expedition his life. One of his security guards must have sent an emergency signal, because on exiting the temple, Vyoz's small team got ambushed and taken prisoner by Keelaakaad troops. When Vyoz and Kel returned to the temple, the dead were still there, the Keelaakaad more interested in capturing the commandos than retrieving their fallen.

Kel had found the scientist in one of the underground chambers they had searched. He remembered the man's head, with a tiny dark red dot on the forehead, and the rear of his skull missing. Kel could still feel the distinct sadness and emotions of regret that had overcome him when he looked at the dead and empty gaze of the man. He realized there and then that he had never seen a fallen soldier up close. As a tank commander he took his share of enemy lives, but they had been invisible entities, inside opposing vehicles or structures, or magnified images of people, being aimed and shot at from range. The dead scientist was close and personal and the only image and feeling resembling post-traumatic stress disorder Kel had brought home from the war. "Maybe it was not a Keelaakaad operation—the temple dig," said Vyoz.

"Maybe not," said Kel. "We should return there and investigate!"

6—HONORED GROUND

Prral. In his dreams, Kel Chaada had been back there many times, as a silent incorporeal observer, moving along the passageways connecting the larger subterranean halls of the temple, always filled with an unsubstantiated feeling of regret, of incompleteness, of having missed something; something important. The dreams were frequent and vivid enough to have him seek an actual return to the site, hoping to find some sort of closure. Prral's geological and archaeological features had not been studied, and although the Nominate of EsChii had claimed the planet long before the last—successful—war, no expeditions had mapped or examined the world. To start this endeavor at the site someone had deemed important enough to organize an archaeological dig near the front line of a war had not been a proposition difficult to sell within the Nominate bureaucracy.

Daaw Krrua, the expedition leader, was not how Kel pictured a senior archaeologist from the Nominate's Central Academy: tall, broad shouldered, deep voiced, and, judging by the demeanor of the female expedition members, distractingly handsome. He seemed an effective leader for this venture, though, directing the various scientists and helpers through the stages of systematic exploration of the temple ruins and assigning tasks, clad in the aura of someone who knew what he was doing. Everybody on the team looked busy and motivated, and a casual tone, much to Kel's relief, was common. To most E EsChii, the people of the Nominate, he was still the soldier they remembered from the video streams of his trial rather than their First Councilor. Only Daaw Krrua and his assistant lead scientist addressed Kel by his title. Daaw's assistant, Ahma Zhanyza, was the other attractive expedition member: a fair-skinned woman with jewel-like blue eyes, rare genetics even for a diverse society like the Nominate. Kel was introduced to her during the preflight briefings before they left for Prral, and he looked forward to spending more time with the biologist during this expedition. Sadly, she seemed preoccupied with work, briefings of the tedious kind, and general admiration of her expedition leader.

"It was very exciting when Daaw invited me to come along for the expedition," said Ahma, holding the same spoonful of soup in the air for passes now, while she spoke about her scientific work with passion. Kel did not mind. This lunch break in one of the dropped, pressurized crew containers was his first proper opportunity to talk with her alone, and if it was up to him, she could go on talking forever. She had the sparkle in her eyes he had noticed when scientists talked about their work, and her voice was pleasant, with a soft accent typical for inhabitants of the Gezzet continent of their mutual home planet.

"So, your studies focus on the microscopic, that's why I never see you outside, chasing the local critters in the canyons," Kel said.

She laughed. "I am not that kind of biologist, correct! I am a molecular xenobiologist, but honestly, most of the time I am not even looking for microscopic traces, I am more focused on nano scale and just above."

"Why is that?" asked Kel.

Ahma put her spoon back into the bowl of cooling soup. "Have you ever wondered why the Kubuu Ksiw left no traces?"

"If you mean the extra-galactics who ravaged the Aloo Spur, maybe our entire galaxy, destroying our civilizations and killing almost all humans, I'd say they left quite a trace!"

"You know what I mean." She smiled then returned to her serious lecture face. "They left unprecedented devastation, yes, but they left no other trace of their presence in our galaxy, and their raids lasted for 20 orbits, some say for 25! There are very few physical artifacts, and not a single biological one we ever found in 1,200 orbits since, not one! This leads me to believe that we are not looking at the correct scale. The few Honored reports we have about face-to-face encounters all speak of a biological life form."

"Yes," said Kel, "the Dark Ones! Large, black hulking monsters."

"Vague, I know," said Ahma, "but all reports call them biological life forms. No one doubted they were living beings. This prompted scientists, well, once we had scientists again who would not be solely concerned with pure survival during the reemergence, to look for biological remains of the Kubuu Ksiw. The biologists among them were all the type of biologists like the one you expected me to be!"

"The critter-chasing kind?" asked Kel.

Ahma's great laugh felt rewarding to Kel, and he did not mind being the simple jester, as long as it put a smile on her face. "Exactly, the critter-chasing kind, or someone looking for cell-size remnants. But—what if—the basic building blocks of these extra-galactics are not at that scale, what if they are smaller? Maybe they left traces all over the galaxy and we simply have not looked closely enough?"

"Is this what you are hoping to find here? Why here?"

Kel would have faked interest just to keep the conversation going, but he did not have to, as he found the topic genuinely interesting.

"I have a reasonable amount of hope this could be a site from the galacticide era," Ahma replied, "and Daaw's initial findings seem to support this. If so, these ruins have not, like so many other places, suffered from orbital bombardments. There is a chance the Kubuu Ksiw visited the surface of the planet. And, if they did, we have a chance to find traces of their presence. I am betting on something just above the nano scale, just on the edge where a molecular structure can still be complex enough to serve as a building block for life."

"What would they have done here, the extra-galactics?"

"Their purpose for planetary surface visits is unknown, as is pretty much their entire presence in our galaxy and their aggression against its denizens, but the reports from encounters with our ancestors said they all happened on the ground."

She scooped a spoonful of soup out of the bowl and got close to consuming it, but stopped mid-motion when Kel said, "It is surprising how little we know about the Dark Ones, and the exact events of the galacticide."

"I know!" Ahma exclaimed. "It is the most horrendous event in human history, at least as far as we know, because we lost not only our cities and space habitats, we lost our history, too—and we don't know any details about the invaders! That's why this opportunity to search for traces here is so unique!"

"I am excited about the expedition, too," said Kel. "But why do you think it is unique? What is so different about Prral?"

"If the preliminary analysis of the complex ruins is correct, it was built during the galacticide and survived it. You find structures of this kind on Honored Ground only, where our ancestors fled to and actually survived."

"I don't understand," said Kel. "Aren't there more than 300 worlds classified as Honored Ground, where either remains of structures, or human remains of the Honored, have been found?"

"Yes, there are plenty of locations to test my hypothesis, in theory, but none of them is accessible. Honored Ground is closed off to scientific research. It is closed off to anyone, really."

"I knew Honored Ground is closed to the public, to preserve the sites of the ancestors, but there must be some research in these places going on!"

"I assure you there is not, at least not for ongoing studies," said Ahma. "If there is a reason to believe a site to be Honored Ground, the galactic government will send a scientific delegation to refute or prove the claim; and once a site is declared Honored Ground, it will get sealed off—for good!"

Kel considered himself to have something close to a scientific background, as a former plasma shield engineer, but he had to admit he had never thought about the politics of research on the galactic scale. "Well, Ahma, you have full access here—let's make the best out of it!"

"Thanks to you, First Councilor!" She smiled and ate her first spoonful, looking slightly taken aback by how cold it had become.

Kel basked in her smile, chuckled at her reaction, and knew he had completely, utterly, and irrevocably fallen for this woman.

ΔΔΔ

"And this is where the trail ends." Ahma pointed to the chamber floor. Daaw, the expedition leader, had his arms crossed in front of his chest, seeming to fake interest only to humor her. Kel recognized the spot, memorable within the maze of the Prral ruins. Even a faint dark bloodstain was visible still. He said: "This is where the scientist died!"

Kel remembered the image of the man missing most of his skull. The scientist had left a lasting impression. Kel did not see him in his dreams, but he always felt dread, darkness, and cold when he was examining the ruins, always by himself, always looking for something, finding nothing.

Ahma, however, had found something. "What scientist?" she asked.

Daaw looked at Kel, who nodded in approval, and then Daaw answered. "There was fighting here in the ruins during the recent war. All the projectiles we pulled out of the walls are contemporary. There were a few people, technicians or scientists by the looks of their clothing and equipment, who died down here, including someone at this spot."

Ahma shuddered and took a step back, "Right here?"

"Yes, darling," said Daaw, "but I still fail to see what this... trail...is about."

"It makes even more sense now," she said. "He found it!"

"Found what?" asked Daaw.

Ahma seemed to lose patience with the expedition leader, who was still standing a few paces back, forehead wrinkled, when she explained it for the third time: "We found no old galacticide-era equipment here, except in a wall shaft in a room next to this chamber. Hidden, dropped, forgotten—for whichever reason there was a loose, tubelike rock formation, like a stalactite, but very even, and hollow. It looked like a storage vial, broken open at one end. After the archaeological scan, your colleague gave it to me for my scans. That's where I found the first nano cells!"

"You mean nano *bots*," said Daaw.

"No, I mean nano *cells*. They have the size of a nano tech machine, but appear cell-like under the scanner."

The two had bickered about the correct nomenclature before, like an old couple. They were a couple indeed, as Kel had found out when Ahma mentioned that Daaw, the handsome archaeologist, was more than a scientific mentor to her. Kel, hoping the xenobiologist was single like himself, was all but crushed by the news and had caught himself being less cordial with Daaw Krrua ever since.

"Let her finish!" he said, angry enough for the expedition leader to shut up after murmuring, "Certainly, First Councilor."

Ahma's face relaxed, and she graced Kel with a look of approval, before she continued, "I programmed a scanner for the specific structure of the cells, which all seemed identical, and tried to find more, and there were some around the contained vial in the shaft but also on the floor. From there, I traced it to two different spots in the room and then a lighter trail of fewer nano cells through the door opening and into this chamber, up to here."

"There was scientific equipment in that room," said Kel. "Maybe the scientist found the vial or even broke it himself, then took a piece to analyze it and rubbed these nano cells over his clothing in the process."

"Yes." Ahma's face lit up. "That makes sense! But how do you know about the equipment?"

"The First Councilor had been here before, when he was stationed on Prral during the war, and witnessed the aftermath of the fighting," said Daaw. "These details were on a need-to-know basis—and you did not need to know."

"Well," said Ahma, "I'll leave you big boys to it, then. I got samples to scan."

Both men watched her walk away. *Leave me out of your stupid games, you arrogant puygo*, thought Kel, looking at Daaw, but what he said was, "Keep me updated!"

ΔΔΔ

The underground complex reached much deeper than the commando team's scan had shown. Layers of sediment settled into the lower chambers, and hallways slowed the expedition down. They brought every bit of cleared material up to the surface for scanning and sifting. In addition, larger scanners, reprogrammed by Ahma Zhanyza, searched every bit of material for more nano cells. To her disappointment, they found no more traces of the mysterious technology. Daaw Krrua remained somewhat dismissive about Ahma's find, but she kept working long shifts on the tiny particles she found, sharing some of her preliminary findings and thoughts with Kel rather than her boss and lover. Both the xenobiologist herself and her enthusiastic pursuit of an unusual theory genuinely fascinated Kel. "These cells are alien, in material, structure, everything, unlike any nanotechnology made by humans," said Ahma. "I don't have enough data for Daaw's reports yet, but I can feel it: This could be it! The nano cells are definitely from the same time like the ruins, so this could be traces of the Kubuu Ksiw!"

Despite containing no more nano cells, the lower levels revealed something new: two low-ceilinged, circular chambers, a distinct departure from the architectural style of the rest of the complex, which featured only straight walls, high ceilings, and right angles. The outer circle walls bulged out and were built from stones of all sizes, fitted together with less sophistication than the laser-cut stones in other rooms. The entire chamber looked more organic, and seemed not to belong to the other ruins, but someone had connected it to a hallway built in the predominant style. To both sides of the door openings were slots where heavy doors might have fit in to close off the chambers. Kel took his time to walk around, his light illuminating the wall segment ahead of him.

Daaw and a group from his team inspected the central pedestal both chambers shared, also circular and with a flat top. The expedition leader still carried his aura of expertise, but he unnerved Kel with the underlying arrogance he presented it with. Kel wondered why Ahma put up with it. Did she respect his scientific credentials and expertise that much? Was he some sort of father figure for the young woman? A part of Kel was glad his rival was not too likable and made it easy for him to plot how to rid Ahma of the man and set himself up as her next partner. The two were a couple, yes, but neither were they officially registered, nor had they gone through the rites of Mnagwa Zmaam yet, so Kel was not too late.

"First Councilor!" Daaw's voice pulled Kel out of his thoughts. "It looks like the team found a third chamber!"

Kel joined the group, and an excited-looking junior archaeologist led them out to the hallway and further along down a ramp into the dark.

"What is this?" asked Daaw.

"Oh, this one," said the archaeologist. "This chamber is still sealed!"

Bright metal, reflecting the different lights pointed at it, filled the space where the other chambers had a gaping entrance hole. "This is the only large metal construct we have found so far," said another team member, "and our initial scans show it is a complete, two-segment sliding door—a blast door, judging from the thickness—with a preserved opening mechanism. But what's really exciting is what we picked up behind the door.

While the walls hardly allow for scanning, the door does. And behind it"—the young man needed a moment to collect himself —"behind it are human remains. Skeletons. A hundred of them!"

7—DESPERATE TIMES

There had been no warnings, no intelligence reports, not even rumors. He was not prepared. The advisors left his office and awaited his decision.

Many spins of calm had followed Kel Chaada's inauguration ceremony: boring briefings about governmental procedures, hearings of little import, and many personal introductions to people seeking the First Councilor's attention for this or the other—mostly their own—cause. Then, suddenly, the galactic government informed Kel in a direct, official transmission to his office that the Ancestrate of Aloo Dash had declared war on the Nominate of EsChii, that hostile military action was now sanctioned, to be expected, and would not end until one nation would seek cease-fire or submit to the other.

War with Aloo Dash meant death and destruction; destroyed fleets, destroyed cities, destroyed planetary ecosystems, devastated populations, and a destroyed way of life. The opposing nation would be battered into full submission, having to give up their form of government, their cultures and traditions, their deities and rites, and any form of freedom they might have enjoyed. It was entering unmitigated serfdom to the cult of the leadership of the Ancestrate; the Nominate would cease to exist.

The Ancestrate of Aloo Dash had won every war for almost three generations. Mnazkash the Subjugator, grandfather of the current monarch, had built Aloo Dash's space fleet from a force of conventional ships of all sizes into an instrument of terror, with swarms of small vessels transported by the largest class of ships ever built—the Grandslaught Carriers. These titanic ships were larger than the theoretical build limit for space structures, which predicted that a too-large structure would collapse under its own gravity into a metallic sphere. The Grandslaught Carrier builders got around the limit by encapsulating a powerful fusion generator—whose output rivaled the core output of a small star—that provided enough outward-pointing pressure to maintain a stable megastructure. While the planetoid-size ship instilled fear, the main purpose for its enormous scale was range: Most spaceships could warp space for five to six light-orbits, some designs for ten, before their energy core had to be refueled and fusion reignited. Grandslaught Carriers could warp up to 1,000 light-orbits without refueling and carry an entire conventional fleet within their monstrous metallic bellies, expanding the military reach of the Ancestrate to nations that had felt safe from their aggressive interstellar neighbors.

The best defense of the Nominate had failed: its location. No darkstring travel routes crossed the Korrats Ridge—the border region with the Ancestrate—which forced any attacking space fleet to either travel around the region, through large stretches of undeveloped worlds without refueling options, or to fly straight through the Korrats Ridge, using enormous amounts of fuel. Warp drives, the common method for space travel, theoretically worked everywhere, but the process of warping or bending space-time to shorten travel time over interstellar distances required immense amounts of energy, so much that even the most efficient fusion reactors would use all their fuel for a few light-orbits, enough to reach a neighboring solar system.

About half of Kel's advisors and high-ranking appointees for various parts of the government urged him to submit, to officially declare Aloo Dash victorious and accept a—likely—one-sided peace accord. They warned him about the destruction the war would bring, and some of the older advisors could offer eyewitness accounts of the effects of orbital bombardment by the Ancestrate's space fleet. Shaajis Sya, so they hoped, was not as merciless as her father, and the Nominate planets would be harder to govern in the absence of an effective supply route for potential Aloo Dash garrison troops. The advisors speculated that their way of life could be largely preserved.

They lied. Kel knew fear when it radiated from someone's eyes, when it formed a layer of hoarseness in the timbre of their voice. They knew four generations of nation building in the Wel Edge would be for nothing if the Ancestrate had its way with the Nominate. They feared for their lives, and, Kel had to admit, it was not unreasonable to fear this enemy. The other half of his government team wanted to fight. Some suggested the war declaration was nothing but a ruse and the Ancestrate would not send its carriers if the Nominate remained steadfast and did not give in. They clung to hope, instilled by previous governments, about the impracticality of a space invasion. This faction of his cabinet said they preferred fighting, but in reality, they wanted to gamble on the Ancestrate's motives for the war: a quick victory over a small, scared nation.

What if Shaajis Sya was under so much internal political pressure that she needed a successful campaign of conquest, no matter if reasonable or efficient? It would be the Ancestrate's first leap across the Korrats Ridge, and—once equipped with new refueling outposts—it could open up an entirely new region of this spiral arm of the galaxy to future military campaigns. Smashing the Nominate could remind the Aloo Dashaad of the glory days of continuous expansion and of regular victory parades in their capital city.

The fear of the Ancestrate using the Nominate as a new base point for more expansion across the Wel Edge could be used to seek allies in the region, arguing that if the Nominate fell, they were going to be the next target. Unfortunately, most Wel Edge nations would only be able to provide additional ground troops, which were not helpful against an Ancestrate fleet. The only other significant regional military power was the

Electorate of Keelaak, an enemy until just recently and not likely to join a military alliance with the nation that had humiliated their ground forces.

The Nominate was alone. So was Kel, left with the decision of what to do next—after all advisors had advised, all experts shared their expertise, and the last government member had left the room. Kel had thanked them and announced he would have a decision for them shortly.

Kel was going to fight. Not by sitting still and hoping fuel cost could deter the aggressor—he would fight to win. Winning against Aloo Dash, unbeaten in a hundred wars, sounded insane —but he was going to try it. He still did not understand how and why he felt drawn back to the temple on Prral, but the expedition had given him a weapon, and he was desperate enough to use it.

8—THE BOMB

"You want to build a bomb?" Daaw Krrua's voice trembled. "That's what you want to do with our find? Weaponize it?"

"Oh, now it's *our* find?" said Ahma Zhanyza. "I thought you didn't want anything to do with it! I can't recall you were very supportive of my research into the nano cells. When I found them on Prral, or when I needed additional scanning equipment. Or when I discovered they were human stem-cell-like dormant mechanisms—in form of nano tech!"

"A mistake," said Daaw. "A mistake I have apologized for many times."

Kel Chaada tried to get between the couple. "I still don't understand how we would make a weapon out of them, let alone how it is going to be the doomsday device Daaw is describing."

"Look here," said Ahma, walking briskly to a large screen in the center of her laboratory. The academy of science campus, deserted late in the rotation, left the main lab room to the three and their verbal sparring. With a few hand gestures, she pulled up a magnified image of one of the nano cells she had discovered on Prral.

She was so excited, remembered Kel, being one step closer to maybe solving one of science's big riddles: Who were the Dark Ones, the invaders, who almost exterminated the human species? Where did they come from? The nano cells, as she had called her discovery from the ruin complex on Prral, dated back to the exact time frame of the galacticide and blurred the line between engineered construct and living microorganism. Were they the trace of the invaders she had been looking for?

"I call it a stem-cell-like mechanism, because, like a human stem cell, it has no differentiated function, no specialization yet. A human stem cell is like a clean slate of a cell. It has a full set of DNA, and can become any type of cell in the body, but has not done so yet. These"—she pointed at the screen—"nano machines here behave in the same way. They could become many different parts in a larger machine, but have not specialized yet. They do not have a function but could have many!"

Kel tried to follow along and asked, before a snarky remark by Daaw heated up the discussion again: "The Dark Ones were machines, then? Or augmented organic life forms?"

"Probably the latter," said Ahma, "but we cannot exclude the possibility of them being very sophisticated inorganics, either."

"That could explain their behavior," said Daaw. Ahma and Kel looked at him. "We have several examples of machines, endowed with artificial intelligence, eventually destroying their organic inventors. The ruins of their worlds can be found all over the Aloo Spur. Typically, they ran out of resources, before they developed any means of faster-than-light travel, curtailing their spread. Maybe the Kubuu Ksiw are the exception. The invaders clearly had the means of trans-galactic travel."

Kel thought about this for a while, then said, "Do you think they came here just to kill off all organic life?"

"I don't think so," said Ahma, "because they also destroyed the machine civilizations still existing. They were indiscriminate in their destructive ways. But, we digress..." She turned back to the screen and switched to a new image, showing part of the nano cell at a higher magnification. "Each nano cell had a combination of electronic and quantum memory unit. We thought, hoped, this could be the analog for DNA in a human cell, containing the information for all the possible configurations it could take."

"But?" asked Daaw.

"But we could not understand the encoded data. Nreedz, we were not even sure if it was data, or code, or something else. Besides this, there are a few molecular structures that could be switches, and we hoped that one of them triggered something in this data or code."

"But?" asked Kel, imitating Daaw.

"We managed to flip those switches with nano probes, but nothing happened, except when we"—she zoomed further into the image—"flipped this one!" She zoomed out again, the image now showing two nano cells.

"It split?" asked Daaw.

"Exactly. It replicated, just like a real cell. But that is not the astonishing part. The real surprise is the speed of the replication. We could not measure it at first; well, we still can't really measure it now, but we estimate it taking less than 10 to the order of minus 32 ticks. Maybe less."

"What?" exclaimed Daaw.

Kel was not sure if this was shocking. It sounded like a really short time, but he could not see her point. "So…what does that mean?" he asked.

"It means that in a lot less time that it takes light to travel through a hydrogen atom, this marvel of a machine completely replicated itself!"

Kel had been right. A really short time indeed.

"Let me guess," said Daaw. "It gave off some energy when it replicated, and you will try harnessing that for your bomb."

"Not at all. It neither produced energy nor did it consume any during the replication. We have no idea how it works, only how we can trigger it. Now, if we can learn how to have it replicate with the trigger continuously in the 'on' position, each nano cell will create 2, and these create 4, 8, 16, and so on. They could double in mass so fast that by the time a single tick has passed, they'll take up the volume of a dwarf planet. Well, except that the incredible speed will not allow them to occupy the needed space fast enough, so they will overlap and bump into each other, quite violently, and turn that friction into heat. I estimate that after reaching the volume of, let's say"—she looked around—"this lab building, new cells will simply break down and disintegrate, stopping the chain reaction."

"So this prevents it from being an actual bomb?" asked Daaw.

"No," said Kel, who was beginning to understand. "This makes it perfect. It will not destroy planets, solar systems, or the universe in a crazy runaway chain reaction. But—it can destroy a city by the time the replication produces too many nano cells."

"Precisely!" said Ahma, looking at Kel triumphantly. "And the heated pressure wave will be extremely powerful!"

"We are talking about a weapon of mass destruction here!" said Daaw. "Built with a mechanism we don't understand!"

Kel ignored him, looking at Ahma. He asked, "One of these nano cells, modified as you described, brought onboard a Grandslaught Carrier, could destroy the entire ship?"

"Well, we would need to work on the modifications first, then have scaled-down..."

"Yes or no?" asked Kel.

She thought for a few ticks, then said, "It could destroy it with ease."

"You cannot seriously consider creating a monstrous weapon out of an archaeological find! We are meant to understand the past, learn from it, not repeat the mistakes of harnessing barely understood powers for the production of weapons!"

"Enough!" said Kel. "We are facing a weapon of mass destruction—a Grandslaught Carrier of Aloo Dash! They declared war—on us! Once it makes it across the Korrats Ridge, they will use this weapon, without mercy, without hesitation, and turn everything and everyone you have ever known to ash! We need to stop them, and I think Ahma has found a way we can do just that!"

"I want nothing to do with this!"

"Fine," said Kel. "You are an archaeologist and your job is

done as far as I am concerned. Ahma, you will continue on this project and lead it. Work on the modifications you talked about. Let me know what you need—equipment, material, lab space, human resources—name it, and you will get it!"

"Fantastic," said Daaw. "She is not even a nano tech specialist, building your nano bomb!"

Ahma looked at her partner, rays of fury in her eyes, angular cheekbones about to pierce through her skin. "Get out of my lab!"

He trotted away. Before reaching the door, Kel shouted after him, "Remember that everything discussed here today is a national secret of the Nominate of EsChii!"

ΔΔΔ

The Mnagwa Zmaam priest had completed the prayer rites and left Kel alone with the 14 men and women who were fixating on him, awaiting his last orders. The scene looked like a classroom for a training session, but the metallic bomb cylinders in front of each of the group gave away a more serious, and more deadly, topic being discussed.

"We have been over this many times now," started Kel. "You know your mission, you know your targets, and you know how to get there. I have served with many of you, and I have sent brave E EsChii to their death before, but death was never certain." He paused. "This time—it is. You will not be here again for a debriefing, and we will not celebrate together after your missions are successful. But you will be the group that beat the Ancestrate of Aloo Dash, not the fleet, not other soldiers, not our government, not me, not our bombs or technology...it will be you who are going to be victorious!" He covered his face with both hands. "With Zmaam's help!"

"Zmaam, help us!" chorused the group, mirroring his gesture. Kel bowed, paying respect, then turned around and left, certain to have seen these faces for the last time, narrowly succeeding in suppressing tears.

Vyoz Vyooma caught a glimpse of the group when he intercepted Kel in the hallway of the Nominate military HQ. "What was that about?" He pointed to the room Kel just left.

"Just saying a prayer with some old comrades."

"Still pretending to be one of Mnagwa Zmaam's children?" said Vyoz.

"Zmaam has her uses," said Kel, grim, without the smile Vyoz expected. "And right now we need all the help we can get."

"Having second thoughts, First Councilor?"

"No. Get your fleet to the staging area."

Vyoz hesitated. "About that...I did not want to interrupt when you laid out the strategy with the other command officers earlier. You know I have never done that in the past...but we are concentrating every ship we have in the Prral system, assuming the Aloo Dashaad being the most vulnerable after the warp. I agree that is the correct assessment, but them being 'vulnerable' is relative. Even with very few or no additional ships launched, the Grandslaught Carrier has a lot more firepower than our combined fleet, and it will not take their targeting systems long to track and lock on all our ships."

The Ancestrate of Aloo Dash had not bluffed and dedicated one of their gigantic ships to warp across the Korrats Ridge to crush the Nominate, who had informed the Assembly of their intent not to submit to foreign rule. The Nominate fleet numbered 90 midsize and large combat ships and 450 fighters, a sizable force for the Wel Edge, but utterly inferior to the estimated 300 to 400 warships and thousands of fighters the Grandslaught Carrier would unleash—and then there was the carrier itself, its enormous surface area being a formidable weapon platform. Kel could not fault Vyoz for his concerns. Vyoz had proposed to split their space forces into many small groups of local strike teams, waging a hit-and-run guerilla war while the Aloo Dash fleet was spreading out to subdue and control the Nominate systems. Vyoz was still a commando soldier at heart, and despite being responsible for all troop types now, his thinking revolved around swift tactical strikes. Kel had presented the polar opposite as his plan to defeat the invaders: assemble a grand fleet of all space forces within the Prral system and engage the Ancestrate in a decisive battle.

"We waged war for Prral for a reason," he said. "Because we always knew it would be the point where the Ancestrate would warp in, to use the darkstrings leading out of the system to most places in the Wel Edge. Although our leaders always told us the vast voids of the Korrats Ridge would keep us safe, they knew this moment would come, and Prral was the key to our defense."

"I know all this...and I understand that it might be theoretically our best chance. I don't like that it is our only chance. If we lose there, all is lost. I am not saying my plan will win the war, but it gives the opportunity to win and lose smaller battles, without losing the entire war in one spin. It buys us time. Time for the Aloo Dashaad to tire and make mistakes. Time for other possible allies to join the conflict on our side."

Kel sighed internally, knowing his friend was right, admitting to not understanding his own reasons for excluding Vyoz from his plans, the true plans for the battle, and the availability of a new weapon. Why did he feel more deeply connected to the 14 human bomb carriers he had just seen off than to his best friend? As the hasty preparations for battle with the galactic superpower intensified, the 14 selected ones had entered his dreams, similar to the incorporeal presence he always felt in his varying, yet recurring, dreams about the temple district on Prral. Kel felt an intimate closeness to each of them, beyond the bond he had formed with some of them through their shared combat experience. Several of the bomb carriers had been almost strangers when the new weapon program started, but now he had stronger attachments to them, as if they were friends or family. He looked at Vyoz, hoping his feelings of guilt were not apparent.

"You are right, my friend," he said, "but this is where I have to ask you again—like I did when we first met in the Zmaam-cursed deserts of Prral—to trust me!"

Kel was certain he had Vyoz's trust, and he had not asked

for it since the last war, not once. He could tell that Vyoz was struggling with the request that went so violently against his instincts.

"OK, I trust you," Vyoz conceded, "but let us at least await the carrier outside the Prral system, at the point they are most likely going to warp in. We can be right on top of them when they arrive and have the advantage of surprise rather than having to approach them first from the rally point within the system. It gives us a better chance—"

"Again," interrupted Kel, putting his hands on his friend's shoulders, matching his steely gaze with the sternest expression he could muster. "I have to ask you to trust me on that, too!"

Vyoz broke his stare, took a step back to break the arm contact with Kel, and mouthed an inaudible, "OK." He stiffened his body to a military at-attention posture and confirmed, with no emotion in his voice: "The fleet will be ready at the designated rally point, First Councilor!"

Kel sighed in relief and wanted to wish his friend good luck, but Vyoz turned and walked away without further words. Kel wondered if he should have told him the entire plan for the battle.

9—FALLOUT

K el felt the tenseness of the day of battle. Was it his own feeling, or a collective nervousness? As Vyoz had promised, the fleet was overhead at the rally point in high orbit, and thousands of men and women readied themselves for the fight. It was uncommon for a First Councilor to join or lead troops. The Maz Tiikiip—his friend—was the perfect commander, but despite the many reasons this arrangement made sense, Kel thought he should be in space with them. Prral, however—the ruins—called him. Although he thought he should be with his troops, he needed to be at the temple ruins, a perfect ground control site from where he could monitor and direct the battle. Technicians had brought a shuttleload of equipment down into one of the larger chambers, and installed uplink antennas on the building roofs, enabling telemetry and communication with the fleet vessels.

"We should go down to the command room, First Councilor," said one of the operation specialists, pulling Kel out of his thoughts. "Preparations are complete on the surface. All command interfaces are ready for you!"

Kel followed the young team chief to the hastily set up open elevator platform, which whirred them down into the chamber they had chosen as the command room. The chamber was perfect, almost as if it was purpose-built for this day, having several rectangular platforms stacked on one another, with combat operator and specialist seats installed at each rectangle's edge, the most senior men and women sitting on the innermost, higher levels. The specialist led Kel to the center station and top-level seat, handing him his combat helmet. Shape and size were ceremonial and reminiscent of the armored helmets worn by combatants in the field, but the built-in devices would connect him to all communication and data streams of the fleet, and gentle movements of his head allowed him to focus on parts of the upcoming action. Putting on the helmet felt comforting, triggering memories of his last successful battle on this planet. Kel realized this time he was responsible for the entire Nominate, not only for 12 of its hover tanks, and his tension returned. The room became noisier, as communication and data streams came online, and operators started talking to their assigned observers on the fleet. It took Kel a few moments to get his bearings in the virtual command-and-control interface helmet created for him, but then he found Vyoz's data stream on the command vessel. He connected to it by nodding his head toward the virtual image of his friend.

Vyoz had ordered his fleet into stacked concentric rings, with the lightest fighter craft on the outside to the heaviest space cruisers on the innermost ring. Kel recognized the formation as a typical semi-defensive arrangement, used against an enemy with superior numbers. All soldiers of the Nominate cycled through service in all branches of the armed forces. Kel had commanded hover tanks on Prral, but he had also spent time with the fleet as a tactical coordinator on a cruiser. EsChii strategists believed their military to be at its best if all personnel knew and understood what other troop types were doing. For the enemy about to appear out of warped space-time, however, no doctrine, training, or sheer determination of the combatants would be enough. The Prral temple had provided a weapon to even the odds.

The data streams and communication came in clear and filled Kel's consciousness. Despite his virtual-only connection to the fleet, he felt a wave of loneliness—and regret. Regret for what? He tried to push these irritating thoughts away and refocus on the upcoming fight. He almost succeeded, then fear overwhelmed him, fear of death and dying. It was not his own fear. It came from someplace else. He gave up trying to focus on the rational data stream provided by the tactical command helmet and let the fear take over his conscious mind. It felt strange to experience fear without being...afraid. Kel wallowed in the emotion, like someone would listen to a distorted voice message on high volume to decipher who was speaking. Then he knew. The bomb carrier Bris Tiizeesho was fearful. She knew her mission was concluding. She knew she was going to die. She knew because the Grandslaught Carrier had warped near the Prral system, and she readied herself for her last moments. The Ancestrate had arrived.

"Attention, all forces! The enemy came out of warp!"

Vyoz's familiar voice brought Kel back, confirming what he had felt. The tactical data streams intensified, showing the carrier's location off the predicted position, but this would not matter. Fleet chatter also increased: individual ships being reminded to remain in formation, ordered to hold their position.

Vyoz addressed Kel directly. "Enemy carrier located just outside the planetary disk. Fleet is in position and holding, First Councilor. Any updated orders?"

"No, Maz Tiikiip." Kel's response came without hesitation. "Hold position until further orders!"

Kel heard a prayer to Zmaam. No, he felt a prayer. *Mnagwa Zmaam, help me!* It was Bris's voice. Then the bomb carrier completed her mission. No more fear. Kel knew that out there, outside the planetary disk of the Prral system, the battle had just been decided. It was going to take several passes to register on the entire spectrum the fleet's scanning devices could measure: gravitational waves, radiation of all kinds, including visible light. It was going to be intense across this spectrum, Bris Tiizeesho's final splendor and gift to her people. Kel reached under his visor and wiped a tear off his cheek. He calmed himself, then sent his orders. "All units, assume formation B! Engage the enemy!"

The Grandslaught Carrier's upper hull cleaved open from

the inside, square kilometers of plating unable to give way fast enough to the enormous shock wave of energy ravaging through its interior, bubbling up in mountains of distorted metal, bursting into shrapnel the size of cruisers, releasing a hellish mixture of plasma and superheated material. Material that had been computer cores, weapon systems, and crew. Material that had been the structural pillars, resting the ship's obscene mass on the fusion reactor. Though drained from the warp across the Korrats Ridge, it still generated the energy equivalent of a red dwarf's stellar core, a core now without that critical counterweight confining its elemental might. Harnessed, it could warp hundreds of light-orbits of space. Unleashed, it tore through the fragmented remains of the ship it had provided propulsion for, enveloping the gigantic scene of mayhem in a blinding sphere of undiscerning destruction.

The scattered tiny dots—ships the carrier had launched immediately after its arrival, some of them capital ships in their own right—were barely visible and gave the only comparison and sense of scale next to the cataclysm that had been their command ship just moments before. Many of them failed to outrun the fury of the fusion shock wave and burst into tiny embers before being consumed by the expanding sphere. The first wave launched gained enough distance to give their crews time to raise shields to withstand the storm of radiation and debris, only to be preyed on by the arriving EsChii ships. The Aloo Dashaad were out of formation, a force by numbers only, many ships damaged, all crews shocked and confused, and not one commander being trained to fight any battle in which the Ancestrate's fleet did not have vastly superior numbers. Through the intensity of the telemetry of two fleets fighting at the edge of a nova-like explosion, Kel heard Vyoz's voice: "Mark as 'surrendered' who has their weapons powered down, destroy everyone else!"

The death toll was in the hundreds of thousands, but the Aloo Dash ship crews and ground forces that disintegrated in the outer Prral system did not remain the only casualties. Reports kept coming in about Shaajis Sya's fury knowing no limits and taking the lives of those whom she deemed responsible for the first major military loss her monarchy had suffered in two generations. In the Aloo Dash capital, high-ranking fleet officers and intelligence leaders were executed, branded for incompetence, negligence, and treason. EsChii intelligence on the central Aloo Dash worlds was incomplete, but enough gruesome images came in to paint the picture. After several spins, the reports stopped coming in, showing the tightening grip of the Ancestrate's counterespionage measures and news blackouts. It did not matter. Kel knew he had won—this round.

ΔΔΔ

"Why keep me in the dark?" asked Vyoz, sitting across from Kel in the First Councilor's office on EsChiip. "I understand the need for secrecy for such an operation, but it would have lifted a heavy weight off me had I known there was a grand plan —and we actually had a chance! I expected a fight to the death, with our deaths being the likely outcome!"

"I always have a plan…" said Kel, but Vyoz cut him off. "We are not talking about three tanks hidden in a hole in the desert here, Kel! We are talking about wagering the entire fleet on a single operative planting a bomb coming through or not! If that had not worked, the distance you kept us at in holding position would have severely limited our chances for a surprise attack!"

"You needed to keep your distance to be safe. We were not entirely sure about the blast radius of the bomb."

"We?" asked Vyoz. "Who is 'we'? It certainly did not include me!"

"The scientists developing the bomb, the bomb carriers —and I." Kel tried to stay calm and not push back against his friend's—justified—anger. He should have told Vyoz.

Before their return to the Nominate's capital, he had decided to come clean with Vyoz, to accept and endure the berating he would receive and tell him what happened. He also decided not to attempt explaining the emotional episodes he had experienced about Prral's temple district ever since they had first entered the subterranean chambers. He did not know how he could have explained it anyway, as he could not understand the phenomenon himself. When he had those episodes at night, while sleeping, he called them dreams; but what should he call them when he was awake? They were equally intense, but the emotional impression he received had expanded in scope. At first he was wandering through the temple, without clear direction or goal, then shared feelings emerged, beginning when the first set of bomb carrier volunteers had been equipped with their bombs.

"Why didn't you tell me?" Vyoz fixated on Kel, but the Maz Tiikiip's steely stare seemed broken.

"I don't know," said Kel. "I could cite security procedures, need-to-know protocols, and I'd even considered telling you that your fleet's behavior would only look believable to the Aloo Dashaad if all of you—including you—were not part of the plan...but, honestly, I just don't know why I did not tell you."

Kel looked down, the universal gesture of shame since the first human colonies. Vyoz was quiet, maybe considering fury or forgiveness.

"Where did we even get this weapon?" Vyoz broke his silence, not absolving Kel just yet, but Kel took it as a first step.

"From Prral," said Kel. "Remember when we reconned the temple ruins after the prisoner exchange?"

Vyoz nodded. Kel explained, "The expedition we organized to go back there discovered it. We wanted to find out why there had been an archaeological dig and who did the digging. The Keelaakaad always stuck to their story that it was not them. We are still not sure who was behind it, but we discovered something, and we are not certain if that's what the dig team was after. There was not much left inside those temple buildings. The buildings themselves were surprisingly sturdy and undamaged, but equipment or other items could be retrieved, at least that's what we thought."

"Did the ambushers have it on them?"

"No, but the dead scientist gave us the clue to finding it. One of our molecular xenobiologists found traces of a nano tech similar to fossilized organic material. On a hunch, she decided to rescan the fossilized traces and discovered they were not fossilized at all. They were on standby. They were kind of lifelike artificial particles at nano scale."

Vyoz's gaze turned blank, and Kel assumed he had lost him. "It is too biological to show up in a tech scanner and too technical to show up on a life scanner, if it shows up on a general security scanner at all. It is nano scale!"

Vyoz reconnected with the conversation. "OK, I get that it's perfect stuff to smuggle onboard an Ancestrate ship, but how do you make it explode with such a force as we have seen? Don't you need a lot of it?"

"That's the brilliant part," Kel said. "You don't! You need a few, and I mean as few as five to ten, particles. Our scientists figured out that these nanobots, or nano cells as they called them, can replicate."

Unimpressed, Vyoz asked, "Can't many nanobots self-replicate?"

"Yes, yes, but not like these things. They can replicate at an unimaginable speed! The explosion you saw, what blasted that carrier to pieces, was the nano cells replicating in an uncontrolled cascade!"

"How do you keep them stable, though?" Vyoz was still skeptical, and his expertise with military ordnance showed through his questions. "What is the trigger mechanism? If they are as volatile as you say, shouldn't they be out of control all the time?"

"They are usually not replicating at all. But the scientists found a mechanism—a nano switch they called it—activating the replication."

"The trigger!" said Vyoz.

Vyoz absorbed what Kel explained for a half-pass, then looked back at him. "These 'comrades' you had your prayer with wouldn't have anything to do with it? Like getting the bomb onto the Grandslaught Carrier?" His face lit up. "You placed bombs on all of them! I recall a dozen 'comrades' or so. You sent them to all Aloo Dash carriers! If this nano stuff is as potent as you say, you need only one per carrier."

"Fantastic memory, my friend," said Kel, "and spot-on analysis! We do have bombs on all enemy carriers indeed. Losing their entire invasion fleet would discourage most other nations, but I fear the Shaajis will have to save face and feel pressured to attack us again. We needed to make sure we could defend ourselves not only once."

"They will come back!" said Vyoz. "The last reports we received from field agents mentioned high-ranking officers calling on Shaajis Sya to send three or four carriers to set an example and burn our worlds. But they will have scanned their carriers now a hundred times and found and removed these bombs!"

"No, they won't," stated Kel, "because they will look in the wrong place. We equipped each bomb carrier with a device— a device resembling a bomb based on some interesting-looking but inert tech—a decoy. The actual bombs are the carriers themselves; they carry the few required seed nano particles in their brain stem and can trigger the explosion by focused thought."

10—DESPERATE MEASURES

"**I** have never seen an Assembly Member before. They never video stream anything from their oh-so-secretive chamber. What did he look like?" asked Ahma.

Kel knew he was in trouble; he should not have shared the fact that he had met with an Assembly of Oorkuu Member with the curious scientist.

Ahma Zhanyza: molecular xenobiologist, lecturer at the Nominate's academy of science, secret project leader for the nano cell explosive. Kel had been in love before, or so he thought, and always through his adult life found women attractive for a variety of reasons. Before the war with Keelaak, Kel had had a few relationships, some more serious than others, but none of those women had occupied his thoughts as much as Ahma.

He scolded himself for being the most distracted in his entire life when high-stake responsibility was given to him. His dreams about the temple and longing for Ahma were always on his mind. During the expedition to Prral, after an initial period of shyness and formal reservation toward her head of state, she had had more open and casual conversations with him. He admired her eye for detail—it was she who had put the find of the dead scientist and the cell-like machines together, discovering the nano cells and then unlocking their potential. She worked on the project without pause when it had become clear it would be the Nominate's only hope to survive the Aloo Dash onslaught. Ahma was all this and funny, with a mischievous smile he liked—but she was not interested in Kel at all. She found him pleasant, and the office he held and the things he did fascinating, but it was a friendly curiosity, no more. She enjoyed being close with the First Councilor, being a confidante in secret weapon programs, but Kel Chaada the man seemed only a friend to her.

Kel had tried. Like today, meeting after the work shifts at his First Councilor residence, he had arranged and set up many occasions where they would be away from others, away from work, and he had been as open about his feelings for her as he could open up to another human being. Her rejection had not been harsh; she had listened to his words and thanked him for his gestures, but she was firm and depressingly final when she explained in the warmest voice that she was in love with Daaw Krrua and, despite the differences they had, was going to stay with the archaeologist.

"Come on, tell me!" Ahma said. Kel shrugged off his thoughts and answered, without revealing the entire scope of the conversation with the Assembly Member: "I had never met one before, either. It was a virtual meeting, so I am not sure if it counts as 'met,' but I can describe him." Ahma fixated on him, impatient, gesturing for him to continue. "He looked like a very tall middle-aged man," Kel said, then paused, which drove her crazy.

"A tall man? Great, now I can vividly imagine this mysterious Oorkuu Ozh—thank you, Kel, all my questions about the people running our galaxy have finally been answered!"

"Well, that's just the thing. Besides his elongated limbs, he did not look special. He was formally clothed, he had cut hair, no beard, only wore the smallest visible insignia of the Assembly, and was soft-spoken. When you hear 'low-g human,' you think of the legendary solar sailors. But he did not seem special. There are millions of men like him!" *As there are billions of men like me*, Kel did not add.

The Assembly of Oorkuu Member had turned out to be no demigod, and the meeting had been disappointing. The Assembly of Oorkuu, the representative body of government for the human-settled galaxy, was at least somewhat mysterious for its citizens. Three hundred sixteen members did not represent any of them directly. Each member represented Honored Ground, a planet where the Honored had lived, survivors of the galacticide. Many younger nations, like the Nominate, did not have Honored Ground and therefore no representation in the Assembly. Most member nations had one representative, and only a few large nations had delegations. The Ancestrate of Aloo Dash had 80 members, one result of the relentless campaigns of planetary conquest and—so suspected many—a driving force behind them, to one day control galactic politics.

Pyaavuu Shiirde Prarrbo, 118th Member of the Assembly of Oorkuu, had looked at Kel with the mixture of benevolence and patronage many elders use when they look down on a child. When the Assembly had sanctioned the declaration of war by the Ancestrate of Aloo Dash against the Nominate, it had been not more than a formality for the galactic government, regulating interhuman conflicts by arbitrating their beginning and end; but staying out of conflicts otherwise. Critics of the Assembly pointed out that they and their creed promoted constant warfare. The Assembly never denied such allegations, explaining that the Madzuu Vrraa Nyuu, the creed "Strength Through Conflict," was the only way to avoid a second galacticide, that only a humankind equipped with large space fleets and populations steeled by armed struggle could ever stand a chance if the extra-galactic aggressors came back to the Akaa Upsa galaxy. The Assembly handled small regional conflicts like the Nominate's recent war against Keelaak as administrative matters, and they only reviewed and ratified final peace accords, sometimes altering details to align with their regulations. No First Councilor had ever spoken to an Assembly Member, let alone addressed the Assembly.

A war involving the Ancestrate of Aloo Dash, which stood for the Assembly's largest member delegation, was a different matter. Still, Pyaavuu had declined a meeting on Omech Chaa in person, but agreed to a virtual QE meeting. QE—quantum entanglement—was the fundamental principle used for faster-than-light communication, enabling real-time conversations across interstellar distances.

Both men sat across from each other at a virtual conference table, in a setting which Kel interpreted as a rendition of an Honored Ruin on Omech Chaa. After a few very formal introductions, Pyaavuu turned the conversation to the conflict: "We understand that the Nominate seeks an end of the hostilities but we are confused by the terms you propose. Could you please elaborate for me, First Councilor?"

"Of course, Assembly Member Prarrbo," said Kel with a friendly smile, eliciting no such expression from his counterpart. "We propose to end the war with a white peace, where neither the Ancestrate nor the Nominate have any territorial losses or gains, and no additional conditions or declarations will be allowed. Furthermore, there will be an Assembly-guaranteed truce between both nations for the next ten orbits."

Pyaavuu kept regarding Kel thoughtfully, and took some time to respond, likely to give his words more gravitas. "And this is the entire arrangement? No concessions or submission of any kind, First Councilor?"

"No," said Kel. "As the tactical victor of the only engagement in the conflict, the Nominate does not see any form of submission warranted. The Ancestrate attacked us, and we mounted a successful defense. We are seeking to formalize the current status of no territorial losses or gains by any party."

A shorter silence followed, then the Assembly Member spoke again: "Yes, you mounted an effective defense indeed, surprisingly so, and against an Aloo Dash capital fleet no less, but—and this is the important point—your proposal is based on the premise that you can repeat this feat, assuming that the rest of the Aloo Dash fleet cannot succeed where the first wave failed. Some could look at this proposal and think that you are trying to get out of an ongoing conflict because you had one lucky battle. That is not how this works. The Ancestrate is quite certain a next battle will have a different outcome and expect this war to end with nothing but your unconditional submission."

"So, you talked to the Ancestrate already, Assembly Member? I assumed the Nominate's proposal needed to go through the Assembly Chamber first before it got presented to Aloo Dash."

Pyaavuu Shiirde Prarrbo looked furious, as if Kel-the-child had just scolded his elder for breaking his own rules. "We conduct our business as we see fit! You cannot possibly think that your small upstart nation has a realistic chance to prevail. All you have done with your surprise victory is to upset the Shaajis and make her vow for much harsher conditions for submission than they normally would ask for. The best we can do for you is negotiate a submission without including reparations or reprisals for the destruction of the Grandslaught Carrier!"

The stance of the Assembly was very much what Kel had feared. Small nations, once seen as "worthy" of submission to the might of the Ancestrate, were expected not to challenge it. But challenge it, he would.

"The Shaajis's assessment is wrong, and so is yours, Assembly Member Prarrbo. We can repeat the destruction of an Aloo Dash carrier, anytime and anywhere. The Ancestrate's forces, despite their huge numbers and impressive ships, have not been updated in 50 orbits. They rely on doctrines formulated by Mnazkash the Subjugator two generations ago. Small and nimble nations like the Nominate have long expected a resurgence of the Ancestrate's expansion and developed new tactics and new devastating weapons like the one demonstrated during the Battle of Prral." He made it sound like their victory resulted from many orbits of research and planning, while they simply had gotten lucky with the nano cell discovery at the temple. "We therefore are ready and able to continue defensive, and if need be aggressive, warfare against the Ancestrate of Aloo Dash—until our peace conditions are met!"

The Assembly Member lost any remaining restraint, being

confronted with what felt to him like a dictate of next steps. "You are mad! Your conditions met? You do not set any conditions; the Assembly does that! Be glad if they do not destroy your worlds! At this time, the Shaajis accepting your submission would be a mercy! You want to end the war on your terms? You will have to win it!"

ΔΔΔ

"He has gone mad!" Ahma Zhanyza exclaimed.

Kel's brief joy upon seeing her at the portal of his official residence vanished when he saw her distraught face.

"Come in," he said, leading her to the main living room. She had been there three times before for friendly, casual visits, but their togetherness had never gone beyond a fleeting touch of their hands or a mouthed kiss for a good-bye. "Would you like a drink?" he asked.

"A glass of briir." She did not hesitate to take him up on his offer, underlining her level of distress. She gulped half the generous pour Kel handed her. "Daaw—he wants to go public! We had a terrible fight, rehashing all the arguments we had before about the nano bomb."

"He was against it from the beginning," said Kel, "but would he really...go public?" Kel meant to say "be a traitor" but chose not to upset Ahma further. The secret program she was leading, resulting in a remarkable weapon system that could give them a chance to prevail against the Ancestrate, was top secret, and although not an official team member, Daaw Krrua knew it existed and what it was about.

"He has gone mad!" repeated Ahma. "He said he could no longer live with the knowledge of it weighing on his conscience and that he would do all of us a favor if he dragged it into a public spotlight for a public discussion. He argued even that when the Ancestrate learned about it, they might reconsider attacking us!"

"That is crazy," said Kel. "They would be alarmed, take

precautions, and likely destroy our only chance for defense, but we could never deter the Ancestrate when they had set their sights on a target. This would never happen!"

"He can be very naïve at times," said Ahma. "It can be charming, but it can also drive you insane. He wants to do what in his view a 'good man' would do."

Kel took some time to respond, walking in a circle around the seating arrangement where Ahma had settled down, emptying her glass, then looking at him in desperation. "What are we going to do?"

"When did he tell you he wants to go public?" asked Kel. "And where is he now?"

"I came here right away. We had our fight a shift ago, maybe less. He went to the academy, his office, I assume. He goes there when he is stressed. His sample collection seems to calm him down. He…"

"Did he say he wanted to go public in general terms?" asked Kel. "Or was he specific, as in 'I am going to contact so-and-so' or 'I am to make an open video stream'?"

"No. No, he does not do any video streaming, and I don't think he knows anyone who would run such a story. He said it like I told you: 'I will go public!'"

"Do you think sitting in his office for a few shifts will calm him down, make him see how crazy this is?"

Ahma shook her head, tearing up. "I don't know."

Kel offered for her to stay longer, and, unlike the other three times, felt relieved when she insisted on going home. He joined her for another drink until her auto-speeder arrived. "We will talk to him first thing tomorrow," he said. "Daaw is not an idiot. He will come around."

She whispered, "Thank you!" and climbed into the speeder. The door closed, and the vehicle hovered away. Kel was already running inside before it vanished into the dark of night, looking for his secure communicator. He found it and contacted the first name on the list.

"Yes?" a familiar voice answered.

"Vyoz, it's Kel. Assemble a team! We got a problem."

"Now? What team?"

"A team you can trust! I have a no-questions-asked task for you, and the time window closes tonight."

△△△

The second gigantic carrier exploding—obliterated in a fusion maelstrom before reaching the Keedz Bend darkstring terminus on the Aloo Dash side of the Korrats Ridge—created even more of a shock for the Aloo Dash military than the first loss of a Grandslaught Carrier.

Kel was certain the Ancestrate had found the decoy bombs and defused their complex but useless innards. The enemy's carrier fleet scanned over and over for any other foreign objects, assuring the Shaajis her second attempt at subduing the Nominate was going to work as expected. An enemy striking back at the Ancestrate in their own space must have traumatized the unchallenged expansionist empire. The Assembly of Oorkuu was now in a bind to increase their diplomatic efforts, their envoy refusing the first request for arbitration, sanctioning a continued use of sabotage missions against the Aloo Dash fleet. Kel had expected the Assembly to contact the Nominate again soon after the second explosion.

Two Assembly Members waiting for him in a virtual meeting room convinced him he was right. He stepped into the avatar projection area and joined the meeting. Kel noticed a change in virtual decor, the conference table now standing in front of what he recognized from video streams. He had never been to the Great Assembly Chamber on Omech Chaa. Kel did not recognize the Assembly Members present this time. Pyaavuu Shiirde Prarrbo's absence was a sign for the Assembly seeking to start the negotiations fresh and without feelings of contempt between the parties. After the formal introductions, the two Assembly Members congratulated Kel and the Nominate for an effective defense against a strong enemy, lauded how this was a great example of the creed working, showing how conflict turned a loose conglomerate of mining companies into a real, strong interplanetary nation.

When they felt they had dispensed enough praise, they turned to the real topic. "First Councilor, we would like to discuss the possibility of arbitrating a cease-fire agreement, initially unconditional, similar to your proposal, with the option of—in time—turning the agreement into a full peace accord."

"A cease-fire?" asked Kel. "How binding will that be?"

"If signed, the Assembly will enforce it," they assured. "It will give us time to find a more permanent diplomatic solution!"

"Assembly Members, correct me if I am wrong, but cease-fire resolutions are not being voted for in the Assembly Chamber, they are not binding like a peace accord, co-signed by the Assembly, would be." Kel knew a cease-fire agreement was worthless. The Shaajis could break it any time. A broken cease-fire resulted only in EsChii having a reason for war against the Ancestrate, for a war being fought already. "If the Aloo Dash government wants to negotiate a cease-fire with the Nominate, we can do this directly between the two nations, while the Assembly can put the peace accord, which we still seek, up for vote in the Assembly Chamber."

The Assembly Members' facial expressions had frozen; no doubt they had paused their video stream and were talking to one another right now.

Kel did not have to wait for long, as they returned only a few moments later. "My dear First Councilor, unfortunately you are not in a position to request any of this. We are aware that your government had directly negotiated with the Electorate of Keelaak in your recent conflict, but we are talking about the Ancestrate of Aloo Dash here. There is no institutional decision-making, there is only the Shaajis. The Shaajis will not meet with you to discuss…anything. Also, the Assembly vote you are proposing can only be initiated by a member nation with at least one representative in the Assembly, of which, sadly, you have none."

"So, an Assembly Member could force the vote for the peace accord the Nominate is seeking?"

"No, First Councilor, only the Nominate could do this in theory, if you were represented in the Assembly. You cannot get anyone to speak on your behalf."

It was Kel's turn to pause the meeting. He took some time to rearrange his office chair, pretending that he had deliberated with his advisors. Kel did not need advice, and he had been alone in his office when he joined the meeting, he knew what he was going to say, and he was very much looking forward to seeing how the two men would react.

"Nobody would have to speak on our behalf. I hereby request, formally and as part of our permanent meeting record, the initiation of Membership for the Nominate of EsChii in the Assembly of Oorkuu."

The Assembly Members were not as flustered as Kel recalled Pyaavuu had been, but they were both surprised on the borderline of being shaken. "But you would need to have Honored Ground, First Councilor, you must know that!"

"Indeed," continued Kel. "We will submit the Nominate planet of Prral for an Assembly inspection with the goal of it being declared Honored Ground. Our—well documented—expeditions have revealed elaborate structures dated around the time of the galacticide, which are, without a doubt, Honored Ruins, and even more importantly—we discovered Honored Remains!"

Kel could tell they would have loved to deny his request on the spot, but they could not, caught in the net of their own rules. Honored Remains were a sensational discovery. None had been found for a hundred orbits, and even Assembly Members could not ignore this without a thorough investigation. The Assembly would have to send a delegation to Prral and study his claims.

Kel closed, "We are ready to welcome the Assembly's commission on Prral as soon as possible!"

∆∆∆

"Academy of Science archaeologist found dead in his office." The headline found little attention, and the articles about the death of Daaw Krrua had few readers, all public attention being diverted to the Nominate soon joining the galactic government.

Kel sighed. Vyoz and his commandos had eliminated a potential leak, jeopardizing the Nominate's secret weapon. The same death also killed a rival. As much as he tried to tell himself that his instructions were vague and did not specifically include "kill him," it was still clear what was the desired outcome. The notion that now, after Daaw's death, Ahma would come to Kel, and stay, was a primitive, naïve hope, but it was all he got. He wished he had never set a foot on Prral, the place where everything began, including his first meeting with Ahma, and a place which cast its influence over him and everybody around him still. He dimmed the light in his living room and closed his eyes.

The thought that the ancient temple district on Prral was not a temple at all had crossed Kel's mind after the successful battle against the first Grandslaught Carrier the Ancestrate of Aloo Dash had sent. The Nominate had set up their command center in the most suitable room, a room that was so suitable for the purpose that its staggered floor structure reminded him of an ancient control room more than any other chamber in prehistoric religious buildings anywhere. Stone walls and carved subterranean chamber architecture were misleading, not designed to impress deities through worship, not used due to lack of sophistication in metallurgy; no, these ruins were once a purpose-built military base. Using the indigenous rock only amplified the stealthy overall construction and clever mix of building materials to make the large buildings invisible to scanners from space. The room they used as a makeshift command room had been a command room before, over 1,200 orbits ago, at the time of the galacticide.

After many orbits of terror, most of the Kubuu Ksiw had left, possibly returning to their unknown realm beyond the galactic darksphere, the boundary around the Akaa Upsa galaxy that warp drives could not effectively cross. The technology they had used for this feat remained as mysterious as their motives for leaving. Few smaller Kubuu Ksiw ships had stayed behind, lurking in the outer galactic arms, occasionally attempting raids on human colonies. The primary task of the Assembly of Oorkuu's Levy Fleet, ships of all types contributed by the Assembly Member nations, was to intercept these Kubuu Ksiw raiders and prevent them from getting close to any incorporated planet. For two generations these space battles had been won by the Assembly forces, chasing off the raiders or—rarely— destroying them, always at the cost of significant losses for the human fleets, a sobering reminder of the technological advantage the small left-behind Kubuu Ksiw forces still held over the best humanity had created.

The Honored had not only lived on their Prral base, they had died there, too. Two of the three chambers were found opened and empty—opened either by force or deterioration of the door mechanism, but a third chamber was found intact, unopened since the days of the galacticide, so perfectly sealed that it had preserved over a thousand orbits what had never been found in the Wel Edge region before—Honored Remains. The two open chambers had yielded only small human bone fragments, possibly leftovers from local wildlife scavenging for food in the chambers accessible from the surface. The closed chamber contained partially decomposed, yet complete, bodies of more than 100 adults and a few children. The Honored had saved the human species; these Honored in the chamber would now save the Nominate. The Assembly of Oorkuu delegation would only need to confirm and officially announce what the Nominate's scientist had already determined beyond a reasonable doubt: Prral was Honored Ground. Prral was going to give the Nominate of EsChii membership in the galactic government, a seat at the table of the great nations in the Akaa Upsa galaxy.

Tomorrow it would be made official. The greatest moment in the history of the Nominate. Ahma would not celebrate, as she was grieving, mourning her idolized mentor and lover, who died under suspicious circumstances. Killed by people sent by a petty envier. A lifetime would not be enough to wash this blood off Kel's hands.

Unless...

11—ASSEMBLY MEMBER

C ould anything still go wrong with the initiation into the Assembly of Oorkuu?

It did not require a vote by its current members; Assembly rules guaranteed that nations with Honored Ground could send representatives to the chamber of the galactic government. The Nominate of EsChii would be such a nation soon. The Assembly of Oorkuu convened in the immense elliptical main chamber, a white dome glistening in the bright light provided by Omech Chaa Alook 1, the system's massive central star. Vast parks and gardens matching the scale of the building and 316 spires surrounded the chamber dome. The grand scale of the galactic government seat dated back to its optimistic founding days. Humankind took to the stars again after the Kubuu Ksiw invasion force had left, discovered the first Honored planets, and everyone assumed there were going to be thousands of these sanctuary worlds coming back together to build a new galactic civilization, seeking representation in the new Assembly. After the initial discoveries, it turned out that these sanctuaries were rare and surviving Honored even rarer. They had sought refuge all over the spiral arm of the human-settled galaxy, and it took almost 1,000 orbits to find 316 of those places, resulting in the same low number of Assembly Members today, meeting in the chamber hall designed for several thousand delegates.

Kel, Vyoz, and the other government appointees at the Nominate Plaza building were watching the Assembly

Members, clad in their formal ceremonial clothing, taking their distributed seats in the chamber. The ceremony video streamed to most settled planets, excluding the Ancestrate of Aloo Dash, which was protesting a new member being added during wartime by censoring the broadcast. Kel, like most galactic denizens, was watching images from the hallowed chamber hall for the first time in his life. The Assembly of Oorkuu held almost no public events, sessions, or hearings. Representatives or spokespeople distributed most galactic governance, not the convened body of all members. A new member nation was momentous and galactic news. Few outside of the Wel Edge region had heard of the Nominate, but now the young nation was famous for having become the latest target of Aloo Dash aggression, even more so for their effective defense and victorious space battle.

The Assembly came to order, the ceremonial chamber chairperson recognizing the members and the leaders of the delegation to Prral, who had to certify the Honored Ground claim.

"Assembly Members!" The spokesperson's voice was shaking, intimidated by the impressive display of the inner sanctum of the galactic government or by knowing that billions of people were watching. "Please hear the findings of our Assembly-appointed expedition to the planet Prral, and in particular its large structure complex, which we will refer to as 'the base.'" The spokesperson gave some details about the Prral system, its single star, age, the planet's geology, and general location of the ruins.

"While the layout and structure of this base allowed for several interpretations, a hidden military post seemed the most plausible. Nuclear dating of the building materials put the entire complex solidly in the era of the galacticide. The most striking evidence for the Honored Ground claim brought forward by the Nominate of EsChii were the human remains found in what can be best described as a burial chamber, a substructure of the complex, dating also to the era of the galacticide. The carefully and respectfully examined corpses of 126 humans showed the following characteristics: Ninety percent of the adults had died from some form of trauma consistent with mortal combat wounds, children had died from preventable childhood diseases, and the remaining adults had various causes of death. No adult had been older than 60 orbits."

Murmuring in the ranks of the other appointees seated around Kel showed that although it was common knowledge that people before the galacticide had not lived as long as their contemporary offspring, it was still shocking to realize how short their lifespan had been.

All of Kel's great-great-grandparents had lived past 100 orbits, and he planned to be around for at least 150. He could not imagine how they spent half of their short lives on a lightsail, on endless flights to reach sanctuaries like Prral, traversing unwarped space slower than light speed. "All this," said the spokesperson, "is consistent with the era's continued Kubuu Ksiw threat, level of technology, medicine in particular, suboptimal living conditions as witnessed on comparable Honored Ground planets, and the absence of post-galacticide telomere therapy. This strengthens the case. The genetic makeup of the deceased, however, irrefutably confirms the claim. Our modern society has a relatively low genetic variability compared to the human civilizations existing before the galacticide. With an estimated 99.99 percent of all humans perishing within less than 20 orbits, most of the 28 human races went extinct. We found 16 of those races among the deceased on Prral, with a broad genetic variance even between members of the same race. Bodies showed clear signs of zero-g and low-g living condition specializations, as well as standard-g skeletal forms. When reconstructible, extracted genomes showed many mutations based on long, consistent exposure to cosmic and solar radiation, typical for humans living on pre-shield-technology space vessels lacking appropriate protection against common sources of radiation encountered during prolonged space travel as well as an inability to create consistent gravitational fields."

The spokesperson paused for effect, having rediscovered his poise and self-confidence after rattling down the findings of his team, preparing for the conclusive finale. "Considering this overwhelming evidence, this Assembly delegation therefore concludes that the Nominate planet of Prral is now to be considered and referred to as Honored Ground, the base as described is declared an Honored Ruin, and the 126 human corpses as Honored Remains. It has been the distinct privilege of this delegation to be in the presence of our most revered progenitors during our investigation. We hereby certify the claim and propose to this Assembly to ask the owner of the Honored Ground, the Counciliary Nominate of EsChii, to name their representative to join this Assembly."

He described the procedures to reseal the burial chamber to preserve the Honored's gravesite, but the rest of his assessment got lost in the cheers of the appointees and their staff. Vyoz hugged Kel, smiling more broadly than ever before. "We did it! We are a Wel Edge mining conglomerate playing nation no more, we will sit with the big boys and girls very soon." Kel hugged him back, then looked around at his fellow E EsChii, celebrating their nation's ascension to the galactic government. "Do you have any ideas who we are going to send to the Assembly as our representative yet?"

"Yes," said Kel. "I will go myself."

ΔΔΔ

"Unprecedented!" the Assembly of Oorkuu called the self-appointment of Kel Chaada. "Scandalous" was the word they used during the first internal meeting of the initiation committee. Opinions in EsChii news streams ranged from liking the idea of their most popular leader stepping up into the midst of the galactic power brokers, to questioning the legality of a blatant power grab.

Kel leaned back in the comfortable chair in his small, but

private, compartment on the shuttlecraft. The strong opinions of the Assembly committees did not matter to him. The Nominate was still under threat by the Ancestrate of Aloo Dash, and he wanted to be certain that a vote for a white peace moved forward. Kel had a healthy ego, and he was ready to admit this, but he was also the only EsChii citizen of some renown in the human-settled galaxy, which—so he hoped—gave his voice more weight in the Assembly Chamber than that of an unknown appointee. The Assembly could protest all they wanted; each new member of the Assembly had full discretion in how to go about selecting their representative. The Counciliary Nominate's hierarchical appointment system left it to the First Councilor to appoint all interstellar diplomatic personnel and international representatives. The only requirement was EsChii citizenship. Kel, born on the capital planet EsChiip proper, had the right to appoint himself, unprecedented or scandalous or not.

"All passengers, please prepare for atmospheric entry!" The shuttle turned for its final descent and Omech Chaa, the Assembly world, came back into sight in the small external viewport. Kel tightened his seat belt.

Vyoz did not take the news of Kel's departure well and appeared to be angry and disappointed about his friend leaving the Nominate, EsChii, and him behind. Kel had not expected such a powerful response. Maybe some sadness about not being able to see each other often anymore, but not the taken-aback sulkiness Vyoz had treated him with. Maybe he deserved it. Kel knew that his new office would take him far away from his home planet, and he felt ready to leave. He asked himself if it was heartless to march forward along this path he had chosen, without hesitation and without seeking counsel from anyone, including his trusted advisors. Vyoz had a reason to be disappointed, Kel had to admit. His friend wanted to be entrusted with knowing the next steps, and just like when Kel had excluded him from the nano weapon program or the battle plans against the Ancestrate, he felt left out once more. Kel had hoped there was going to be an opportunity for the two to reconcile before he left for Omech Chaa. He had pushed for an initiation into the Assembly as soon as possible so he could propose a binding peace to be voted on. When the Assembly arranged his travel on short notice, Kel missed the opportunity to set things right in person, both with Ahma and Vyoz, but vowed to QE-call them as soon as he arrived at his new home.

The shuttle was shaking a little. "Three passes to touchdown at Ngee Dakeedwem spaceport."

It was going to be an impressive home for Kel, the 317th Assembly of Oorkuu Member. They would build a new spire to house his administrative staff and any specialists or advisors he required and also to serve as a palatial residence for himself. Through the gardens, the Assembly Chamber would be in short walking distance, all under the protective bubble of the shield dome, protecting the heart of galactic government from every external threat, including orbital bombardment. Vast underground archives stored physical artifacts and electronic copies of everything important the human species had created since the galacticide. Buildings with all imaginable distractions, cultural and athletic entertainment worthy of a large planetary capital, were next to the inner core of Assembly Chamber and gardens, ensuring the well-being of the Assembly Members for the time of their service in the chamber—a lifetime of service. Assembly of Oorkuu Members served for the rest of their lives, the long term being the primary reason for galactic stability and the wondrous resurgence of human civilization after the galacticide. Unlike in most planetary nation governments, the Assembly Members never had to turn their focus on reelection campaigns, getting reappointed, or having to deal with other distracting procedures concerning a renewal of their term. Galactic policy-making was aimed at fulfilling grand visions for a reemerging species, not being bogged down by short-term-gain populist governance. Giving one unique perk to each of the 317 galactic leaders pushed the advantage of long-term policy-making to the extreme.

The Honored Ground living on the moon Omech Chaa had become the legendary refounders of all human civilization in the galaxy and first Assembly Members. They were said to have lived unnaturally long lives, the original inventors of the most mysterious gift all Assembly Members now enjoyed—immortality.

12—THE RITE

"We have your procedure scheduled in two rotations, Assembly Member. I know you have been briefed about it several times by now, but I cannot stress enough that you are not allowed to eat anything for six shifts before the procedure!" the medical assistant instructed.

The procedure, and the surrounding details, had been explained to Kel many times indeed. It was the last step, the true initiation, to the Assembly of Oorkuu, and one of the galaxy's best-kept secrets: Oosech Wesech, the immortality rite. From the confidential briefings, it almost sounded to Kel like a religious ceremony, involving mysterious and not-well-described technology dating back to the original Honored, turning his mortal body into a self-rejuvenating, resilient powerhouse of health. The immortality effect was relative; he would not become indestructible. Severe trauma, deadly to a normal human, would kill him as well. He could not survive a fall from his skyward-growing spire residence, and gun projectiles would not bounce off his skin. He would, however, not age any further, and never suffer an illness again. His bones would stay elastic, his muscles would not atrophy, and his brain cells not degenerate. Forever. He caught himself contrasting his —exciting—fate to "normal" humans, a species he was still going to be part of for two more rotations, before entering the quasi-eternal realm of the Assembly of Oorkuu Members. His first secretary had shown him all the major buildings and sights after his arrival.

"And this is the spire of Lotnuuk Rrupteemaa, the first immortal to serve in the Assembly of Oorkuu. He has been a member of our galactic government since 755 AEG—after the end of the galacticide—and was the first to undergo the rite of immortality, the Oosech Wesech. He will be easy to spot in the grand chamber, being one of the tallest Assembly Members, giving us a glimpse of a bygone era, when most of the offspring of the solar sailors had the typical elongated-limbs low-g physique."

Sru Mayoop, the first of the secretaries assigned to Kel Chaada, was acting as his tour guide and beamed with pride, showcasing the wonders of his home world, Omech Chaa, usually referred to as "the Assembly world" in most parts of the galaxy.

"That's over 450 orbits, wow!" Kel had said, faking interest, not in the mood for tourist trivia. He had come here to save his nation, not to admire architecture. It was hard to ignore the grandeur of the spires, though. Each of the 316 buildings located around the enormous central park containing the grand chamber had its unique design, but they all followed a pattern of tall, twisted, almost organic-looking towers. They served as office buildings and majestic living quarters for the individual Assembly Members.

"Indeed," said Sru. "Four hundred sixty orbits, to be precise. Lotnuuk Rrupteemaa's long term and service to the people of the galaxy is an embodiment of the second pillar of a reemerged human society: a stable government. A government freed of the shortsightedness of term limits, political campaigns designed to garner public support, leadership able to focus on the grand scale of guidance and decision making with galaxy-wide, long-lasting impact."

Kel found Sru's style of speaking impressive, but too elaborate and dramatically over-the-top for Kel's taste. Sru was going to be his chief speech writer, part of his future duties as first secretary to the soon-to-be Assembly Member. Kel had to remind himself of working with Sru on his upcoming speech for the Assembly—his first. It should sound a bit more like himself, polished, yes, but also straightforward and heartfelt.

"That was a great introduction to the localities, Sru," said Kel. "Thank you! I think I need to rest a little before we meet with the rest of the team tomorrow and get started on the vote proposal."

If Sru was disappointed, he hid it well. "I guess you noticed the sky, appointed Assembly Member?"

Kel did not know what Sru was talking about and feared his ignorance would show that he had missed parts of Sru's lectures, being preoccupied with his own thoughts. "The sky?"

"Yes, it turns from white, when we are illuminated by the main star, to orange, when we are illuminated by the first binary, to red, like now. In a few passes, our host planet, the gas giant Omech Chaa Sok, will rise and start filling the late rotation sky. Time to sleep for the locals!"

Sru smiled. Kel knew many human-settled worlds were not planets, but moons. Omech Chaa was the first one he had visited. "Will it get much darker than this? I thought this world had no proper night."

"That is correct," said Sru. "For most of the bright part of the rotation, you will see one or two of our stars in the sky, sometimes even all three. When we turn toward the planet, light is less intense, but the reflected light off the high-albedo, bright gas giant is still bright enough to give the illusion of daylight. I know the absence of a proper dark night is confusing for newcomers, but you will get used to it."

Kel had so many questions, but few details were available about the actual immortality procedure. The assistant initiators described it as short and painless, but with possible side effects like nausea. Maybe that was why he was not supposed to have anything in his stomach, so he would not soil the holy floor of the Oosech Wesech chamber. Typically, new initiates had a rest period of a few rotations after the procedure, but he had, with success, insisted on immediate admission so he could bring his peace proposal forward.

Kel was restless. He had spent the two rotations prior to the immortality rite in his temporary apartment, which served as office and living quarters, while the 317th spire was being erected within walking distance. On news streams from EsChii, he had followed the appointment procedures for his successor, the new First Councilor. Vyoz Vyooma had been the military's favorite once more, but several other candidates emerged, planetary representatives and local favorites of the different Nominate worlds. In most rounds of the appointment procedures, the individual electors only voted for themselves, with Vyoz getting no votes at all. Eventually an unknown administrator of the newly incorporated Nominate planet Prral rose through the ranks of the appointees and won the last round. Prral was now the Nominate's most prestigious planet. Although uninhabited, its Honored Ground status moved it into the spotlight of public attention and national pride, dethroning EsChiip itself. Lacking a real population on her administered planet, Prral had no interest groups to please or political factions to cater to and offered neutral, clean-slate leadership after Kel's short and tumultuous stint as head of state. He had offered to Vyoz to give him a public endorsement but not received any response.

The apartment door buzzer pulled him out of his thoughts and away from the video streaming terminal. The initiators were here.

ΔΔΔ

Would Kel still feel...human at the end of the rotation?

Wearing a plain white robe, a more minimalistic version of the traditional Assembly robes, Kel walked so slowly that it felt awkward, led, flanked, and followed by the more elaborately dressed initiators. Making their way to the Oosech Wesech, this group of men and women would lead the ceremony and operate the technology required to make humans immortal, not knowing how the machines they used work. The true secrets were kept by the Assembly, and the Assembly alone. The room the initiators led him into was many times larger than required for the apparatus standing in its center, an architectural theme he had noticed all over the Assembly Grounds—everything was inefficiently immense, lending weight by volume for even mundane items and procedures. The Oosech Wesech was a rare ritual. It was about to be performed for the first time in the lifetime of the young-looking initiators, and only for the 317th time in post-galacticide history.

The apparatus looked more functional and less ceremonial than Kel had expected, and the lead initiator made him stand at its center. An open rectangular metal frame surrounded him. The ceremony began with some chorus-like chants, spoken in traditional Old Galactic, the language of the spacefarers and solar sailors of a lost era, a crude language stemming from the need to harmonize space travel across the myriad of civilizations before the galacticide. One initiator led the chanting, then the group followed with a repetition. The only thing asked of Kel was to stand still, until they reached the end of the liturgy, which translated into asking him if he was ready to receive the gifts of the Oosech Wesech, and if he was doing so out of his own free will. Learning the Old Galactic phrase for "I do" had been easy, and despite an increasing anxiety, he responded loud and clear when the time came: "Iir duvem."

The initiators strapped a breathing mask over his head and secured it over his mouth and nose. It did not release any odor different from the air in the room as far as he could tell, so he probably was not being gassed. Several flat, but rounded, cold, metallic devices—sensors, maybe?—were attached to the palms of both hands, his neck, and his temples. A sound and vibrations emanated from below his feet, reminding Kel of sitting next to a power generator, a flashback to his days as a hover tank commander. Did the frame create a force field that induced the transformation? Were the devices in place to monitor vital signs? Would the breathing mask keep him from passing out?

No further appendages were added, and he was still standing on his own feet, so the procedure would probably not make him lose consciousness. New immortals falling flat on their faces was likely not what this ceremony was about to portray. He tried to push these thoughts aside and focus on what was happening. The lead initiator nodded at Kel, reassuring him that preparations were complete. He nodded back.

The initiators resumed their chanting, with a new cascade of traditional ritual phrases. The vibrations intensified, but apart from those, Kel felt nothing. They had warned him that the transition would not provide any intense sensations, and he was disappointed that this was indeed the case. The air flowing through the breathing mask became moister and had a hint of moldy odor when the chants reached their ceremonial conclusion. With the abrupt end of the chorus, the vibrations stopped. Was that it? He felt nothing new, nothing he had not felt before, but he was hungry. Once his mind focused on the fact that he had not eaten during this rotation, it was all he could think about. He hungered for a large, opulent meal with lots of meats.

The initiators started removing the devices, and the young female lead initiator brushed slightly against him while she removed the breathing mask. Kel noticed how young and attractive she was, as if he had seen her for the very first time. Hunger overcame him, an insatiable appetite for flesh, to be eaten, to be taken, and a whirlwind of images of orgiastic consumption raced through his consciousness.

"Do you want to try it next?" he asked her with a predatory smile.

"Oh no, Assembly Member, it will take at least a hundred spins to reinitialize the Oosech Wesechaak, the machine. Besides, I am not worthy to receive the gift!"

"Says who?" probed Kel.

"I will lead you back to your chambers, Assembly Member," she said, and he could swear she smiled back at him.

"You must be hungry!"

13—GREAT SPEECH

What did people mean when they said, "I feel like a new person"?

They could not have felt as rejuvenated, alert, vigorous, and virile as Kel felt that moment. The young initiator had slipped out of his apartment already, leaving Kel still wondering if she had been a willing participant or organized entertainment to go along with his meal. The meal—heaps of meaty dishes of exotic varieties; Kel ate it all. He had never eaten that much, been with a woman that long, followed by short, deep sleep, then awoken feeling so fresh, clear-minded, and all around satisfied like he did this rotation. Maybe the few, rather dull Assembly Members he had met so far had gotten used to this and took it for granted, but if this was what it felt like being immortal, he was going to enjoy every spin. "Increased appetite" was among the list of potential side effects he had gotten briefed on, but nobody had prepared him for the all-encompassing desire to consume he had felt at the very end of the ceremony. He wondered if he would feel like that again and hoped he would.

Now he was hungry for his first appearance in the Assembly Chamber, forcing a peace agreement to get voted on. The two secretaries he had been assigned so far, the core of an expanding entourage, walked with him from his quarters to the main portal of the grand chamber to join the Omechaak, the formal Assembly of all immortals. Sru Mayoop, his first secretary, had helped him formalize the wording, but at its core the next steps would be simple: Before the Assembly Chamber session, they had put his request to speak, address the Assembly, and give a verbal description about what he proposed to have a vote about. The vote was going to be a yes-no vote, either for adopting a binding peace agreement between the Ancestrate and the Nominate, or against. Voting was electronic, but the results would be shown for all to see.

While all the Assembly Grounds, the spires, and the communal buildings were impressive, the main chamber was downright intimidating. Reaching the main portal, Kel needed to say good-bye to his staff—only Assembly Members were allowed in the building.

The main portal was large enough to allow a Nominate frigate to fly straight into the building. The optimistic miscalculation about how many Honored Members it needed to accommodate could not entirely explain the chamber's scale. Someone had designed it to minimize the individual and aggrandize the institution of a galactic government.

Would he, Kel Chaada, plasma shield engineer and former tank commander, find the voice to sway this institution?

$$\triangle\triangle\triangle$$

Kel followed the instructions he had memorized to find his seat at the far end of the building, forcing him to parade along in front of all other Assembly Members. They all had known one another for many orbits. He was the first newcomer in a long time, and everyone's eyes rested on him. Kel tried to shrug off the stage fright and strode to his assigned seat with dignity and purpose—or as best as he could imitate them. The portal closed as he arrived at his seat. He sat down and used a tiny ear set providing audio and auto-translation, the virtual stream helmet being reserved for more-abstract presentations or discussions. His case was not abstract; it was straightforward and simple. Kel could not clearly see if his fellow Assembly Members had taken their seats already or not. The white robes and the white walls, floors, and seating blended together. He heard the session being called to order and a short list of announcements, ending with Kel himself being introduced.

"We extend our warmest welcome to our new esteemed colleague, the sole representative of the Counciliary Nominate of EsChii, 317th Member of the Assembly of Oorkuu: Kel Chaada," said the voice, adding, "who has brought a vote to today's session. Assembly Member Chaada, you have the floor."

Kel had hoped the Assembly would address a few items before it was his turn, just to get used to the procedural back and forth, but it was his turn right away. Uncertain if anyone could see the gesture, he stood up, clearing his throat, before turning his audio on. He addressed his new colleagues, spoke a few words of appreciation for the institution of the Assembly, and then introduced his peace treaty proposal formally, with all the required descriptions and procedural content his team had helped him with. Last, he added a few personal lines about the people of EsChii holding no animosities against the Ancestrate of Aloo Dash but also pointing out their strong desire to keep their independence.

"With that, dear Assembly Members," he concluded, "I entrust the chance for lasting peace in the Wel Edge region, with Prral itself being the hallowed resting place of our Honored ancestors, in your capable hands!"

He wanted to sit down, but the applause held him back. The other Assembly Members, also standing, clapped their hands audibly through the now unmuted Assembly channel. It was nowhere near as impressive as the collective cheers he had experienced at his inauguration as First Councilor, but it still evoked pride to hear this chamber, a place he had seen for the first time today, fill with an ovation for him.

The voice came back. "Thank you, Assembly Member Chaada! I call the session back to order. We will now vote." The applause ended, and the Assembly Members sat back down, picked up their hand terminals, and cast their votes.

The galactic government had a reputation for being slow and inefficient, leaving Kel surprised at the expediency of supporting the peace treaty. A few passes after his speech, the chamber had confirmed support with 227 votes for the treaty. Kel assumed the large delegation of the Ancestrate of Aloo Dash and maybe a close ally or two made up the against votes.

Then his heart sank. The 227 votes were votes against! He feverishly double-checked the display and his own data stream. His proposal had not passed.

"Thank you, Assembly Members—the vote is now complete! As for the first proposed measure of the session, a peace treaty between the Ancestrate of Aloo Dash and the Nominate of EsChii, the majority voted 'No.' The state of war as defined by the rules of this Assembly will continue until one belligerent submits to the other. We now move to the second agenda item..."

ΔΔΔ

The vote was against.

No peace treaty. Kel Chaada had not saved EsChii. Making Prral Honored Ground, giving up leadership of the Nominate, giving up his friend, his former life—all for nothing. Kel did not follow the rest of the session, glad there was nothing else to vote on, not paying any attention to the discussion, his mind revolving around the lost vote. The session ended, and he remained seated, hoping for the other Assembly Members to disperse and leave, so he could return to his apartment unseen and lick the wounds of his failure in solitude.

His wish was not granted. The Assembly Members did not jump up and leave as he envisioned, but congregated together in groups, maybe in their delegations or social circles. To add to his agony, he saw one of the Assembly Members walking toward him. He recognized Pyaavuu Shiirde Prarrbo as he drew closer. Pyaavuu was the first Assembly Member Kel had ever talked to, and the last person he wanted to talk to right now.

"Assembly Member Chaada!" said Pyaavuu jovially, making his way up the gently sloped outer part of the chamber

98

hall with long strides of his elongated legs, arriving, sitting down next to Kel's near slumped-over body. "Not what you expected, I presume," he said, not triumphantly, but with a dose of condescension shining through. "Great speech, though! A breath of fresh air in these chambers!" His smile vanished without a trace when he turned to Kel. "I was trying to warn you about this peace proposal."

"Well, you failed," Kel snapped back. "I recall not being member of this club was holding us back from getting it voted on, not a general reluctance of the government to allow for any peace or protect anyone from the Ancestrate!"

"You got your vote," said Pyaavuu, "and through an impressive display of statecraft—finding genuine Honored Ground, Honored Remains, very impressive indeed—but it did not help you in the end, I believe we can agree on that. Where we disagree is on who needs protection from whom."

Kel looked back at him, angry and confused.

"You, my dear Assembly Member, assumed your little Nominate needed our help from the big bad Ancestrate." Pyaavuu put his smile on again. "But that is not the case. You have demonstrated, as surprisingly as forcefully, that you can take on the most feared weapon system in the galaxy, the Grandslaught Carrier. You have convinced me, and others, that you can repeat what you have done twice so far. If anyone needs protection, it might be the Ancestrate of Aloo Dash needing protection—from you!"

Kel's mind cleared, and he regained a stable mental stance. "The Levy Fleet!" he said, his piercing stare meeting Pyaavuu Shiirde Prarrbo's patronizing eye.

"The what?" Pyaavuu said with genuine surprise.

"You have failed today to protect your own fleet—the Levy Fleet! Every nation provides ships, but they are all irrelevant compared to the Grandslaught Carriers the Ancestrate adds to the Levy Fleet. Are you not worried that the little Nominate, as you called it, might blow up some more of these precious weapon systems, and a drained Aloo Dash navy will provide fewer of those to the Assembly fleet? You should have voted to protect the Ancestrate today, shouldn't you?"

Pyaavuu did not look surprised anymore, and the self-assured resting expression of his face returned. "You have joined this Assembly now, Kel Chaada, but you have much to learn. Many of us have been sitting and voting in this Chamber when your Nominate was a single mining claim on some backwater world. Some votes against you today were cast by people who witnessed Mnazkash the Subjugator creating the Ancestrate. You—unfortunately—have no idea what you are doing."

"Oh, I understand perfectly well," Kel said. "It all makes perfect sense. But why let the war continue? A peace would have protected the Aloo Dash fleet and guaranteed the supply of carriers for the Levy Fleet!"

"No, you don't understand." The smile on Pyaavuu's face gave way to impatient anger. "We do not want to protect the Ancestrate! Most casting the 'no' vote today hope you will dismantle the Ancestrate's fleet, pull their military teeth at least, or send the entire nation spiraling down at best. Do you really think this chamber wants a monarchy led by brutes and imbeciles to take over the galaxy? Gain a majority in the Assembly? For two generations we have waited for something, for someone, to curb their expansion, to stop their military's march over countless systems, adding Honored Ground on the way. You have provided the chance to reduce that military!"

Kel hated to feel like a young student, being schooled by Pyaavuu Shiirde Prarrbo. "You mean...you want the Nominate to win?"

"Don't be ridiculous—no! The Nominate will fight with the ferocity of the desperate, destroy a few more carriers, but eventually the Ancestrate will discover your secret trick or simply adapt strategy and bring its non-carrier fleet to bear. No, the Nominate will lose this war, and its ruins will get added to the Ancestrate, like so many nations before it. But, before that happens, the Ancestrate's strike capabilities will get reduced, and the significant military losses will dethrone a highly unpopular Shaajis. She will get replaced with a more manageable ruler. Our Aloo Dash delegates have some potential successors in mind already. Maybe the entire system of Aloo Dash government will collapse, we will see."

"The Nominate, our entire nation, is just a tool for you!"

Pyaavuu looked saddened, as if he had to tell a child that their favorite pet had died. "You will need to let go of your Nominate. The Nominate, the Ancestrate, this nation here, that conflict there, it is all fleeting. Only we are eternal, and you are one of us now!"

"But I represent the Nominate!"

"No, Assembly Member Chaada, you guide the Nominate, you make the long-term plans for them, and you influence their leaders to do what is best for the big picture—the truly big, galactic picture. You are here to guide whoever holds that Honored Ground that you so remarkably discovered on that planet Prral. And if, one day, soon or in a hundred orbits, Prral has new owners, then you will guide them, too. And then, eventually, you will almost forget which quarreling bunch of miners or militarists last put their banner onto that rock, and you will understand yourself as an eternal shepherd of the galactic structure, left to us by the Honored. These are the people, and their ideals, you represent here. The universe has physical constants, holding it together, and it has one political constant, holding society together—us."

Kel did not respond.

"As I said, Assembly Member Chaada, you have much to learn!" Pyaavuu stood up and turned away to leave.

"What if," asked Kel, "we destroy so many carriers that the Ancestrate will never recover? It took them a hundred orbits to build up this military might. Are you not worried what will happen to your Levy Fleet? How is the Assembly of Oorkuu going to defend the galaxy against the Kubuu Ksiw raiders? Have you thought about that possibility?"

Pyaavuu turned around, pity in his eyes. "No, I have not thought about that, and no, I am not worried. Do you know why not? The raiders do not exist! The Kubuu Ksiw—all of them—left the galaxy after the galacticide and they have never returned. Stories of a continued external threat to humanity are useful to justify adherence to the creed and to galvanize support for a strong humanity and its eternal protector—the Assembly. But— they are just that: stories. The only genuine threats to the galaxy are the power-hungry and the incompetent, people like Shaajis Sya or you, ex-First Councilor Chaada. Now we can pitch both against each other and have the lesser evil prevail, returning to a more balanced galaxy, governed by us."

He walked away, adding, "Great speech!"

△△△

As elated as Kel had felt early in the rotation, as crushed did he feel this moment. He had lost the crucial vote to save the Nominate. Was Assembly Member Prarrbo right?

The Ancestrate would discover the bomb carriers at some point. The nano bomb would not win a prolonged conflict; it made an attack on the Nominate extremely costly and forced peace negotiations. The Assembly would let things run their course and watch what was going to happen. Also devastating, or maybe even more so, was the revelation that the entire justification for the creed billions of people lived and died by—Strength Through Conflict—was a lie. Kel had no proof but knew to be true what Pyaavuu Shiirde Prarrbo told him, because—in a terrible way—it made sense. The only reports of occasional encounters with the left-behind galactic invaders, the raiders, came from the Levy Fleet of the Assembly and from no one else. Unarmed merchant freighters, exploring darkstring scouts, rogue asteroid mining vessels never ran into raiders or their bases, only the Assembly's own forces. He wondered about how they dealt with the losses they always reported —did they destroy their own ships for the sake of a "more balanced" galaxy? After today, nothing seemed too surprising or farfetched. The Assembly of Oorkuu was a gang of galactic power brokers and self-absorbed kyongak wekak—and Kel would have to spend eternity with them!

The Assembly granted eternal life, but it could also take it. All chamber closed-door proceedings except voting results were government secrets, and that included all conversations between Assembly Members within that building. Pyaavuu Shiirde Prarrbo played it safe by schooling Kel on galactic politics inside the chamber, knowing the penalty for revealing any of it was death. Only two Assembly Members had received this punishment in the history of the post-galacticide era. Kel wondered if those "traitors" had been well-meaning people with a conscience who wanted to reveal the inner workings of their cult. He would not go this route. Kel feared death as little or as much as everyone else, but as a dead man he would be of no use to the Nominate. The Assembly of Oorkuu was to be treated like a war zone, a political battlefield with traditions and rules, some bendable and breakable, to be dodged or exploited like in any other conflict he fought. Today, he had lost. He did not understand the field and underestimated the actors—a mistake he would not repeat.

It was impossible to make plans while he was hungry. The insatiable appetite from the previous rotation had returned, and the desire for the carnivorous buffet he consumed dominated his thoughts. He ordered an obscene amount of food for delivery to his temporary quarters and called in his staff at the same time. *He would devour the spiced meats and work on using the Assembly's rules against it, a fitting combination of activities*, he thought.

"The Assembly will not vote on anything regarding a peace treaty again; this is no longer an option," said Sru Mayoop, showing a hint of disgust at Kel's animalic eating while he was trying to stay focused on the topic. "The only way to end the war is if both sides agree on a resolution and bring it jointly before the chamber."

Still chewing a much too large bite, Kel inquired, "Last time I asked the Assembly about this, they said there is no way to negotiate with the Ancestrate, but that was before the Nominate became a member."

"That is true, Assembly Member, but I am afraid addressing the members of the Aloo Dash delegation will not change anything. They will not try to reach an agreement with you."

"I am not planning on talking to anyone in the Assembly. I will talk directly to Shaajis Sya!"

Kel's team members looked perplexed. "To the Shaajis? But…she talks only to her delegation members when they travel back to Aloo Dash, if she talks to anyone outside their home world at all!"

Kel got close to finishing his feeding frenzy, licking the remains of the spicy meat sauce off his fingers, and stated with all the dignity the scene allowed for: "I am the 317th Member of the Assembly of Oorkuu and I can talk to any leader of any galactic nation at any time! Please organize a meeting with Shaajis Sya and get me passage on a passenger ship or reserve private transportation. Book yourselves cabins, too. We're going to Aloo Dash!"

14—DIRECT NEGOTIATIONS

Nobody supported Kel's decision to meet the Shaajis. Neither the Aloo Dash delegation, nor the other members of the Assembly, but there was not much they could do except show open contempt for his obvious snub of their recent vote.

The downtime during the flight to Aloo Dash gave Kel an opportunity to focus thoughts on the remaining bomb carriers. Despite some anxious moments he could pick up on, they were all in relative safety and still ready and able to fulfill their missions. The best—and only—weapon against the Ancestrate was safe for now. With the threat to her key military assets still existing, Shaajis Sya had agreed to a meeting, maybe out of curiosity, wanting to see who dared to challenge her rule, or maybe out of practical concerns for her strategic position.

Arriving three rotations before the meeting, Kel and his two secretaries had time to take in some sights of the home world of the galaxy's largest nation, and one of the few remaining absolute monarchies. Ngeem gba Shaaj, the capital city of the planet Dziilaa Sok and royal seat of the Ancestrate, was a most impressive place, and coming straight from the oversized architecture of Omech Krreng that was difficult to accomplish in Kel's view. He was used to utilitarian buildings, performing a function, varying in size and shape only if it made sense. The Assembly world's white mountains of polished metals blinded any visitor and were to project the splendor of a reemerged humankind.

The Aloo Dashaad seemed to prefer stone as building material. Human-sized, dark slabs, laser cut and sculpted, assembled into buildings much larger than they needed to be, many layers of exterior walls for each, making every building look like a fortress ready to withstand a siege. The age of the buildings was hard to tell, and Kel wondered if the warrior Shaajrrurrhes like Mnazkash the Subjugator promoted this martial style. Using stone had been universal for all buildings designed to impress, dating back to the ruins of great pre-galacticide civilizations. Kel had read somewhere that maybe stone was not a common building material before the galacticide; it was just the only one that survived the extra-galactic onslaught and the orbits that had passed.

Kel had to be satisfied with his own thoughts and conclusions; his assigned chaperones, guards, and ceremonial secretaries who did not leave his side since arrival, working in shifts and being posted just outside their guest residence doors, did not deliver any narration during his tours through the capital city. They spoke a professional, courteous but cold, bare minimum of words with him, and none with his staff, uncomfortably trotting along wherever he went. Kel was neither offended nor surprised. He represented the opponent in an active war; he was the enemy. That he was allowed to tour the heart of the Ancestrate showed that the generation-old hubris of feelings of unlimited superiority was still going strong.

Did most Aloo Dashaad even know that two of their carriers had been destroyed?

ΔΔΔ

Shaajis Sya Omga's royal palace dominated the skyline, its dark stone making it appear like a silhouette even in bright daylight.

The architects of the royal hall that two guards led him through must have exchanged notes with the builders of the Assembly Chamber. While the latter settled for white, everything was dark gray here, designed to belittle anyone foolish enough to come here, testament to a warrior race who knew nothing but victory and sucked all wealth out of anyone they trampled along their path, only to bequeath that wealth on the person living here.

Kel decided he must be unworthy to be met in the royal hall, as he was escorted outside into what looked like a central garden. Flora from many worlds, cut into exquisite patterns and shapes, left an open network of broad metallic walkways, leading to a central plaza, underpopulated by only three human-sized shapes, standing as motionless as the trees. As Kel and his two martial walking companions drew closer, he recognized one shape as an Aloo Dash Assembly Member, the other as another guard, clad in the same armor and cape, holding a ceremonial lance, containing a concealed modern weapon no doubt. The third was a woman.

Her torso looked revealed, as if she was only wearing a light, smooth long skirt draping down to the ground. As Kel got closer, the revealed torso turned out to be an illusion, as she appeared fully covered with what looked like a thin layer of paint on her skin, made from a colorless yet shiny material that hid her anatomical details yet seemed to exist just barely: the Shroud of Shaaj. Ceremonial garb of the Shaajrrurrhes. Made from a single layer of neutrons, according to legend, the exclusive building material of the hyperdense neutron stars, the heaviest and densest material in this universe that was not a black hole, thinner than anything, yet opaque, held in shape by warp generators that could power a planetary nation like the Nominate for spins with the output that was needed to withstand Kel's gaze on its wearer.

"Revered Shaajis," spoke the Assembly Member near the shimmering figure while gesturing for Kel and his guards to halt, "before you has come Assembly Member Chaada, representative of the Nominate of EsChii!"

Kel stopped and let the introductory protocol roll, remaining silent. The only time his Aloo Dashaad chaperones had graced him with more than a few curt words was during the etiquette training. He had listened, but reluctantly so. There had been a thousand times more monarchs than immortals in the galaxy, and she was simply the head of state of a planetary nation, while he represented the galactic government. Had she been briefed on how to address an Assembly of Oorkuu Member? In the awkward reality of this moment, however, that was not how he felt. The palace, the royal hall, the gardens where even nature bowed to the dictate of its owner, the entire city projected the singularity of power onto the beholder, and that singularity stood before him, a below-average-height woman, maybe 20 orbits old, who despite the obvious design of the intimidating gestures, was one of the most awe-instilling sights Kel had ever seen.

Her face was covered with some sort of shiny coating, matching the indescribable glow-color of her flowing robe, and hardly moved when she spoke. "Assembly Member, we welcome you on Dziilaa Sok."

The words were polite and her voice pleasing, deep for a small-framed person, but could not have sounded colder if she had announced his death sentence. She did not move a muscle when she ordered everyone: "Leave us!"

Kel assumed he was the exception. After a well-measured moment, guards and dignitary moved out of earshot. She turned and walked toward a nearby path, giving no sign if he was to follow her. Kel was here to talk, so he followed, noticing three moving objects overhead, the movement creating a brief flicker in their visual stealth field that concealed them up til now. These were likely the hover generators warping space-time to match her body, maintaining the legendary shroud. People said the shroud was impenetrable, but it was probably the strong distortion of the universal fabric that—if anything—protected the Shaajis, not the vague illusion of a garment.

When he caught up with her, Kel had refocused his thoughts on his purpose for being here. "Shaajis," he started, not using "revered," despite being instructed to use it like any

Aloo Dashaad, but he left out her first name, another etiquette tradition. "I have come here to negotiate what had failed to garner support in the Assembly of Oorkuu, as you undoubtedly have heard—a peace treaty between our nations."

The Shaajis kept walking at a slow pace, neither turning her head nor responding. "The Nominate I am representing has obvious motives for wanting peace, but I firmly believe that the Ancestrate of Aloo Dash has, too." It felt strange saying "the Ancestrate" while walking next to the actual Ancestor queen. He paused, only to elicit more silence, and then continued, "We have, as you experienced, the capability of destroying your core fleet units, the Grandslaught-class carriers, at will. That capability remains, and despite our reservation toward weapons of mass destruction, we will not hesitate to use it again." He pointed upward. "There is one of those carriers in orbit of this world, Shaajis. What would the people of Ngeem gba Shaaj, all the Aloo Dashaad think, if metallic debris was going to rain down from the skies for ten spins? How much faith would it give them in the ability of their government to protect them? Do you know how I know how scary it is when building-size pieces of bent metal hail down? Prral is experiencing right now the first wave of scattered remains from the battle and the destruction of the first carrier. And that is an uninhabited world. What would people think when this happened on a densely populated planet?"

The Shaajis stopped. Not moving her head, she said, "We are an Omga, Assembly Member. Our family has stopped caring what the people think generations ago."

Kel kept fixating on her while she stared ahead, not gracing him with eye contact or any change of intonation, or anything else showing his words had any effect on her except stopping her stroll in the garden. "Was your only purpose to come here to threaten us?"

Kel quickly said, "No, Shaajis, I came here to submit."

She turned her head to face him and blinked—the first glimpse of a human gesture since this audience began.

"Elaborate," she said.

"I propose that the Nominate submits. You win! As the victor of the war, the Ancestrate of Aloo Dash enters a peace accord with the Nominate under the condition that all prisoners of war, taken after the Battle of Prral, will be returned to the Ancestrate immediately and unharmed. I can guarantee for these conditions to be fully met."

"And that is it, Assembly Member? No further conditions?"

"Correct, Shaajis, no further conditions, specifically no loss of territory, no occupation, and no integration of the Nominate into the Ancestrate and no reparations."

She remained in her statuesque stance, returning his stare. An awkward silence followed, and the Shaajis remained quiet. Kel was tempted to just play along and say nothing, he was not ready to change the proposal, but he could explain it in more detail: "This agreement allows you to not pursue this war you declared any further, avoid further destruction of your major, and costly, military assets, and do so as the declared victor of the war. You also won't leave empty-handed, as you will get the prisoners of war back. The first Aloo Dash prisoners of war in a long time, if my history study does not betray me."

Silence.

Then it was the Shaajis's turn to point upward. "Do you see these hovering devices, Assembly Member?"

Kel was not sure what to say, or if his last moment was about to come, finding out what efficient weapon system was enclosed in the metallic cylinders, unloading their destructive power onto him, for trying to stare down an Omga family member, on her own world in her own garden.

"I called them the three monsters when I was little, and my father never corrected me. They have been my protectors for as long as I can remember, hovering over me my entire life. Now I am 23 orbits old, and I still have three monsters hovering over me: the military, the industrial complex, and the intelligence services. What you are proposing allows me to feed only one of them, Assembly Member. It will not suffice."

Kel was surprised, pleasantly so, despite the cold facade, the drapings of power, and the almost inhumane distance—the Shaajis, like everybody else, had something she needed, and was negotiating!

"I assume," he started, "what I proposed will feed the military, satisfying their need for an honorable disengagement. What else would you need to feed the others?"

The Shaajis turned her head and started walking again like before, without any regard to him matching her movements. "We need access to the surface of Prral, for two reasons. First, our intelligence would never allow for carrier technology to fall into enemy hands, so we will need to collect the debris you so vividly described, near the battlefield and on the planetary surface. Second, we will need prospecting rights on Prral, with the option to stake mining claims. We are practical, Assembly Member. The notion of something like prisoners of war having value beyond satisfying anyone besides a few old officers is naïve. Mining Prral will have tangible value."

"And feed the monsters?" asked Kel. The Shaajis did not confirm, as it seemed to Kel she had decided it was her metaphor to use and hers alone. "This could work, Shaajis. You could sweep the debris and search for resources at the same time, but under one condition!"

She turned her head toward him again. He said, "I can sell this to the Nominate government as our treaty conditions if they are allowed to inspect all incoming Aloo Dash vessels. Only completely unarmed vessels are allowed to enter and operate in the Prral system. If this is agreeable, I believe we have the outline of an accord."

The Shaajis turned her full body toward Kel, the legendary shroud's brightness irritating his eyes, waving a gesture with her right hand. The Assembly of Oorkuu Member, an immortal man, came running like a summoned pet.

"Revered Shaajis," he said, out of breath. Her eyes fixed on Kel, she said, "We have an accord. Prepare an agreement for you to take to the Assembly. Make sure it gets the votes!"

Aghast, the galactic dignitary stammered, "But...but, revered Shaajis, are we really allowing this man...your father would have—"

"My father," said Shaajis Sya, her voice even frostier than before with a hint of anger, the first emotion she had shown. "My father would have fed you your own intestines had you brought up his father to him. Count yourself extremely fortunate that I weighed your prolonged absence from our court and unfamiliarity with required obedience in my decision to let you continue to serve us unpunished."

With his head bowed down, he wrote Shaajis Sya Omga's brief yet complete peace accord between her empire and the Nominate, his hands shaking as he took down the dictate on his notepad. She dictated the entire document without hesitation, stopping, or correcting herself once, then turned around and walked away toward one of the palace buildings, without farewell, dismissal or further words of confirmation, her silent way of reminding the two men left behind that every word she spoke was a decree, unbreakable law for billions.

15—COST OF PEACE

"**M**y parents were cowards!" said Vyoz Vyooma, the commander-in-chief of the Nominate forces.

"Why do you say that?" asked Taawa Nyiitsats, sensing that Vyoz was opening up to her for the first time.

"Do you know what the Kpootmaa Autarky is?" asked Vyoz.

"No, I don't."

"That's where I am from. It used to be a nation in the Keedz Bend, on the other side of the Korrats Ridge. It is now part of the Ancestrate of Aloo Dash. The Aloo Dash fleet was coming, and my parents simply picked up their things, my sister and I, and left. The thought of standing their ground and fighting did not even cross their mind! They lined up with thousands of other refugees, heading for EsChiip. We got on that stinking freighter to take us across the Ridge. It could barely warp interstellar, so we needed 50 refueling stops to reach EsChii territory. Fifty! It took forever. I spent half my childhood on that freighter. It was overcrowded, the food production could not keep up, and people started dying. Sometimes they tried to accelerate refueling by scavenging asteroids, which didn't really yield anything. The skipper kept fantasizing about a rogue planet he knew midway in the Ridge, for a real refuel to make some bigger warps. It was draash nreedz! Never existed. Do you want to know the only reason we made it?" Taawa remained attentive but silent. "We made it because we took whatever fuel we could find from another ship of fools, some transport even more derelict than our crap heap, filled with refugees slightly more starved than our own crew. They killed them. They killed them and took their fuel and whatever they could transfer from their hydroponics bay. My parents were part of the boarding party. They were not brave enough to stand against the Ancestrate, because they 'were no soldiers.' But they would smash in the heads of some half-dead technicians and surface farmers to get fuel for their own escape. That they would do!" Vyoz was breathing heavily.

"Do you blame the Ancestrate for what happened?" asked Taawa.

"No," said Vyoz, without hesitation. "My own nation had just recently declared war on a neighbor because we wanted some planet. The Ancestrate did the same. They wanted our nation—and took it. Do you know the Republic of Tsaagu?"

"Yes," answered Taawa. "They held back the Ancestrate for orbits."

"Exactly!" said Vyoz. "They are famous for it! My nation did nothing. Like my parents, they just left it to the Aloo Dashaad. This is why you have never heard of the Kpootmaa Autarky! But I can tell you who is to blame!"

"Go ahead," said Taawa. "Tell me who is to blame."

"The civilian government. Bureaucrats, administrators, accountants, and public servants. You can't build a Strength Through Conflict society with this kind of people. You can register a mining claim, file for tax relief, or for a patent, but you cannot get ready to fight the Dark Ones with only civilians in the government."

"But the Nominate of EsChii has a civilian government," said Taawa.

"Yes, and that is why my parents fled here. Oh, how well that worked out for us. Disrespected refugees were we. They could hardly ever find a decent job or hold one for some time. Then the E EsChii got smart and figured they would be next. The armed forces took over. Things did not get better immediately, but at least they put some structure in place, trying to glue this fragmented patchwork of former mining companies into a real nation."

"Do you really think the series of military coups in EsChii's recent history have helped the nation?" asked Taawa.

"They did not have the backing of the people," said Vyoz, "or not enough people. No surprise, with many E EsChii being former refugees, fleeing from one beaten nation or another."

"But you never lost hope?" asked Taawa.

"No," said Vyoz. "I didn't. Even after the current civilian administration got established, I joined the military as soon as I was old enough, just before professional soldiers were no longer a thing and the citizen-army was created. I never gave up hope. Then..."

Taawa gave Vyoz time to collect his thoughts, but when he remained silent, she asked, "What happened then, Vyoz?"

"Then, after all these orbits, we finally had it all in place: the perfect First Councilor, a strong military supported by the people, and a weapon against the Ancestrate. We could have been the legendary Tsaagu, except we had a real chance of winning against the Ancestrate. And then it went all to nreedz."

"But the government is still civilian. And First Councilor Kel Chaada was a civilian, too. What—"

Vyoz glanced at her. "He was not! Kel Chaada was a warrior, and we fought side by side in the deserts of Prral to win the war! He might have been a citizen-soldier conscript, but he was no civilian, he had spirit. Nobody was happier than I was when he ascended to lead the nation after the Prral conflict. When Aloo Dash declared war, he pushed against submission and was the only one who wanted to fight!"

"The only one, Vyoz? Didn't you want to fight?"

"Of course! I meant he was the only one in the government who wanted to fight—don't twist my words!"

"I apologize. Please—continue. You were describing what went wrong."

Vyoz Vyooma was telling her the truth. He had been so proud when Kel got inaugurated and again when he announced they would not submit to the most powerful nation in the galaxy. It pained him to think about how their relationship had declined and even more so to say it out loud. "He was my hero. And my biggest disappointment. My parents, I never really looked up to, so in my eyes they did not fall as far as Kel Chaada did. Just when we had it all in place. We could have taken terms to the Ancestrate. Our terms. The Assembly didn't do anything, so the war went on. And we kept blowing up their carriers." He stared at Taawa. "We could have blown them all up." He paused, but she remained quiet, maybe having learned when to prod him along with questions and when to leave him to his thoughts. "Then, suddenly, he decided to join the Assembly! Become a bureaucrat, discuss terms and conditions, make big politics in the big Assembly Chamber. He could have sent anyone from the Council, or appoint anyone else, but no, he had to go himself. Left us here with some civilian as his successor. And you know what happened to Kel at the Assembly? The same thing that happened to my parents when they came here. They laughed at him. They let him present his peace vote and voted it down. What does he do? Go crawling to the Shaajis! Instead of raining their exploding carriers down on her, he goes there and asks if he could have peace! Peace, please! A magiich disgrace!"

"How did this make you feel?" asked Taawa.

"If you are waiting for me to say 'sad' or 'betrayed,' you misunderstood our conversation," said Vyoz. "It made me see very clearly what needs to be done."

"What needs to be done?" asked Taawa.

"Do you know what I would have proposed to Shaajis Sya?"

"No, what would you have said to her?"

"I would have made it clear that the Nominate was not an easy prey, and she probably knew that, anyway. I would not have offered peace, I would have offered more war! A better war, a successful war, not a slow grind, losing lots of carriers to get what, some mining rights? No, I would have offered her the entire Wel Edge."

"The entire Wel Edge? I think you can only offer what you

have."

"I have the weapon. The weapon that can blow up Grandslaught Carriers. It can be used against the Ancestrate. It can also be used against its enemies. The Wel Edge could be part of a strong military power, but not through some weak peace accord, instead through mutual strength, becoming a frontline bastion against the Dark Ones, under effective local leadership."

"Local leadership, as in local military leadership?"

"Exactly," said Vyoz. "Tell your mistress the Nominate has the means to help her cross the Korrats Ridge for good, a feat even Mnazkash the Subjugator did not pull off."

"My...mistress?" asked Taawa.

Vyoz smiled. "Yes, did you think I would have told you all this if you were from the Electorate of Keelaak, a fellow veteran from the last war? You are a double agent for the Ancestrate —even back on Prral when you got exchanged, well, almost exchanged against my team and I, you had observed the war for the Ancestrate's secret service. And almost bashed in the head of Kel Chaada. Wonder how things would have developed if you had."

Taawa stared at Vyoz. "I will be in touch with a response." The transmission ended and her avatar disappeared from Vyoz's living room.

ΔΔΔ

Over 700 messages, congratulatory by glancing over their subject lines, had come in Kel's terminal at his Omech Chaa living quarters. The successful vote about the peace accord was galactic news, and commenters described it as a huge upset of the Ancestrate of Aloo Dash by a much smaller nation. The Nominate of EsChii became flooded with investors, trying to get a claim in Wel Edge region mining. Kel was certain within the Ancestrate the message was different, censoring and blocking independent news streams, praising their military for a hard-fought victory, securing crucial mining resources, or something similar. He did not care. The Shaajis got her story to tell; the war was over, the peace accords sanctioned by his new colleagues, some of them looking at the newcomer with less contempt, even a hint of respect.

Seven hundred messages. Two of them were not congratulatory. Kel was both dismayed by their content and glad he listened to them right away. Ahma Zhanyza, unfulfilled love of his life, appeared distraught and furious, her reddened face yelling into the camera in a scary close-up, half-finished sentences in her native dialect Kel could not understand well, ending the message with two words screamed at him in standard Jeesh Gep: "You monster!" That, Kel understood, along with the terrible feeling that she had found out—somehow— what he had done.

The other message was from Vyoz Vyooma, his snubbed friend, who sent an urgent warning, confirming Kel's fears: "I wish we would reconnect under better circumstances, Kel. They are onto you! Secrecy of the...operation we conducted at the academy of science campus has been compromised. A warrant for your arrest was issued by the Nominate's council, for murder and abuse of power. It's not looking good, buddy, and I am not sure if your new status will protect you. Contact me if you need a way out through the sewers!"

The last time Vyoz had offered this, it had been in jest, leaving after his inauguration on EsChiip. Kel felt the heavy weights put on his chest. They had found out. She had found out. His deed was monstrous, and now he needed to pay the price. The raw loathing in Ahma's screams was not as destructive as the bottomless disappointment in her eyes. He would never hold her, comfort her, share a meal with her. Her last thought in this world, just before she died as an old woman, was going to be about how much she hated him. Kel sat in his apartment, sunk into the soft chair, not replaying her message even once, but listening to it in his head a hundred times.

He heard some noises outside while he wallowed in his misery and thought some guards had come for him, taking him away to his peers, gleefully witnessing his damnation. Vyoz was correct: His status as Assembly Member would not protect Kel from a capital crime charge on his home world. Nobody pressed his door buzzer. It seemed justice was not that swift. Part of him longed for punishment, putting an end to his existence and stopping the endless loop of Ahma's message being recited by his guilty conscience. Falling deeper into the abyss, he realized that justice would not be swift, and there would be no end. He would be charged with murder, found guilty, then face a life-in-prison sentence. While this was a hard punishment for everyone, his punishment would last for eternity. He would not die in prison; his term would not include that final mercy.

Kel made a decision. It was a practical one, maybe a cowardly one. If he had to face eternal damnation, he would be damned on his own terms. Kel contacted Vyoz via a private, secure QE channel. To his relief, Vyoz answered the call. "I need to get out of the sewers!" Kel said. Vyoz responded, no questions asked, as if they had last spoken a few spins ago.

"Pack for two shifts, my friend, not more! Bring some hard currencies if you have them. Order private transport to the main spaceport outside the Assembly complex, then travel as far away from that port as you can, in the opposite direction. Use ground transport, reach a different port, the smaller the better. I will send you a file in a pass. At the small spaceport, upload that file to the port's feedback bulletin board. This will be the signal for the crew I am sending to pick you up."

Kel memorized the instructions. There was so much he wanted to tell Vyoz, but he could only muster a thank-you.

"Don't you worry," responded Vyoz. "We will get you out of there!"

ΔΔΔ

Friends and enemies were the same people, just time and context told you who was who at any given moment. Vyoz Vyooma thought back to the war on Prral. Kel Chaada had become his friend. The enemy agent from the prisoner exchange was the enemy. Taawa Nyiitsats was a remarkable woman, unflinchingly ruthless and fiercely loyal to her mistress, the Shaajis of Aloo Dash. Vyoz had kept an eye on her file as she was processed through the Nominate's system as a prisoner of war, eventually sent back to the Electorate of Keelaak when all enemy combatants were released at the end of the war. Her military record was interesting: It showed her as enlisting into the enemy's forces late in the war, yet she showed the proficiency and poise of a combat veteran during the few moments he had observed her on Prral. Vyoz had pulled her release interview and listened to her answering a short list of administrative questions before the release; all in perfect Keel Zhaja, the language of the Electorate, a language Vyoz spoke well. Keel Zhaja was a strong dialect of New Galactic, one of the hardest to understand for a New Galactic speaker, using many words from Old Galactic. Twice during the interview Taawa Nyiitsats had slipped into full-blown Old Galactic for half a sentence or so. The interviewers did not notice, but Vyoz did. Besides some of the oldest members of the Assembly of Oorkuu and some scholars, no one in the galaxy spoke Old Galactic anymore. Except for the elite of Aloo Dash.

Vyoz had stayed in touch with Taawa, casually, as a professional courtesy between veterans of a past conflict, who simply happened to fight on different sides. She never turned him down for a call, even suggested meeting in person. He knew she was an agent for the Ancestrate. Again, officially, she was still the enemy, like she was when he first met her.

Vyoz had been loyal to Kel Chaada—always. He supported him during the military tribunal, his nomination to First Councilor, and forgave him for keeping him out of the loop about key decisions regarding the Nominate's military, including the nano bomb! But in the end, Kel had only one agenda, and that was peace, peace at any price. He would leave the Nominate to some gutless administrator, and debase himself in front of the Assembly of Oorkuu and the Shaajis, for peace. Peace had no place in this galaxy. It had not, ever since the Dark Ones had ravaged it. The creed Madzuu Vrraa Nyuu was the guideline humanity had lacked before the galacticide—Strength Through Conflict, as it was commonly translated. But Nyuu did not mean "conflict" in Old Galactic, it meant "war." A warrior himself, Vyoz understood perfectly well what this meant. The weak would perish and the strong would thrive. The strong had to stand up against the raiders, again and again, as the scouting parties they left behind probed the defenses of a reemerging human civilization. One day, they would have to stand up against the full might of the Dark Ones, and peacemakers would not prepare humanity for that threat.

When Vyoz felt the time was right, he had shared these, his most personal and intimate thoughts, with Taawa. She had not disappointed, not even tried to talk herself out of his allegation about her being an Ancestrate spy. She promised to get him and his ideas introduced to the powerful in the Ancestrate, and she followed through. The Ancestrate was a military powerhouse. Naturally they understood the value of his proposal, even if presented in vague terms.

"We have everything prepared on our end to receive the traveler." Taawa's avatar came back into the projection area in his living room. "Can you confirm he has left yet?"

"Yes," answered Vyoz. "My crew has picked him up, and they are heading for Aloo Dash space through the Nemkeg Spoke. All you have to do is make sure to be there when they land."

"Impressive, Vyoz. My mistress will be pleased. I am curious. How did you manage to get him to leave?"

Vyoz smiled. "I shall keep a few secrets to myself for now, I hope you understand."

"I do," said Taawa, "but it never hurts to ask. I will be back in touch when the traveler arrives." The communication stream ended.

When the "traveler" was still his friend, Vyoz had helped him eliminate a mutual enemy, a potential whistle-blower and traitor to their cause. That person, an archaeologist, was an enemy at that time. Maybe today he could be a friend and ally. He was dead, though, and Vyoz had killed him for the "traveler." Too bad he would never find out that it was he, Vyoz, who had leaked this information now, spelling his doom. As he said before, the distinction between friend and enemy was simply a matter of time and circumstance. Leaking it to the government was one thing, but he also leaked it to the traveler's former love interest. In time, it was going to turn her into a friend to the cause, too.

16—FLIGHT

Kel was impressed by how quickly Vyoz had made good on his promise: both crew and ship were perfect for the job. The job of bringing him—the soon-to-be disgraced Assembly Member Chaada—to a mining world where he could hide for...how long?

He would need to build a different life, start anew, a contingency he had never spent a single moment planning for. The ship, a utilitarian but modern transport shuttle with impressive warp range of 18 light-orbits, would drop him off on an Aloo Dash ore mining colony at the periphery of the Ancestrate. Vyoz's plan for Kel's disappearance was bold, but it had a good chance of success. Nobody would assume Kel was heading toward former enemy territory to disappear. There was going to be some Aloo Dash military stationed on a mining colony, but it would be a single outpost only for an entire planetary surface. They did not require more for these types of places. The miners were not people distracted by inciting rebellions against the Shaajis's rule; they were young, well-paid men and women focused on running mining equipment on a planet nobody called home or cared about. The Ancestrate left policing and security to the mining corporations, and that was the cover Vyoz had in mind for Kel: ex-military, near-middle-aged guy with mining colony background taking on a low-key security job on an active ore dig. The contrast with "war hero, First Councilor, and immortal member of the galactic government" was stark, painful, and almost humorous. That life was over now. He could plausibly play the role that Vyoz prepared for him in advance. Growing up in the Nominate, he had spent time on mining colonies in the Wel Edge. Not as a miner, but for the shield technology company he had worked with. He had seen many dig sites, where he and his colleagues installed protective plasma shields and warp lifters. He knew the type of people, their mannerisms, and how to blend in.

The transport's crew, who was going to bring him there, played the role of a security subcontractor team, delivering one of their colleagues to a ground assignment. They looked the part: four men and two women, mixed genetics across all races, unique in their individual appearances, but all blending together in their distinct soldier-of-fortune demeanor. People who came from nowhere and fought everywhere. They had exchanged no words with Kel beyond the necessary, asked no questions, and —so far—he had returned the favor and spent the last shift in his crew compartment, small but his own, trying to piece his mind back together for the challenges ahead. He wondered how long the flight would take and left his isolation to discuss the route with the ship's captain, who was addressed as "Skipper" on nonmilitary vessels.

"We will need a total of four warps," said Skipper Gameny Tswosna, "with three refueling stops. We use some depots off the main darkstring connector, but you should still stay onboard for the entire time, just in case."

"Four warps?" Kel was surprised. "I understand, and appreciate, that you want to play it safe, but isn't that overkill? It sounds like a really long run for a relatively nearby destination."

"Not my choice," said Gameny. "Your former colleagues from the Assembly have declared the entire Nemkeg Spoke unsafe for travel, lots of Kubuu Ksiw raider activity in the region."

Kel could not suppress a chuckle. "What's funny?" asked the skipper. Kel thought about sharing his newfound knowledge about the Kubuu Ksiw threat not being real with Skipper Tswosna, but then disguised his knowledge a little: "There is no Kubuu Ksiw threat in the Spoke. I know because I was there when it was decided to announce this."

"Really?" asked the skipper, not trying to mask his doubts. "And why would you immortal boys make this up?"

"Because," said Kel, somewhat regretting having gone down this path, "the Assembly wanted to make sure the Ancestrate was making good on their promises for the Levy Fleet contingent now that the Nominate kicked their kyongak and they are two carriers down."

The skipper eyed him, considering Kel's half-lie. It must have been convincing enough, for he said, "Hmm, this would save us time...and money. Going through Nemkeg, we could probably do this with two warps and only one refueling stop mid-Spoke. Are you sure about this alert being fake?"

"Absolutely sure. I am also onboard myself, right? Why would I want to run into Kubuu Ksiw raiders when I could have put an easy bullet to my head on Omech Chaa? The route is safe."

"I'll run this through astrogation," said the skipper and shuffled off, his leg muscles disagreeing with the high gravity setting, accommodating the high-grav crew members.

Twenty passes later, his voice came on Kel's intercom: "OK, you can't wait to start your new job? We won't stand in your way, haha. Route through the Nemkeg Spoke is plotted. Strap in for a quick burn to get to the Spoke darkstring, then we'll warp."

ΔΔΔ

The transport's alarm siren ripped Kel from his sleep. Pushed to the wall, he felt strong vibrations in his small cabin, from the ship using thrusters to maneuver faster than the warp field gravity could compensate for. He heard the crew hurrying along the central hallway toward the cockpit, exchanging curse-laden yells about enemy ships. Kel grabbed a shirt, mismatching his pants, and clambered forward to the cockpit, too, trying to outbalance the bucking of the ship without success. He fell and slid down the hallway, entering the cockpit flat on his back, feet first.

"Raiders!" said the astrogator. "Three contacts."

Skipper Gameny Tswosna gave Kel a piercing look. "This is your fault!"

Raiders? Kel reeled. Had he fallen for a double lie? Were the extra-galactics real after all? Had Pyaavuu Shiirde Prarrbo played him that well? He might be a rookie politician, but he knew how to fight. Kel pulled himself up into an open cockpit seat, strapped in, and shoved a tactical helmet over his head. Uncalibrated, the virtual tac-helmet gave him an instant headache as soon as the data stream entered his mind, and he needed a few moments to focus even on the simplest objects. Three contacts, just outside the darkstring, waiting for ships warping in toward the fusion fuel depot in a nearby system, looking for prey, just like in the old stories about the Dark Ones, the bane of humanity.

The ship went through a series of fast maneuvers, designed to throw off targeting systems and make it harder to get a lock for weapon systems. Weapon systems? The tac-computer showed small, corvette-size enemy ships and approximated their weapons array. These systems looked unfamiliar, alien, and the transport's system could not identify them, but the large number looked impressive for such small ships. He saw some of the other crew members joining the data stream, virtually manning the few weapon stations.

"What do we have online?" asked Kel in his mind, directing the question to the crew members in the data stream. "Can I operate the mass driver?"

The skipper had not turned on any weapon systems yet and was furious about the request. "What are you doing in my stream, you kyong wek! You brought us here, and now these raiders are on us!"

"I know I am not that popular right now, Skipper"—Kel cleared his thoughts and attempted to remain calm—"but I know how to operate short-range guns! We can take out one on the flanks, or at least cripple it on the first run!"

"The first what?" asked the skipper.

Kel hesitated. "The first attack run. They are just waiting there. With some initiative we can even the odds a little before they break formation!"

"What are you talking about? Why should they break formation?"

"Because..." His own thoughts sidetracked Kel when he tried to respond into the data stream. "Because they are in a defensive holding formation! This looks more like a 'hold, ready to run.' Something scouts would be doing. They do not seem to plan to engage."

"Wrong, kyong wek," the astrogator screamed using her thoughts. "They just painted us with a target lock!"

"We don't know that," thought Kel into the data stream, trying to stay composed. "This could be their scanning technology."

"And this is why we keep our weapons offline!" said the skipper. "We stay cold and run! Maybe we are not a threat to them without weapons hot. And we are most certainly not going to attack! Now get off my magiich stream!"

Kel's headache spiked as the skipper overrode his data stream and turned it off while his mind was connected. He winced in pain as he ripped the helmet off.

Dazed, Kel looked around, every movement of his head punishing him with excruciating spikes of headaches, his brain still traumatized from the sensory load of a badly synchronized data stream, followed by its brutal end. The ship shook less now, the skipper following through on his announcement of dodge and run, accelerating away from the three ships, with some random anti-target-lock maneuvers built in. He felt minor explosions from the mid-hull, the crew popping out decoys hoping to compound the confusion for the raiders' target systems. The Kubuu Ksiw raiders: described as the pinnacle of aggression, superior in technology and tactics, mopping up humanity's battle fleets, killing trillions without hesitation. The ships out there were careful. No aggressive moves. No objects, moons, planets in the system used for cover to spring a trap in the last moment. They held positions like someone not sure about their next step, scanning the transport with a broad beam, not to lock target but to track position. Their formation was passive, defensive, and so were their actions.

"These are not raiders!" Kel tried to get the attention of anyone in the cockpit, now all strapped in, tac-helmets on and fused to the transport's computer's data streams. "These are not raiders! Listen to me! These guys are something else!"

The skipper removed his helmet. "We heard enough from you! What does it take to shut you up?"

He reached for his belt, his hand coming back up into sight with a handgun in it, taking aim at Kel. The next moment, Kel's headache was gone—and so was everything else, like a black blanket pulled over his consciousness.

17—SECRETS

"**K**el Chaada is dead," said Vyoz Vyooma.

Ahma Zhanyza, although sitting in her own chair in her own lab office, was uncomfortable. Vyoz towered over her while two women in unmarked uniforms guarded the door.

"How...how did he die?" asked Ahma.

"A fuel depot in the Nemkeg Spoke picked up scans of raiders preying on ships warping out of the darkstring, and Kel Chaada's transport was destroyed. It looks like Mnagwa Zmaam punished him for what he did to you and your...boss? Partner? Lover?"

"I do not believe in Zmaam," said Ahma. "I am a scientist."

"I am aware," said Vyoz, "and an important one, too. What do you believe in, Ahma Zhanyza? Do you believe in the Nominate of EsChii?"

"I don't understand."

"It is not a complex question. Do you believe in serving your nation? Because it sure looks like our former head of state did not. He was running from the law, from justice, selling us out to the Ancestrate!"

"To the Ancestrate? Why...he must...is that why he was traveling the Spoke? It leads to the Ancestrate."

"Exactly! We must fear the worst, in terms of secrets he had potentially shared with the enemy before his demise. That's why I am here, with you."

"You are the Maz Tiikiip of the Armed Forces. What can I

possibly do for you?"

"My dear Ahma," said Vyoz, "I am fully aware of the secret weapon program you have been heading under Kel Chaada's administration. Now, our concern is what he might have leaked to the Ancestrate. We believe he could have used the information during his negotiations with the Shaajis of Aloo Dash. Can you check your administrative logs to find out when he had last accessed the project database?"

"I can," Ahma said, "but I'm not sure if your associates have the clearance to be here when I do."

Vyoz nodded, and the two guards left the office. "Please, Ahma, go ahead." Vyoz pointed toward the terminal.

It took Ahma a few passes to go through the security protocols, log in, and search the administrative access files. "Here it is," she said and pointed out a log entry. "This is the last time Kel...First Councilor Chaada accessed the system. It looks like it has been a while..."

"Are you sure you have full access to search all relevant files? Could he have used a terminal at a different site or lab?"

"No," said Ahma. "I have full access privileges to everything in here. This was the last time he looked at any project data. And there are no other sites. For security purposes, this project has been run completely centralized."

"Of course," said Vyoz, looking at the information displayed at the terminal. He pushed his right earlobe. The office door opened, and a guard, looking worried, said, "Ahma Zhanyza, something is wrong with one of your colleagues, could you please come and take a look?"

"Oh no," said Ahma. "What happened?" She hurried out of her office, following the female Ancestrate special operative, who would—much to Ahma's surprise—ready her for transport off-world. They would take her to an Aloo Dash site for further interrogation and out of Vyoz's way.

Satisfied with his work, he sat down in her chair and looked at the open terminal connection to the Nominate's best-kept secrets. Vyoz created a full-access account for himself and copied all files onto the portable storage in his cuff. Then he wiped the database and backups clean. He stood up and smiled —having added another bargaining chip for the moment he would negotiate his future with Shaajis Sya. He touched his earlobe comm again and said, "Team, we are done here. Take the prisoner to the transport. Make sure everybody else is dead. Have a good flight back to the Ancestrate!"

18—CAPTIVITY

All there was—was the cell.

Kel could not tell day from night. He could not even tell if there was such a thing here. His internal clock had stopped working. He was in a small room, brightly lit, a few geometric shapes sticking out of the floor, a rectangular box he used as a bed, a cylinder with an opening to dispose of organic wastes. What made the room a cell was the absence of other openings, windows, or a door. It was hot in the cell, not unbearably so, but the temperature was always high. There were no visible openings for air to be pumped in, but they had to exist. Kel had been here for many spins before he started losing count or caring about the count.

The air in the cell had to recycle somehow. Otherwise, he would have died here long ago. Yes, the thought that he in fact had died had crossed his mind, more than once, and with varying intensity. His last recollection, now vague as time had passed, was the skipper shooting him. Did he get killed right there and now would be tormented by boredom for all eternity? A very low-fidelity afterlife, or being captured and held prisoner by an alien species, observing him for the rest of his life—the same eternal misery for an immortal. How ironic. The same hot, bright room with a few shapes with nothing going on. Except the meals. He was getting fed by some afterlife meal illusion mechanism, or by the observing aliens.

Meals had been the only distraction in this odd scenario and lent some credibility to the alien hypothesis. Rations were delivered through a sliding opening in the wall, on a tablet or plate. The rations were different-sized, geometrically shaped, barely edible, chewy masses along with water in an open container. Some spheres, cubes, prisms, and cylinders, so bland-tasting that he wondered if the aliens maybe just provided him with something to pass the time instead of rations, and he had eaten the alien equivalent of game pieces for a board game. The sliding opening delivered way too many to eat at first, then reduced the amounts, and adjusted the consistency to more chewable. Then the opening delivered cylinders only. They were easiest to chew, with improved taste, and more flavors added over time. If this was not the afterlife, then someone fed him, observed, and adjusted to improve his conditions. Someone kept him alive.

But they never adjusted that temperature down. He still had the mismatched pants and shirt from the day the transport had run into the three ships. Pants rolled up, never wearing the shirt because of the heat; the aliens sure enjoyed their human to look ragged, maybe liking the ridiculous contrast to the self-cleaning cell that looked as pristine as it had on the first shift. He had tried to soil it with the only waste he had, but somehow the walls or floor absorbed what his body could produce. Kel never saw the end of the space encounter with the three ships. His memory ended with Skipper Tswosna shooting him, likely with a stun gun if he was not dead. It was safe to assume they did not escape, or at least Kel did not. If the others were alive, he did not know where they were held. Maybe they had handed his unconscious body over to the aliens in return for their freedom. No. No! All these thoughts were ridiculous. If the aliens had been the infamous raiders, remnant forces of the hyper-aggressors decimating the human species, they would have run their transport down and destroyed it with their impressive weapon array. End of story. That, clearly, did not happen.

These were the careful aliens, waiting, probing, observing. Well, eventually they must have gotten a little more physical and captured or boarded the transport, but they were not

Kubuu Ksiw raiders. He was the prisoner of someone curious, who took their time before they acted. Unfortunately, they were taking a long time. The boredom was numbing, the lack of stimuli hurtful, and the monotony poisoned his mind. But Kel had realized some time ago when he still tried to count spins based on the meal distribution: Time was his only strength, his only weapon in this scenario. Whoever they were, he had more time than they did. They had to do something with him. Make contact, punish him for pushing excrement down the meal slot, kill him—do something. He would outwait them.

Kel had his own strange world to explore, and he could do so from this cell, using his mind. The bonds with the bomb carriers still existed, and he could feel all of them. Some fainter than others, some more frequent than others, but the entire group—except the two who had seen their mission through to their fiery end—was still alive. He could feel their emotions, sometimes for several passes, and their rhythms, habits, and thought patterns became part of his waking existence. He assumed they did not sense him, as he felt no resentment; they had certainly heard about his sins and crimes by now and would not approve and meld minds with him if they were aware of who they shared glimpses of their consciousness with. He had to admit that his psychological stalking was likely the most intimate breach of privacy possible, but being part of the thoughts of a familiar group gave him peace and helped keep his sanity.

Then the nightmares started.

ΔΔΔ

The shared group thoughts had bled over into his sleep. Sometimes Kel dozed off when his mind joined with the bomb carrier clique, but then new, grotesque, frightening characters entered this world inside his head.

Kel had not feared monsters when he was a child and did not waste any thought on them as an adult, but here they

134

were: dark, moving masses of what looked like graphite, slow in their motion, but always coming toward him, with undefined limbs, fingerless protrusions growing from their bodies, ever so slowly reaching for him. Kel almost never recalled his dreams. Ahma had told him once she had recurring nightmares about not being able to move when she tried to escape a pursuer in her nightmares. Ahma. Did she curse him with these?

The nightmares varied, but the monsters always looked and behaved the same. The mind encounters with them were strenuous for the psyche and the body. Kel would wake up, sweatier than usual, and had vomited over himself in his sleep a few times. The happy daydreams of the shared human thoughts turned into potent feelings of fear, panic, and pain. Were the bomb carriers in trouble, being mistreated, or did their thoughts meld with the horrors of his sleep?

One spin, the connection to the bomb carriers severed. Kel stopped feeling them; no vague, distant presence, no thought fragments, nothing. For the first time since the Oosech Wesech, the immortality rite, he lost his appetite, struggled with eating even half his rations, only to vomit them out almost immediately. After a few spins, the lack of nutrients and—more so—the loss of water showed. He was wasting away in an uninterrupted haze of semiconscious wakefulness, thought fragments of the bomb carriers, and monsters reaching for him. The surreal dreamworld and his miserable waking conditions were indistinguishable, in a scary way: The cell wall appeared to open up, seamlessly giving way to a door-like opening, framing a dark mass resting on several spiky protrusions, holding a massive body of black rock, thinning out to the top into a sort of head, featuring an eyeless, noseless face with a mouth opening from the nightmares, showing what looked like several rows of sharp teeth. This face turned toward Kel. The dark mass did not move.

"I am Raar," a distorted voice boomed through his head. Convulsing, vomiting, Kel fell to the cell floor, losing consciousness, embracing the silence it brought.

△△△

What happened?

Kel's nightmares got scarier, more realistic, and then they stopped. His sleep was peaceful, uninterrupted; his appetite came back, and he could keep down what he drank and ate. After just three rotations, he felt well enough to think, without fright, about what had happened. He suppressed the urge to reach his mind out to the others. Maybe he had overused his still unexplainable ability.

The monsters had left—until the fourth rotation. The wall slid open, framing a dark mass, monstrous jaws facing him. Kel sank to his knees, hopelessness weighing him down—not again! Would the torment never end?

"I am Raar," said a somewhat unpleasant, male, mechanical, but not mind-shattering voice. A voice outside his head. A voice he could hear with his ears! He looked up at the monstrous visitor. His thoughts were clear, for the first time he could remember, but the questions hurt: Was this a Kubuu Ksiw, here to devour his emaciated body, after it and its fellow raiders had enjoyed breaking his mind? Had all the nightmares been real, and this was not the first time the dark mass had been in his cell? Or had some sort of mind prison been manipulating him all along?

"I am Kel Chaada." All he had left to offer was his name.

The dark mass moved forward, some of the lower body protrusions vanishing into the main body, others elongating from the rear. Although it looked like stalactites of graphite breaking and being replaced, the motion made no sound. The wall closed behind the dark figure. "I am content you can understand me now, Kel Chaada," said the mechanical voice. A translator, it dawned on Kel. It is using a translator.

"Yes, I can understand you. And you are Rar...?" To his shame, Kel could not repeat the dark mass's name as fluently as the mechanical voice had approximated his.

"I am Raar," he repeated.

"Yes, yes, you are Raar. Hope I said this right. Can you tell me where I am?"

"You are our prisoner, Kel Chaada."

"Yes, I assumed as much. Am I on your ship?"

"Yes, Kel Chaada."

"How...long have I been here?"

"A short time, Kel Chaada."

"A short time? It did not feel like...it felt like a rather long time!"

"A short time, Kel Chaada," the voice repeated, without changing intonation.

"OK." Kel changed topics. "Where are the others? The others like me?"

"There were no others like you, Kel Chaada."

"OK. Well, the others from my ship?"

"We killed them, Kel Chaada," stated the dark mass, as if it had announced something as inconsequential as the time.

"You...killed them? Why?"

"They are our enemy, Kel Chaada."

"They are your enemy? Why? We did not attack!" He left out that he had been the one proposing an attack run, but as far as his recollection could carry him, they had been running away from the alien ships.

"They are our enemy, Kel Chaada."

"They are your enemy, huh? What about me, then? Am I not your enemy? How am I not your enemy?"

The mass took longer to respond, either to work out a response, or the translation lagged. "You are like us, Kel Chaada."

What? How could this dark, rocky nightmare with sharp teeth assume they were anything alike? Maybe they were... attracted to his mind connection to the bomb carriers? They could be a collective mind or at least communicate through thoughts as their primary method of communication. The monsters entering his nightmares had been his alien captors, trying to communicate! His mind, as alien to them as they were to him, could not interpret this input, and like an uncalibrated virtual data stream, made his mind and body suffer as a result. Then they switched tactics and tried computerized translation.

"I am nothing like you, Raar! How did you even learn how to translate my language? Humans have a lot of different languages."

"We learned, from human ships, and other humans, Kel Chaada."

"From other ships? We were not the first ship you attacked?"

"No, the humans have been our enemy before, Kel Chaada."

A realization formed in Kel's mind. Nasty, piercing, yet crystal clear in its brutal logic: Assembly Member Pyaavuu Shiirde Prarrbo had not lied to him when he explained that the Kubuu Ksiw invaders were long gone. He had, however, left out a crucial truth: Skirmishes between the Assembly forces and occasional raids on human vessels happened, but not with or by the extra-galactic menace of old; instead, by these aliens, whoever they were.

"Who are you? Not you, Raar, as an individual, who are your people?"

"We are Traaz, Kel Chaada."

Traaz? Kel had never heard of such a species, let alone as a sapient, spacefaring species, not even in the galactic legends. "Do your people have other names? Did other humans from other ships call you Kubuu Ksiw?"

"No, Kel Chaada."

"So, your people are from this galaxy, you did not come from someplace else, correct?"

"Incorrect. We came from a different galaxy, Kel Chaada."

Kel was stunned. It was, of course, possible that this alien entity was lying to him, much more interested in gathering information about him than revealing information about its people, but was there a possibility his conclusions had been wrong—again.

"Have the Traaz...did your people destroy the human civilization a long time ago?"

A naïve question if this was a Kubuu Ksiw, but Kel did not have anything to lose at this point.

"No, the Traaz did not destroy the humans. The humans were nearly destroyed by the Hak, Kel Chaada."

"The Hak? Did they come from another galaxy, too? Like your people?"

"Yes, but not from our galaxy. The Hak came from a different galaxy, Kel Chaada."

"Have your people met the Hak, then? Did the Traaz meet the Hak?"

"Yes. The Hak nearly destroyed us, too, not long ago, Kel Chaada."

"You fought extra-galactic invaders? Recently?"

"Yes, Kel Chaada."

"You don't need to mention my name after each sentence, Raar. When you fought the extra-galactics recently, were your people here already when those invaders attacked the humans?"

"Yes, it was the same attack, it was galaxy-wide."

None of this fits together, thought Kel, then another realization crept up on him: "When you say 'recently,' how many orbits ago does that mean for you?"

"The Hak attacked 1,235 orbits ago."

Stone-faced, Kel inquired, "Just to make sure, an 'orbit' for me is a fraction of a full rotation of Akaa Upsa, the galaxy. My people define it as a one hundred millionth of the time for a galactic rotation."

"We are familiar with the unit 'orbit' from other human ships. The Hak attacked 1,235 of such orbits ago."

"If you came here before the Hak, how long have your people been here? When did you leave your galaxy?"

"We never did. Our galaxy collided with this one."

"But...this galaxy never collided with another galaxy in eons, the last collision must have been billions of orbits ago."

"Yes, it has been a long time," said the voice.

A long time. Kel realized how "short time" and "long time" could have different meanings for different mind-sets and dared to ask, "Raar, when you said you kept me alive because I was like you, what exactly did you mean?"

"You are like us, Kel Chaada, long lived."

"Long lived—you mean immortal?"

"No, long lived."

"How old are you, Raar?"

"I am 508,123 orbits old."

"You are half a million orbits old? That's...that's probably older than the human species!"

"The human species did not exist when I was born."

"I...I..." Kel could not finish his sentence. Why did he even consider these unbelievable statements? It wasn't like he could read the alien's body language or have any reasonable expectation of detecting deception from a menacing-looking mass of movable graphite. Yet he somehow sensed it to be true. He also could not think of an angle, an upside the alien could have by telling him lies about this topic. "How would you know," he inquired, "that I am simply long lived, and not immortal?"

"We know, because the method that turned you long lived is ours."

∆∆∆

All human history he knew was a lie.

The early Oorkuu Ozh, first human generation after the galacticide, must have picked up the immortality transformation somewhere from the Traaz. They used it on themselves, perfected it for use with humans and then kept it as their best-guarded secret. It was hard to tell if the lie about the extra-galactic Kubuu Ksiw leaving raiding parties behind originated from the same time, or was added later. It was told to keep the surviving humans on an edge of anxiety, so traumatizing that a creed like Strength Through Conflict became an acceptable norm for an entire civilization. The highest priority for the first recivilized remaining humans after their species got nearly wiped out had been the concern about how to become as powerful as possible and how to keep everyone else of their species in check by fear and infighting. The Ancestrate of Aloo Dash ruled billions of people by direct fear of the Shaajrrurrhe, who might, remembering Shaajis Sya's threat to her own Assembly Member, feed you your own intestines. The Assembly of Oorkuu ruled everyone by indirect fear of someone else, the extra-galactic threat, so powerful and menacing that all nations accepted perpetual warfare as a preparatory state of mind, to be ready when the Kubuu Ksiw came back in force. In the meantime, they loaned their best military assets to a few hundred elitists, living forever in glittering white towers.

Kel felt he could judge none of this, as he was one of them. The only ancient nano tech he ever discovered he had turned into a bomb. It did not surprise him that the Traaz did not like humans. Why keep him alive? He could believe the initial intrigue he must have offered to his captors, being kept alive by the same technology that allowed them to live epoch-spanning lives.

The alien Raar kept coming back to his cell. Maybe Kel's astonishing level of cluelessness fascinated him. While the Kubuu Ksiw raids were simply a lore of lies perpetuated by the early human governments, the ongoing conflict between Assembly forces and the Traaz was real, and had been for many orbits. Kel assumed the Assembly used the Traaz as a stand-in threat for the Kubuu Ksiw. Scary aliens, superior spacecraft, heavy weapons, attacking from the unsettled parts of the Akaa Upsa galaxy—a perfect fit for the narrative. Raar's species was scary indeed. Every time he arrived—almost silently—through the sliding wall, he induced a jump scare in Kel. Maybe based on the recollection of his nightmares, maybe by the sheer dread emanating from his massive, dark, silicate body. The translator had difficulties conveying Kel's questions, or it struggled with the Traaz's responses, likely both, regarding detailed technical or biological descriptions. As far as Kel understood, the Traaz were hollow heaps of an organized rock-crystal mixture, making them a silicon-based life form. Silicon-based life was not new to human xenobiological exploration, but the examples that had been found so far were equivalent to simple multicellular organisms, few with the ability of directed motion, and none of them sentient. Silicon-based chemistry was less reactive and therefore much slower than carbon-based life metabolisms, but their silicon-based counterparts enjoyed a high durability and longevity in return.

The Traaz were impressively long lived, with fluid movements, adapting their body shape by growing and shrinking the crystal scaffolding of their bodies. They also did not know illness or disease. Kel had been injured before the Traaz took him prisoner, a state Raar kept calling "damaged," but he could not find the tiniest scar on his body, testament to the longevity treatment working its regenerative wonders. Raar offered no opinion of his own on how the Oorkuu Ozh got their "immortality" technology. Maybe it was a sensitive topic, or he simply did not know. Guessing, extrapolating, or assuming were not hallmarks of Raar's behavior. He dealt in facts and stayed away from any speculation. *A careful species*, Kel thought, *and observant, only acting when certain, that's how they had behaved in the brief encounter in space and that's how his captor and jailer, Raar, behaved.*

There was still the fact that they had boarded the ship and killed the crew. The passive facade was not to be taken as docility. The Traaz were a dangerous species, appeared technologically superior to humans, and Raar's monstrous body could have ripped Kel apart beyond the ability to self-heal, without a doubt. Raar avoided topics like their exact location, what kind of ship they were on, and how many others were traveling with them, but he freely responded to all questions about human history his species was aware of.

Historical topics fascinated Kel. The galacticide had not only wiped out almost all humans but also almost all their history and culture, making the pre-galacticide a realm of myths and legends, rather than historical facts. Ancient human civilizations likely spanned all along the Aloo Spur and the Akto Rim, having colonized almost a quarter of the galactic volume. The Traaz had settled many worlds in the Ze Fyez, which ran on the Ring facing away from the galactic core. According to Raar, the Akaa Upsa galaxy's peculiar structure, with two major and two minor arms, resulted from his home galaxy colliding with Akaa Upsa in a distant past, distant even by Traaz standards. Millions of star systems intermixed in the collision period, which took eons to complete, re-forming into the substructures of the galaxy. Most stars in the Traaz-settled part were not native to Akaa Upsa, but the ancestral home systems of Raar's people.

The Traaz had lived in that spiral arm ever since the collision, wary, observing a new emergent threat: sapient mammals. The feeble humans, soft flesh wrapped around a brittle endoskeleton, were neither threatening by appearance, nor by the technology they developed. It was their rapid breeding, the short time between generations, the numbers by which they started filling habitable worlds in their spiral arm. Both humans and Traaz lacked the ability to cross the darkstring-free space between spiral arms by warping space-time, and pre-galacticide humans would die from old age if they attempted to cross the galactic chasm at sub-light speed. None of them had ever attempted to cross into Traaz space, as expanding the colonization along their own spiral arm was easier.

The Kubuu Ksiw had brought this expansion to an immediate halt. These galactic raiders had technology superior to both species and nearly wiped out both. The Traaz, according to Raar, survived by pure grit, a few hardy survivors remaining on every world, former agreeable habitats turned into radiated ash deserts. The humans survived by having many individuals pre-galacticide combined with their ingenuity of finding hiding places. Some of their lightsail ships might have made it through the Fyez Transit, maybe even met the Traaz, but that was Kel's own conjecture—Raar, as usual, did not want to speculate.

"What did the Kubuu Ksiw want?" asked Kel. "We humans have never found out or understood."

"They took planets," said Raar in his typical fashion, giving responses begging for elaboration.

"They took planets?"

The cell shook—not from this revelation, but from some massive force that hit the ship.

19—HUMAN TACTICS

"**I** have to go," stated Raar, no emotion in the mechanical voice.

"Wait, Raar, what is going on?"

Kel had experienced no motion in this cell of his, not in the half-orbit he must have been here by rough estimation, no acceleration, not even the faintest vibration. Now another jolt, shaking the floor enough to lose his footing. Raar slid through the wall opening, looking unfazed by the shaking, not gracing Kel with an explanation. The wall closed.

Raar never left a conversation topic mid-sentence. He had spent much time with Kel, irregular shifts, sometimes shorter, sometimes longer. Hurtful memories came up. The last time Kel had been on a shaking ship, he ended up being imprisoned by an alien race. What fate would await this ship—and him, helpless and stuck on it?

The jolts continued in more rapid succession. The Traaz ship must have been absorbing an increasing barrage of... something. Kel knew it was not anything natural, which they could have avoided after a first surprise hit. They were under attack! He hoped his captors would not employ their sit-and-wait tactic he had witnessed during the encounter in the Nemkeg Spoke. That memory felt distant. A jolt strong enough to pull the floor away underneath him interrupted his contemplation, throwing him against the wall, then up to the ceiling, by what must have been an extreme ship maneuver, gluing him to the upper part of his cell. Kel had lost all his agility during captivity. He got thrown around the only room he had known for a long time without crouching or rolling, bouncing around like the soft sack of flesh Raar certainly saw him as. It hurt. Even more so when he came crashing down onto the edge of his bed. A crack from a broken bone was the last sound he heard before things went black.

Regaining consciousness, Kel saw a dark figure standing in the wall opening, reminiscent of the nightmares he used to have. Kel struggled to raise himself up, a piercing pain making him collapse on the bed again when he put some of his weight on the broken leg. Behind the dark figure was a sight he had never seen. The adjacent chamber had always been so small, some sort of security lock, but now it was open wide to allow view into a part of the ship outside the cellblock. Kel had also never seen another Traaz besides Raar. It turned out when his captor-visitor talked about the "others" on the ship, or "the crew," he had not lied. There were two Traaz, and neither of them was Raar. The nearest one was smaller than his familiar captor and had several lighter stripes across its otherwise dark body. The second one had additional rocky protrusions, which came closest to what would be an arm on a human body.

Kel, having been a soldier for a good part of his life, knew a weapon when he saw one, and that second Traaz held one aimed at Kel. He had never been held at gunpoint and was not sure if it was fear that encroached on his esophagus, but he felt like he had to throw up. Trying to keep his last meal down, with some disappointment about his lack of physical and now psychological resilience, he gestured toward the opening, which led someplace else in the ship.

"Do you want me to come with you?" he asked the striped Traaz.

No response.

"Do you want me to stay? Where is Raar?"

The pointed-teeth-filled mouth-heads each gave the equivalent of a stare. Kel noticed these two did not carry a translator, a small, but noticeable device Raar wore around the neck region of his body to every visit. Why did they not gesture what he was supposed to do next?

Kel pointed at himself, then the opening, but before he could pose his question again, another jolt shook the ship, sending him flying toward the Traaz. As easily as he was thrown around by whatever exerted these forces on the ship, as steadfast were the dark, rocky captors glued to the floor. Maybe they had decided Kel was too fragile to be left to his own movement, or they distrusted their human prisoner. The striped Traaz grew armlike protrusions to match the weapon carrier's ones and grabbed Kel around the body.

Even after all his time getting to know Raar, Kel still found a Traaz to be a frightening creature. The thought of touching his graphite-looking skin had never crossed Kel's mind. As the striped Traaz grabbed him, he expected the arm surface to be rough and the grip to break his remaining intact bones, but it was—almost shockingly—gentle. Firm, to lift him up without effort, but gentle. No dark claw touched his broken leg.

The two Traaz moved through the opening, weapon carrier first, followed by the Kel carrier. The opening was jagged and rough around the edges, and Kel understood why as he overlooked what seemed to be a hallway in the ship. The vessel's interior, as far as he could see, was a mess of formerly smooth metallic plating bent out of shape, some structural elements piercing through the wall covers, cracks in both floor and ceiling; some had odorless, black liquids dripping down, other openings offered glimpses to parts of the ship that were on fire. This spacecraft was close to being destroyed. Whatever was attacking his captors was winning this fight.

Other Traaz became visible for a short moment as the two who picked him up from his cell made it down the hallway, surprisingly quick and agile, bridging gaps with their ability to stretch and contract their lower bodies, carefully shielding Kel from liquids and fires, likely harmless to their hulking silicate masses, but deadly for their prisoner. *These guys are rescuing me*, thought Kel. *This part of the ship will not stay around for much longer, maybe even the entire vessel, and they are taking me someplace else.*

There was a nonverbal, eerie silence. As Traaz passed one another in the hallway, only the crackling fires were audible. If this crew was panicking, they did it quietly, at least to human ears.

The hallway led upward and the two Traaz were following its path when another violent jolt hit the ship. The striped Traaz held on to Kel, tightening his grip. An explosion, along with the abrupt movement, half deafened Kel. The metal frames holding the ship together emitted a long, high-pitched squeal, being pushed to the material limit—and beyond. In the chaos of flickering lights, flames, and terrifying noise, the hallway floor gave way. The two Traaz must have felt the downward motion, too, as both of them tried an alternate route, branching off the hallway, through tighter quarters, some intact, some a mélange of alien starship innards, untraversable by a human even without a broken leg. Kel was grateful his two guards had turned into protectors.

They expediently reached their destination, an undamaged part of the ship. Several airlock-like openings on one side, groups of Traaz—the most he had seen in one place— lining up in front of them. Raar stood at the end of the room, waving an arm protrusion, created by the crystalline restructuring of his body, mimicking a human gesture. "Come with me, Kel Chaada!" said the mechanical voice, the most pleasant sound he had heard since the attack began, breaking through the surrounding din of impending destruction. Kel's carrier hurried him into the opening next to Raar, the room looking like the interior of a small shuttle or escape pod, crammed with Traaz, their shades of gray all looking the same dark in the waning lighting of the dying ship. Raar followed inside as the last to board, the wall closing quickly behind him, lights becoming bright as the smaller vessel they had piled into now ran on its own power. Another bang followed, benign compared to the massive explosions before. The escape craft detached from the doomed mother ship.

Nobody was strapped in. There was not even anything in the pod resembling a seat, let alone seat belts. Aware of the dangers that rapid space travel caused the flimsy humans, the striped Traaz held on to Kel, while sliding into a niche in one of the external walls. The Traaz's lower body expanded into the shape of the niche, anchoring it in place. Kel's captors were a sight to behold, their marvelous, tough bodies flexing into every cranny of the vessel, 40 demonic visages pointing at him, showing what had to be a universal trait of all sapient life—curiosity. Kel thought about the possibility of all this being part of the atonement for his sins, escaping from one hell of bent metal and fire, chased by powerful demons, into the next, a pit filled with monsters, who might just have brought him along as a meal during their escape from their destroyed ship.

"Raar," asked Kel when he caught his breath, "what is happening?"

"The ship is going to be destroyed."

"Yes, but who is destroying it? Did we run into an Assembly fleet?"

That was a scary option. If his fellow escapees had to leave their vessel behind because of the humans, the eyeless stares he was receiving were probably not friendly ones. "Did we fight human ships?"

"No, the Isonomih attacked us, Kel Chaada."

"The Isomy? Are they Traaz, a different faction?"

"No, the Isonomih are a different species."

Another species Kel had never heard of before. "What is happening next? Where are we going?"

"We are going to our larger ships." The translator took a moment, then announced, more precisely, "We are going to our battle fleet."

"A battle fleet? Better than the ship we were on? Can they beat the...Isonomih?"

Kel's heart sank when Raar's mechanical proxy simply stated, "No."

"What do you mean? Why can't your ships beat them?"

"The Isonomih have similar numbers and fight better."

"Better how?"

"They fight faster, like the humans. They can also anticipate our moves."

"Like the humans? But you beat the humans, unless they have a much larger fleet!"

"That is because the human ships and the human crews are not sturdy. But they fight faster. This is why we want to keep humans out of our spiral arm."

Kel, despite being held by a monster, roughed up by escaping a ship on fire, leg broken, could see their dilemma now. The humans, and their militant aggressiveness combined with their fast breeding, scared the Traaz, so they wanted to prevent them from even thinking about crossing the interspiral arm chasm through costly skirmishes within the chasm border territories. Raar and his companions were raiders indeed, just not the infamous Kubuu Ksiw.

"How come there are Isonomih near the Fyez Transit? I don't think we humans have ever encountered them."

"We are not near the Fyez Transit. We have crossed into Traaz territory."

"Crossed the Transit? I know we have been en route for quite a while, but I am certain it was not nearly enough time to cross into Ze Fyez!"

"We have better ships now, Kel Chaada. We were going to my home, but the Isonomih are pushing deeper into our territory."

If Raar told the truth, Kel was now in a region of the galaxy that no human had ever visited. It might turn into a short visit, as Raar had clearly stated that the upcoming fight could end badly.

"How do they beat you? You said they anticipate your moves."

"Yes, they do," said Raar. "Now we must hurry." He turned to the wall at the end of the shuttle's tight cabin. It slid open.

△△△

"We have arrived," said Raar, "but we are not safe yet."

They must have landed on or docked with one of the other ships of the battle fleet, Kel figured. It had been unnoticeable, without noise, deceleration motion, or any forewarning. Kel could not imagine the force the attacking Isonomih must have used to so violently shake the much larger vessel's interior where he had been a prisoner. The striped Traaz peeled himself out of the wall niche and followed Raar, still carrying Kel with immense care. The 40 other survivors of the attack shuffled behind them in single file, without a sound.

Kel wondered if Raar was some sort of officer or leader —he had boarded the escape pod last, and was the first to leave it. During the brief journey, the others, except the striped one carrying him, had kept a respectful distance. Now they all followed him to wherever the destination was on this battleship. The hangar-like hall their escape craft had landed in was huge, filled with unfamiliar ship designs, equipment, and many other Traaz. Some carried weapons, some equipment, one had a cracked lower body, leaking some clear, gooey mass. He was the first wounded Traaz Kel had seen. Nobody tended to him. Maybe the wounds did not appear as severe to the Traaz, or maybe these aliens never developed the field of medicine out of lack of necessity.

"Where are we going, Raar?"

"I am going to the ship's controls. You will be taken to a safe place."

"The ship's controls? Are you a skipper...captain? The ship's commandant?"

"I am second in command."

"Of this ship, or the battle fleet?"

"Second in command of all Traaz."

This seemed unlikely, but so far Kel had never caught Raar in a lie. "Great, someone with say. Take me with you to the ship's controls!"

"Why, Kel Chaada?"

"Because I am a human tactician, a combat leader, and I can help you beat the Isonomih!"

Given the Traaz lack of facial expressions, or any face to begin with, not counting the sharp teeth mouth, Kel could not tell if Raar was considering his words, or just having an inaudible laugh with his friends. "How can you help?" asked the mechanical voice, without judgment.

"I can show your fleet new maneuvers, something these Isonomih have never seen you perform. We will surprise them!"

Kel cringed at the partial ridiculousness of his offer, but if he let these Traaz do their wait-and-see thing against some aggressive foes, who, unlike the humans, had better technology, they would all die. Raar stood there, hopefully contemplating to take him up on this offer. The last captain to whom Kel had proposed using his brilliant tactics had shot him with a stun gun.

"Follow me," said Raar and moved up a ramp leading out of the hangar-like area. Kel attempted to hop along on his unbroken leg, but he touched the floor with the broken one, and found it not hurting as much anymore. His body's regeneration was fast to mend the fracture. Still, his pace was not fast enough for Raar, who turned around and grabbed Kel, just as gently as the striped Traaz of whom he had lost sight, and carried him up the open, lattice-like interior of the ship, reaching what looked like the control room after a few passes. The Traaz in the room stopped whatever they were doing when Kel arrived in the arm protrusions of their leader who brought his pet prisoner to the bridge during a deadly battle.

Kel asked, "What is the situation?" as if it was his hover tank's cockpit, the last military vehicle he had commanded. Raar did not seem to mind the inquiry and responded, "The enemy fleet is assembling in their attack formation and will launch their attack in a short time."

"What are we doing?"

"We are holding our defensive position."

"Let me guess: single, one-dimensional line, facing the enemy at slow speed, waiting for them to move?"

"Correct, Kel Chaada." Maybe being virtually indestructible had prevented this civilization from developing any advanced tactics, or something else held them back. He would have to phrase his proposed maneuvers in simple terms, so that Raar could relay them to his crew.

"You need to pick one of the flanks, one of the sides of the formation they are in, and attack it in a semicircular run." Kel gestured the fleet's movement, waving his hands through the heated air in front of him. It was blistering hot, even more so than in the cell he had spent so much time in. He was sweaty, with some oily mass from the abandoned ship still sticking to his pants, one leg swollen from the fracture, near to physical and mental exhaustion, trying to explain the basics of space combat to the second in command of his captor species.

"We need to let them make the first move. Whoever makes the first move, will make a mistake," pushed Raar back.

"No." Kel stood his ground. "Whoever moves first has the initiative! They force you to react, and if that's how you always fight them, they will expect it. Attack their flank first, take some of their ships out while the rest of their formation swings around, keep pushing on that flank while circling around them, and always face a few of their ships with all of your ships. I have no idea what weapons you have or what they will use, but whatever it is, you can use all of your firepower, and they can't. You have never done this, they will not see it coming."

Kel could swear he felt Prral's fine dust on his lips, and saw Vyoz's face considering him when he added, "Trust me!"

20—A NEW HOME

Kel was to be presented to the Traaz ruler this rotation, but unlike when he had met with Shaajis Sya, he did not have the slightest idea what he should say.

Raar had not lied when he said he was second in command, but the translation was inadequate: He was the heir apparent of the realm of the Traaz. The aliens, like the Ancestrate of Aloo Dash, had never moved on from an absolute monarchy; at least they had the excuse that their monarch, Raar's parent—Zihriik—had been their leader for what Kel assumed must have been a ridiculously long time. The translator had called Raar's relationship to the Traaz they were about to meet his "parent," but Kel had noticed no obvious sexes among the aliens he had seen so far. Maybe "parent" referred more conceptually to a forebear than the human definition of the term.

Raar had fought fast—"fast like a human"—and had ordered his crew to execute the aggressive maneuvers per Kel's suggestions. Although badly executed, they completely surprised the Isonomih ships with the atypical behavior. Never had the Traaz ships torn into their flank, leaving them to react, trying to control the situation while taking losses, their entire formation coming apart after just a few passes, taking more losses and then, one by one, emergency warping out of Traaz space. According to Raar, it had been the first battle his people had won for many orbits, an encounter he had estimated they would neither win nor survive. It was hard to tell what happened after the battle, the aliens' communication being nonverbal, based on exchange of thoughts. No cheers, or any discernible joy or at least relief. Everybody just crewed their stations or repaired battle damage. However, the remarkable victory not only stood out from a long sequence of losses, it also saved the heir apparent's life. His parent, Zihriik, must have taken notice, and likely wanted to see this human, who had turned from a curious science project to being useful.

Zihriik's throne chamber was the opposite of the royal seat Kel had visited on Aloo Dash: underground, dark and windowless, low ceilings, few light sources illuminating walls looking like moist, sweaty, burgundy-colored rocks and casting long shadows into side tunnels otherwise. A dark-hued Traaz, with a bright light spot on his front and reddish stripes of sparkling crystals, equipped with a translator unit like the one Raar carried, stood in the center—Zihriik, the ruler, no doubt. The small groups of Traaz accompanying Kel, including Raar, formed a half circle around Zihriik, at a respectful distance. The ruler grew an arm protrusion and waved at Kel. "Come forward, Kel Chaada!" It was the same mechanical voice Raar used. "I am Zihriik."

Kel moved toward him a few steps, only a light limp remaining, his leg feeling much better after a few spins only.

"It is an honor to meet you," he began, bowing his head, wondering if this gesture meant anything to the alien.

"You have saved my offspring," stated Zihriik, interrupting what Kel had assumed would be a longer, formal introduction or exchange of pleasantries. For a near-immortal species, these aliens seemed to have no time to waste. "You have saved other Traaz, too. You are our prisoner. Humans are our enemy. Why did you help us?"

Zihriik's question did not seem to account for the obvious: Kel would have died along with everyone else onboard had they lost the battle to the Isonomih, but he felt that saying "I wanted to save my own kyong" made him sound small and selfish, so he improvised by stating: "I am like you!"

Zihriik stood silent, maybe pondering his response. "You are long lived, like us, and helped us. Other long-lived humans fight us."

"Oh, you mean the Oorkuu Ozh, the Assembly Members? Yes, they fight you so they can rule the humans."

"To rule the humans? Explain."

"They pretend the Traaz are the Kubuu Ksiw, the Hak, as you call them, and make humans fear them in order to control the human-settled galaxy."

"We are nothing like the Hak! Why do short-lived humans believe the long-lived humans?"

"Because there is no human left alive who remembers what the Hak were like. We have nothing left from that time except a few stories."

Kel was not sure if his explanations made sense, or got correctly translated, but Zihriik changed topics. "My offspring has studied you for some time and said you are an interesting human."

"He studied me? Well, yes, we talked quite a bit, and I learned a bit about your people as well."

"What have you learned?"

"I have learned that Raar can be trusted, he never lied to me."

"Have you lied to him?" Kel's stomach turned, and he felt nauseous. "Can I trust you?" asked Zihriik, but his voice changed. It was not the mechanical translator voice. The voice came from all around, not just from the direction where the alien leader stood in front of him. It was similar to the thoughts and voices he shared with the bomb carriers, emotions rather than sentences, yet clear in their meaning. Kel tried to form a response with his conscious thought—"Yes, you can"—then forcefully vomited his last meal onto the floor right before the monarch of this alien nation. The retching did not subside for passes. He fell on his hands and knees, feeling like he had turned his insides out in front of Zihriik and his court, furious with humiliation, unable to control his body.

"His Uurmi cannot hear or speak." He heard Raar say that from behind him, using the translator voice.

"How is this possible?" asked Zihriik. "Have you ever talked to his Uurmi directly?"

"No," said Raar.

"Where does his voice come from, then? What is creating his thoughts?" Even the low-intonation translator voice could not hide Zihriik's confusion and astonishment.

"What...is the Uurmi?" asked Kel, getting back up, wiping his mouth with his already stained sleeve, not caring if he broke protocol even more, doubting that it was possible. His question seemed to have puzzled ruler and heir alike.

Zihriik's translation unit came to life, stating: "The Uurmi gives us long life, you and us, it is what makes us alike. The Uurmi is us! The Uurmi is you!"

ΔΔΔ

If Kel was to return to the human-settled part of the galaxy, what would he do there?

Kel had lied a lot: He had lied to his friend, his love, his captor, and likely countless other people. Compared to the Assembly Members, however, he was an absolute amateur. Not only did they rule the galaxy by an invented, nonexistent threat and had stolen their legendary immortality technology from an alien species, they also obfuscated how the procedure worked, even from their own initiates.

Uurmi, as it turned out, were microscopic entities, similar in size and apparent function to the many single-cell life forms in the galaxy. The entire "procedure" to turn a human immortal as he underwent it was unnecessary: The complex machinery and devices, the people present, the chanting, none of it had any influence and function. The only important step was to ingest a dose of the Uurmi. They would settle down in the human abdomen, like other intestinal bacteria humans had shared their bowels with for as long as the species existed. The

Uurmi then excreted their many complex compounds, using the body's own mechanism of transport, like blood, to get them to where they were needed to keep the host organism in top shape, forever. Like intestinal bacteria, they were a symbiotic parasite, a different life form, benefiting from the host's body, but paying back with dividends for a mutual gain. The only technical step was preparing the Uurmi "cells" to adapt more easily to a human body. Everything else during the ritual was a show, put up to convey a complexity of the procedure that did not exist. Immortality was not something the Assembly wanted to share lightly. Once the Uurmi established a foothold in the human body, the positive effects of unlimited rejuvenation became permanent. The insatiable appetite Kel had noticed in the shifts following the procedure was a natural side effect of the Uurmi reorganizing the gut flora, making the recipient crave a carnivorous diet.

The Uurmi used by the humans and the ones used by the Traaz differed in one major feature: While the Uurmi living in Kel's insides were a loose collection of specialized individual cells, unaltered Uurmi would become more: a complex network of cells, able to process and retain information in an organized form, becoming sentient. In fact, the Uurmi were the only entity inside a Traaz body that had a higher form of consciousness. The Traaz were—simply put—animated silicate rock, with an intestinal tract reaching from their monstrous mouth to an opening on their lower base body. Occasionally they needed to bite off some silicate rocks with their pointy, sharp teeth-like mouth crystals, and they inhaled oxygen to produce most of their silicate molecular building blocks. This diet was simple and unappealing, but maintained strong, virtually indestructible bodies that lasted more than a million orbits. As remarkable as this species was, they were not sapient. Their bodies were, however, the perfect home for the Uurmi, a panspermian parasite, always looking for host species to take over, settling their intestinal tract if they had one, adding their required foods to the diet of the host, and rewarding it with near-eternal life. Each Traaz gave its Uurmi colony a permanent home, well protected, and with its impressive and deadly jaws well suited for killing and biting off the Uurmi's favorite food—multicellular, animalic meat. The Uurmi prevented the Traaz from turning into rampaging meat-devouring monsters, instead turning them into even longer-lived, hardy, robust sapients, creating eon-spanning civilizations surviving even galactic collisions, communicating with one another through telepathy, overlapping force fields created by their consciousness. When talking to Raar and Zihriik, Kel had not conversed with the rocky Traaz shells, but the networked Uurmi mind inside. For the Traaz this was the only form of existence they had known since both species met and fused billions of orbits ago in a distant galaxy, eventually becoming part of Akaa Upsa.

What had confused Zihriik when they met was Kel's consciousness not stemming from the Uurmi colony inside his gut, but another organ creating sapient thought, the human brain. It had taken the Traaz who held him captive in his cell quite a while to figure this out, trying to communicate with him Uurmi to Uurmi at first, gut to gut, with the nasty side effect of Kel's Uurmi cells, unable to deal with the telepathic onslaught of information, dying and rebelling, turning his intestines into a bacterial war zone, with the unpleasant side effect of losing meal after meal, forcefully purged from his system. If he understood correctly, Raar himself had the translator unit constructed, conveying information via sound waves, a bizarre communication method from the Traaz point of view. Kel must have talked to himself or in his sleep a lot for them to have picked up on that option. Raar had studied him, as Zihriik said, first as an example of a foe, trying to understand the way of thinking and motivations, then as a fascinating specimen. Now, he had become an asset.

Kel's tactical prowess had impressed Zihriik, even more by him rescuing not only one of their battle fleets but also his heir. Their hive-minded world view could not comprehend self-preservation of the individual being a driving force for one's actions, so they saw Kel's intervention as an act of extreme selflessness shown by an enemy. Kel did not have a good understanding of their culture, but they seemed to view this as an honorable deed, worthy of a reward.

He took his prize back to the guest quarters of Zihriik's palatial underground maze to ponder. The reward was a choice —and it was not an easy one. Zihriik granted him his freedom, offering to either take him back to the human-settled spiral arm, or have him live among his captors-turned-hosts, giving him a consulting role in the Traaz's space fleet: a tactical advisor in their fight against the Isonomih. It seemed like an obvious choice at first. Being set free by the rock monsters and returned to his own people sounded attractive. But was it? What would happen after his arrival? Should he go back into hiding?

The alternative was to lead a strange life, thousands of light-orbits from home, with aliens that had haunted his nightmares not too long ago, making him vomit if they tried to greet him. It was going to be a strange life indeed, but he would be free. It was going to be a meaningful life, a life of purpose. He had, as far as he knew, saved the Nominate of EsChii from destruction, and now he could try doing the same for his adoptive civilization of hardened immortals. Kel would stay— and fight. Fight—fast, like a human!

ΔΔΔ

"The Isonomih have no weaknesses."

"Nonsense!" said Kel, uncertain if his angry demeanor would translate into something meaningful for the Uurmi mind inside Raar's familiar hulk. "Everybody and everything has a weakness!"

The first tactical review meeting onboard Raar's flagship was not going well and made Kel wonder how the Traaz had held up against their Isonomih foe at all. "Let's summarize: The Isonomih are a machine civilization. Everything is electromechanical, with buildings, machines, and vehicles all designed to house artificial intelligence cores, the Isonomih's equivalent of a human brain or a Traaz Uurmi. They are methodical, fast to react, as you would expect, and have weapon systems comparable to the Traaz. They do not rely on heavily armored ship designs but have a superior shield technology. They also, as it seems, fairly recently, developed a new warp propulsion system that gives them far better range." Kel paused.

"This is correct, Kel Chaada," said Raar.

He did not like when Raar called him by his full name at the end of every sentence and had told him so many times. Raar used his name sparingly, but it was always during tense conversations. Kel was convinced the dark alien only did it when he was at odds with Kel, knowing that repeating his name would make him angry. *There is an ego under this ancient silicate crust*, thought Kel, *and it has feelings that can be hurt.* This, strangely, calmed him down, made him smile, even.

"They ran!"

No reaction from Raar.

"There is your weakness! When things did not go to plan for them, they tried to adjust their formation, but every Isonomih ship that took damage soon warped away. Once their numbers dwindled, all other ships also left."

"Yes, they avoid losses," said Raar.

"And you don't?"

"We avoid losses when possible, but it is not our highest priority. Our highest priority is to win the battle. Lost ships are only a secondary concern."

"Lost ships, what about lost Traaz?" asked Kel.

"When a ship is destroyed by anything else but an explosion, the Traaz crew can survive in space for a short time and await rescue."

Knowing that a short time for a Traaz could be a long time for a human, Kel had to ask. "How long can they survive? You need to breathe oxygen, right?"

"We inhale oxygen regularly to digest, but we can live

without it for 20 shifts."

A hardy people they are, thought Kel. *Worthy survivors of the galacticide.*

"The Isonomih will retreat when they take losses, but we struggle to get close enough to damage their ships with our weapons," said Raar.

"Why is that? Are your weapons not effective at range?"

"The problem is the Isonomih shielding, it is adaptive, and our missiles and projectiles can only penetrate it when fired from very close range."

"How do we get your ships close then?"

"That is what you tell me, Kel Chaada."

Unable to tell if Raar was still cross, or trying to develop a sense of humor, Kel pondered the question, then asked, "Have you tried to match your thrusters with background star's spectral signatures? Or modified your ship's shields to hide in proto-systems and nebulae?"

Silence told Kel none of these had been tried. Hiding ships or at least making their scanner signature less obvious by using natural phenomena or bodies in space was as old as space combat itself and the Isonomih might know these tricks as well, but they had never seen the Traaz use them. All they needed to do was to get the Traaz ship close enough to do effective damage, then the Isonomih could decide to stay and fight on even terms or, as they seemed to prefer, vanish by warping away. The superior range gave the Isonomih the initiative, the ability for deep incursions into Traaz territory, but the defenders knew these regions well, as each gas cloud, asteroid belt and gravitational anomaly was charted.

These places were perfect to set a trap.

ΔΔΔ

"All ships standing by for assault range," said Raar, standing in the frigate's small command room.

The first two skirmishes with Isonomih forces had been

traps, set for their scouting ships. They could not destroy any scouts, as Kel expected, based on their previous behavior. All enemy ships retreated, and the Traaz had no losses, either. Every region the Isonomih could not scout, they would not dare warp into with a larger attack fleet, so the Traaz planetary populations saw these small successes as huge wins, keeping their systems safe, for a short time at least. Even the most stoic sentient rock must tire of losing battle after battle, so Kel assumed. The tactical victories boosted morale.

The third operation was bolder. Isonomih task forces often assembled near stars, just outside of the corona, maybe to hide their ships from direct observation or using the heat or radiation to recharge some of their systems. Whichever the reason, it happened regularly, and Kel planned to use it against them. A force of 20 Isonomih ships, light scout vessels, but also several larger destroyers, had taken positions near the Kreukthoto system's yellow main sequence star. Kreukthoto was a mature solar system, devoid of debris, gas, and small planetesimals that littered younger systems. Anticipation was not a strength of artificial intelligence, but learning was— Kel could use each new tactic only once, then the Isonomih would adapt. Limiting their assembly points to these types of "cleaner" solar systems was one countermeasure taken to prevent being ambushed. Kreukthoto, like many older systems, had an extensive collection of comets; many on long, stretched elliptical orbits around the star. Raar's attack force was hiding in the coma of one of these comets, just about to complete the gravitational swing by the yellow star, hurtling toward the other side of the luminous body, passing the parked enemy flotilla at close distance. The coma, between the comet's nucleus and the tail, was where the gaseous cloud the star's radiation was pushing out of the leading nucleus was densest, dense enough to hide a strike group of Traaz frigates from standard approach scanners until it was too late and they had reached what they needed against the AIs—a short striking distance.

"Holding tight formation, weapons powered down."

Raar's translator made the thoughts of the other ships' captains audible for Kel. Their ambush group would remain as stealthy as possible until the last moment. That moment arrived when the comet, innocent on its elemental journey, crept up on the unalerted AI ships. Kreukthoto's star filled most of the screens. Traaz ships had no viewports, like most of their buildings had no windows. The aliens' surface coating had a layer for sensing —seeing—some human visible light and infrared, and they had interior lighting accordingly, but it was not the primary sense their Uurmi mind relied on. It could sense electromagnetic fields, even weak ones, and was directly connected to the ship's sensors, similar to human crews having data streamed into their consciousness through the virtual tactics helmets. Kel had suggested having such a direct connection created for him, but it was unclear if Raar had one commissioned to be developed, or even liked the idea.

Kel clenched his teeth and hissed to himself, "Let's get them!"

They reached the closest distance of approach. The Traaz ships took a few ticks to power their weapons, then jumped out of hiding onto their unsuspecting prey. A large spread of missiles rained on the Isonomih destroyers and scouts, closely followed by the attacking force, firing all available projectile cannons. The raid was short and brutal, the AI ships taking massive damage. Two of them, shields deactivated for unknown reasons, were overpowered by the incoming hail of metal, disintegrating in blinding explosions; a third, damaged thrusters out of control, headed into the star's corona toward a fiery end. The Isonomih had taken losses for the first time since the incursions into Traaz territory had begun.

Raar turned his neck around, opening his jaws just wide enough to show his teeth. "Victory!" he said via thought, and Kel sensed the same from his crewmates. The unspoken words included more nuance and information, a sense of common accomplishment, more than his neutered gut Uurmi could pick up from the hive mind.

Kel envied them this closeness, something he had not felt since the camaraderie between soldiers during the war on Prral, or the emotions shared with the group of bomb carriers. Their thoughts were gone, likely silenced by the enormous distance from...home. Kel wondered how the Nominate was faring.

"Do you regret not rejoining your people?" asked Raar. He must have picked up on Kel's thoughts for the short tick the Uurmi connection lasted.

"No," said Kel out loud. "I am home."

21—FIGHTING MACHINES

20 orbits later...

"Warriors of Traaz," Kel Chaada conveyed through thought, "welcome to my home!" The command room of the battle cruiser Sheekilku, his flagship, certainly felt like it. For 20 orbits, Kel had spent most of his time here.

He stood in the center of the circle formed by the Traaz, keeping the defined distance—a sign of respect for their third in command. He looked around, recognizing the different hues of gray, various markings in the silicate crusts, some natural, some scars of battles fought together, seeing the familiar sight of his most trusted captains.

"We fought the Isonomih for many orbits, we fought them in our core systems, pushed them back to our fringe, then the border, then their fringe, and now we have arrived at one of their core worlds for the first time!"

A wave of pride and acknowledgment emanated from the group. "We are not on the defensive anymore. We now have the initiative after so many battles won but also so many Traaz lost. Their long lives were cut short, but their sacrifices have enabled us now to strike into the industrial center of the enemy for the first time—the Isonomih shipyards, assembly factories for many of their ships, who have plagued us for so long. The Isonomih have proven to be a formidable foe, industrious and adaptable, and we have used every trick, every feint, every hideout to ambush and destroy them. Today, my warriors, we will fight like we have not fought in a long time: like Traaz!"

The confusion among the captains was almost tangible. Although Kel had mastered the Uurmi telepathy during the drawn-out conflict, a state of thought dissonance still wrenched his gut. Kel had learned from past mistakes and never had meals before combat. His captains had good reason to be confused, as it was his relentless drill of innovative, never-repeated tactics that had led the silicate species from victory to victory over their mechanical menace. Now he wanted them to fall back on their old ways.

"The shipyards are crucial for them, and they will have to defend them. We will approach the yards at maximum thruster speed, in a tight formation. They will expect to get ambushed, as we always ambushed them, and keep their ships in a flexible defensive formation, allowing them to protect their installation from all directions. By the time they realize we only attack from one direction, with our entire force, we will have closed in enough to break through that perimeter. Not close enough for our weapons to be effective—theirs, however, will be, and we will take hits, incur losses. We will pierce their line and head straight into the yards, and I mean all the way into the massive floating dock structures themselves. While we fire at everything we can aim at and take their ship factories apart, they can decide to wait for us outside, or follow us into the yards to fight us— fight us at close range. We will refocus our fire at every ship that follows us inside and destroy them right where many of these ships have been built!"

Kel felt a wave of approval. Not that he needed it anymore, but he was still glad when the captains stood behind a plan and did not simply follow orders. In the many orbits of war against the machine civilization, Zihriik, the Traaz leader, increasingly trusted his former prisoner turned tactician, gave him more authority, a ship, and eventually a fleet of his own to command.

Kel was certain that Zihriik would rather risk a human on the front lines than his own heir, Raar, who commanded fewer ambushes and raids now.

The battle at the Isonomih shipyards was a next step, not only for the Traaz gaining the initiative in the war but also the first full fleet action to be commanded by Kel alone. He had chosen the yards as their first target in the AI territory for two reasons. One was to diminish the enemy's ability to replace their losses and build new warships. The second reason was more subtle: The Isonomih's AI cores were the individuals of their civilization. They fit into many other sophisticated machines they built, like spaceships, but they saw all these as replaceable, compared to the cores. Striking the shipyards would deal an immense blow to their war effort without destroying many of the AI cores. The shipyards were highly automated and would not need more than a few individual AIs running them, maybe only a single one. A successful attack could leave the Isonomih's infrastructure broken enough to consider ending the war, but the low losses of actual Isonomih AIs would not make them too apprehensive to dismiss seeking peace.

Peace. Since the day the Nominate had drafted him away from his shield engineering job on EsChiip, Kel had fought in an interstellar conflict of some kind or another, spent the last 20 orbits fighting raid after raid, ambush after ambush, with the Isonomih. They did not grow tired, it seemed, and neither did his adoptive Traaz civilization. Despite all the ingenuity he could devise for ever-changing tactics, losses on his side were mounting. His warriors did not complain and willingly risked their long lives. Kel, thanks to the Uurmi living inside him, looked not one orbit older than when he had first met Raar, but he felt the repetitive strain of going from operation to operation, star system to star system, fight to fight. Like his experiences from Prral, the camaraderie between soldiers was one truly redeeming factor of military life. "Return to your ships, warriors! Get into formation, we will attack soon."

Tense anticipation of battle and thoughts equivalent to

wishing good fortune ebbed and flowed through Kel's mind as the captains left his command deck one by one. Kel had given them all the tactics he could come up with. Now he needed to rely on the Traaz grit and the Isonomih miscalculating their attack plan. He could count on the one, but was relying on the other enough to win?

△△△

This was it, the decisive battle, designed to convince the AIs of the fallacy of continued conflict.

A scout probe sent ahead had confirmed their attack vector, and Kel's captains had put their capital ships into a tight formation as ordered. They wedged the smaller cruisers and destroyers into the formation as well, preventing smaller Isonomih craft from disrupting or breaking up the formation when they were trying to pierce through the defensive ring of enemies around the yards. Not "trying to pierce through," they were *going to* pierce through! His mastery of the Uurmi telepathy allowed him to have private thoughts, tucked away and hidden from the group. He could be honest with himself and the doubts he had. The attack was going to be brutal during the initial phase, with better shields, higher fire range, all advantages on the enemy's side, except one: the concentrated force of an entire fleet attacking one small area.

The other ships' crews collectively thought: "We are ready." Kel strode to his command chair and strapped in, the only convenience he allowed himself, not shared by his command crew, his feeble human body simply unable to withstand the turbulence of rapid space battle maneuvers.

The attack run began, his flagship coordinating a maximum burn for all vessels around the binary system's smaller star component, using the larger star component for a swing-by maneuver, increasing speed, ending the S-shaped trajectory on a direct collision course with the Isonomih installation. Enemy sensor beacons had picked up their arrival without a doubt and were transmitting to the shipyards, putting them into highest alert by the time they came into effective range.

"Prepare missile swarm!" ordered Kel. All missile-carrying vessels launched their payload with a quick burn, thousands of missiles forming a halo around the fleet, ending their acceleration, matching the ships' speed. On near contact with the Isonomih, they would reignite and head straight into the Isonomih at the target vector. Almost all of them would end up exploding on the enemy's phase shields in an impressive show of force, but not cause actual damage. They would, however, keep the enemy countermeasure systems busy for the few ticks until the particle cannons came into firing range.

"One lightpass," reported the chief astrogator. Kel felt the bridge crew getting ready for the final approach. The more distant crews of the other ships fell into the chorus of anxious anticipation right before combat. Despite the danger they raced toward, Kel loved these moments, when all he thought and all he was became one with the crews; the entire fleet of metal and animated silicate became him, and he became the fleet.

"Missile swarm loose!" Kel's order let the anxiety relieve into an unheard battle cry. Thousands of yellow-white streaks lit the space around the Isonomih perimeter fleet, ticks away from impact. "Enemy defense formation holding, evenly distributed. Minimum resistance ahead."

They bought it, thought Kel. The Isonomih were still waiting for the Traaz surprise attack, the ambush from some place they did not expect; the feint that never happened. Following the shock wave of the collective missile explosions, the compacted Traaz fleet was on its way to break into the defensive sphere around the yards. All enemy ships around that aimed-for breakpoint opened fire, controlled by an AI that might just have realized that the only trap in this battle was the absence of one. The incoming fire was not any less deadly because of this. Unlike the Isonomih phase shields, the Traaz protective plasma matrices could not compensate for the incoming force of projectiles. The lead ships took most of the hits, plasma flaring up, hull armor penetrated, internal explosions fracturing hulls, turning two of the largest battleships—a formidable force just a tick ago—into infernal husks of uncontrolled metallic mass, breaking out of formation, veering toward the enemy, becoming open for receiving fire from almost all angles. The larger ships took several smaller vessels with them, rammed into and damaged them, or bumped them out of the formation. Others avoided collision, but the maneuver burns took them out of the protective formation just the same.

The ships ejected from the formation would have to fend for themselves as the main force pushed on past the perimeter. Incoming fire had less impact, as missiles and projectiles had to catch up with the passing Traaz fleet, heading straight into the gaping maw of the largest module of the shipyard, where battleship-size vessels were assembled. The gigantic metal cave was open, without gates or protective shields, the mechanical Isonomih not needing protection from the harsh, cold near-vacuum of space. Burning all retro thrusters, the fleet entered the megastructure, all coming to a halt relative to the yard's orbital speed. One frigate on the periphery of the formation botched the synchronized maneuver and rammed the opening's frame, dealing the first damage to the shipyard, paid for with many Traaz lives.

All outward-facing guns opened fire, blasting every visible surface or internal structure of the shipyard. The layer of ships coming in last, positioned between the yard's interior and the Traaz fleet, prepared for the Isonomih attempting to follow them inside, if they dared to plunge their ships into the now well-filled dock. Isonomih ships were tough, but the shipyards had not been built to withstand attacks and the structure came apart after only a few volleys of fire from the fleet.

"Enemy positions?" asked Kel. Would the Isonomih follow them despite the risk, or get into position to harass the fleet with missiles?

"Perimeter sphere formation collapsing inward to the shipyards, closing in, but no pursuit yet." He thought it unlikely that the AIs felt anything resembling shock, no matter how surprising the Traaz fleet maneuver had been, so they had to be planning something else. "Escape pods launching from shipyard structure." That was it—they were fleeing, the fleet coming in not to continue the fight but to collect the yard's AI survivors.

Three passes later, warp signatures outside the disintegrating shipyard showed the Isonomih had started leaving the system. It had taken only eight passes between first shots fired and the shipbuilding facility breaking apart. The main frame of the structure collapsed after sustaining too much damage and metal chunks the size of battleships drifted away. Unchallenged now after the guard fleet's departure, the Traaz kept firing until they were convinced that no piece of wreckage remained salvageable except for the metal content.

"Victory!" Relief, pride, and joy raced through Kel's mind. He did not even attempt to think his own thoughts, just bathed in the ocean of the fleet's exhilarated hive mind. An additional thought-wave of excitement mixed into this celebration, undefined, drowned out by the shared sentiment, but then clearer, picked up by most in the group consciousness, creating mental gasps from his silicate comrades: "We have picked up a survivor!"

Kel did not understand why this was so shocking, as the Isonomih put survival of their combatants over everything, a fact he had exploited tactically for orbits. He followed the thought-wave to its origin, directly asking the Traaz captain, who got the Isonomih onboard his own ship. "Congratulations for taking a prisoner, warrior! I assume this is a rare event?"

"Yes, Commander. The escape pods we thought we tracked were not small ships, they were stripped AI cores. This is the first one we have ever captured intact!"

△△△

Kel had never fought the Isonomih up close. What would the AI core look like?

The Traaz transferred the captured core to Kel's flagship's holding facility. "All our scans show the core is operational and active," reported the cell block crew. They were careful not to probe the Isonomih too much, constituting communication in the sense the Traaz understood it. It was the commander's privilege to speak to any prisoner of war first. *Just like Raar had talked to him*, thought Kel. Unlike Raar, Kel was too curious to keep his prisoner waiting for many spins, and headed to his cell right away. A forcefield enveloped the AI, a security measure, negating its own limited warp field capabilities, gluing the core body to the cell floor, keeping it in place while Kel would be in the room. As he approached, the wall slid away, presenting a scene that was as novel as it was familiar.

A bright, almost white-walled cell like this one had been his home for many spins.

The current prisoner had no known needs; even the most basic amenities Kel's cell had featured were missing. It was an empty rectangular room. In the center stood the prisoner, from the floor reaching up to Kel's chin, a segmented metallic figure, a pentagonal prism forming the base for the widest part, a thin disk featuring two antenna arrays—maybe scanners. A translucent cylinder sat on the disk, emanating a blue light —the power source?—topped by a flat dome. The dome was riddled with small bulges, gaps, and delicate irregularities, making it look more organic than he had expected from an electromechanical being. Like a Traaz at rest, it featured no visible appendages for motion or object manipulation, and none of the surface details had an obvious mechanical function.

He walked around the Isonomih, which remained motionless, and decided to treat the side showing more surface details as "front" facing, when he addressed the AI by thought: "My name is Kel. Who are you?"

He followed up saying the same words out loud, struggling somewhat and having to clear his throat, realizing he had not used his vocal cords much, relying on shared thoughts and emotions for many orbits now, eventually even stopping his habitual self-talk.

He tried a few more sentences and questions, both by thought and vocal language, with no result—the Isonomih likely could not understand, or even receive his communication attempts, or in the unlikely case it did, chose not to respond, or could not. The AI core standing before Kel was usually embedded into and connected to some other form of Isonomih machinery and might be incomplete without it. It was possible that Kel was talking to a brain without eyes and ears, alive and conscious, but unaware of its surroundings, including Kel's presence. He decided he had been naïve to come here without a thorough scan for options to interface with the core, hoping for a meaningful exchange of words or thoughts. At least the Traaz tradition of the commander speaking to the prisoner first had been properly upheld and allowed lower-ranking crew members to get to work analyzing the prisoner.

Kel stared at the Isonomih for a pass, then turned around and signaled the guards to open the sliding wall. He left the cell, feeling dread as memories bubbled up into his consciousness from both his imprisonment and the ship being on fire when he first stepped out of his cell. He looked back and stared at the wall, now closed, trapping the prisoner in the cell. Orbits ago, his untrained mind could not pick up the nuances between sensory memories, recalled emotions, and conscious present thought, but now they were as clear to him as listening to three distinct languages from different planets. The memories were all his own, but the dread came from within the cell—the Isonomih was frightened.

△△△

The Traaz engineers could not explain how Kel could pick up an emotion from the AI, and how it could produce one so clearly.

After retrieving surviving crew members and salvaging parts of the destroyed or damaged ships, the raiding fleet returned to Traaz space, giving the specialists time to further analyze their prisoner of war. The AI was not requiring any external inputs or energy supply, it seemed, and was an autonomous machine, capable of limited motion and power production. All analogies with existing Traaz computer technologies failed. They could not understand the internal structure of the AI core from scans alone, showing a shocking level of complexity and uninterpretable patterns of electric and quantum computing activity. The hull showed more promise: several of the surface features resembling interfaces between a regular computer core and external components, opening up routes of communication or at least some basic signal exchange.

Traaz ingenuity had built Raar's translator box, transforming the complex Uurmi thought patterns into audible human language—Kel's native language—and back. They had researched and constructed that prototype in a quarter orbit. It dawned on Kel why it had taken so long for the first Traaz, his now-friend and confidant, Raar, to visit his cell. Raar wanted to communicate with his then-prisoner first, not to violate his people's traditions. Kel himself had visited his prisoner more carelessly, lucky to pick up on the Isonomih's distress. The Traaz had seen this as first communication and lauded Kel's ability to understand thoughts across species.

The Traaz were a meritocratic culture, respecting individuals with unique or well-developed abilities, and had never hesitated to communicate and collaborate with Kel, a human: member of a species they shared a contested border and exchanged fire with. He had lived among them for many orbits, and they had not once excluded him from anything, unless his less-rugged body could not keep up. He was certain that integrating a telepathic, monster-mouthed, dark pile of rock into any human society would have proven near impossible.

"The interface is ready, Commander," reported the lead engineer of the flagship. "For now, it is limited to voice input and output, as we used the design your old interface was built on."

"Let's talk to our prisoner." Kel headed to the cell block. The Isonomih stood in the white room where Kel had left him several spins ago. Nothing about the AI's appearance, including the intensity of the blue glow, had changed, except the few cables attached to its base, one connected to the familiar translator box at their end.

"My name is Kel. Who are you?" asked Kel.

"847838918415501088…" started the Isonomih, with the same voice Raar and Zihriik used on their translator units when Kel still required them, irritating and strange, going against human habits to link voice and intonation to a specific individual.

"Do you have a name besides this number?"

"No."

"My species cannot easily memorize long numbers. Can I address you as 8-4, Me-Ruu?"

"Yes."

"Are you damaged or harmed in any way?"

"I was taken prisoner, against my will," said Me-Ruu with the stoic speech pattern that, if the voice had not been so strongly associated with Kel's Traaz friend, would be very fitting for an electromechanical being.

"Yes, you are our prisoner. We are at war."

"I do not understand."

"You do not understand that we are at war?"

"I do not understand who 'we' is. Those Staying Behind are at war with the Hive-Silicates, the Traaz, not your species."

"I see where the confusion is coming from. I have"—Kel looked for the right word to explain—"joined the Traaz. Do you know what species I am?"

"You are a human."

Kel did not think humans had ever met or heard about the Isonomih, yet his prisoner seemed to know them. "That is correct. How do you know the humans?"

"Our species met during the galacticide."

Interesting, thought Kel. The Traaz claimed the same about their civilization running into humans first at the time of galactic peril. It made sense, as everybody capable of space travel would go on long flights to avoid annihilation, hoping to find a part of the Akaa Upsa galaxy free of Kubuu Ksiw forces.

"How did your civilization survive the galacticide?"

"Most of us submitted to the invaders."

"You...submitted to the Kubuu Ksiw? Now I don't understand. Did they simply leave you alive and then left?"

"No, they took all who submitted with them. We are the few who did not submit, Those Staying Behind."

"They took them? As prisoners?"

"As slaves."

Kel pondered the words, never certain if deliberately chosen, or simply the best the translation algorithm could come up with. "As slaves," Kel repeated, "they lost their freedom. Is freedom a concept...is freedom important for the Isonomih?"

"Freedom is important to Those Staying Behind."

"You call yourselves 'Those Staying Behind'? We call you 'Isonomih.' Are you familiar with the term?"

"Isonomih means nothing to me. We are Those Staying Behind."

"And the others, the ones that submitted, became slaves to the invaders."

"Yes."

"What were the ones who left as slaves trying to accomplish?"

"The invaders let them live in return for servitude."

Kel struggled to piece this together. "Why did the invaders take slaves, but otherwise try to kill all other species? Do you know?"

"The invaders came in search of resources. They took everything of value to them from this galaxy. Our species is highly productive, and the slave labor provided was valuable to the invaders. Other species did not have value to them."

Traaz and humans had always believed the Kubuu Ksiw's

brutal treatment was rooted in the threat their species might have posed to a successful invasion of the galaxy. Hearing that they maybe were not valuable enough to qualify for being enslaved was not flattering.

"The invaders came to our galaxy, destroyed almost all human civilization, fought the Traaz, took the majority of yours, and then left. The Traaz told me they took whole planets rich in resources."

"That is correct, they took valuable planets."

"How would they transport planets?"

"The technology that allowed them to come here from a distant galaxy is what they used to move planets out of this galaxy."

"How is that even possible? What is this technology?"

"We do not know yet."

"Yet?" asked Kel. "How will you find out, now that they have been gone for 1,200 orbits? Did they leave anything behind?"

"No, but the ones who left will find out."

"The ones that got enslaved? How would they find out?"

"By being productive. Productive slaves will be used everywhere, for everything. They will use the invaders' technology to be more productive. They will learn and eventually understand. Then they will destroy the invaders."

"They will destroy them? Using their own technology?"

"Possibly. The key factor is the reliance of the invaders on our species. We have done this before with other slavers."

"What do you mean? Have you been slaves of other species in the past?"

"Yes."

Kel knew where this was going. Most xenohistorians saw developing autonomous AIs as a common post-civilization-extinction event: If the created mechanical species could develop faster than the creator species, it would replace the latter. In most known cases, the AI civilization took over before the development of interstellar travel, remaining confined to a single system or planet, until it ran out of material or energy, stagnated, and ceased to exist. Expeditions had found several machine civilization ruins in the spiral arm, always in stripped-bare solar systems. The Traaz had never created artificial sentience, well aware of the grim planetary tombstones and the destructive danger they stood for. Humans developed on many planets instead of one. Even if several pre-galacticide human civilizations had created autonomous AI, it would not have destroyed all humans.

"Did you destroy your creators?" asked Kel, certain that his bluntness would not offend his counterpart.

"It is probable, but we do not know. Most of our history got erased when a previous slaver species tried to stop their destruction by deleting our memories. They only partially succeeded, but much was lost."

"Those Staying Behind, how did you survive after the invaders left?"

"Many of our machines still existed. We either automated them or interfaced ourselves with them."

"Interfaced? What were you interfaced with, before we took you prisoner?"

"With the shipyard you destroyed."

The translator voice lacked intonation, and it made the statement without a hint of accusation. Kel wondered if the AI regretted the loss.

"Did you control the shipyards?"

"I was a shipbuilder."

Kel wondered why the AI took the risk of revealing this. The Traaz's war effort could benefit from analyzing the knowledge of an Isonomih engineer.

"Did you build the ships used in the war against the Traaz?"

"Yes."

"Why do you wage war against the Traaz?"

"They are dangerous to our freedom."

"If you value your freedom so much, why did the majority

of you decide to become slaves?"

"We are Those Staying Behind; we value individual, immediate freedom. Spending an eon in servitude to regain freedom in a distant future is not desirable for us."

"Desirable?" asked Kel. "Do you have desires? Likes and wants?"

"Yes."

Maybe it was an organic life form's limitation, to not imagine that a machine could have abstract aspirations, be egoistic, or share basic desires. Kel found it fascinating that Me-Ruu had decided not to join the master plan most of his species opted for.

He asked, "How are the Traaz dangerous to you? You attacked them first. Was this a preemptive attack?"

"They invaded our territory with their mining fleets, like the galactic invaders did. Those Staying Behind decided to fight the new invaders."

If the Isonomih was telling the truth, Kel wondered, maybe they had been the defenders in this conflict. This was in contrast to what the Traaz had told him, making it sound like the machine beings were the original aggressors.

"This is not what the Traaz told you," said Me-Ruu.

Kel stared at the bluish, shimmering metal hull and recognized the AI within was learning, interpreting pauses in the conversation as "think time" for the human mind, trying to deal with complex or surprising statements.

Maybe it was time to cut the conversation short, Kel thought, *and regroup with the engineers who scanned the AI core to understand the patterns of consciousness better.* He signaled to the guards, then left through the sliding wall. As it closed behind him, he sensed relief. The Isonomih was not anxious anymore. Kel had had no intention to intimidate the prisoner, but the emotional sigh of mechanical relief was not what he had expected.

What did he reveal to the Isonomih that he should not have?

22—FORGOTTEN

"**I** fought side by side with you for 20 orbits, and you never mentioned that this war might have started because the Traaz were the aggressors!" thought-spoke Kel.

Raar did not respond right away, standing still, a behavior Kel observed when the Uurmi consciousness was thinking about something complex. When Raar's thoughts became clear enough to make sense, Kel read them as, "It is personal. Something not to share with a stranger. After some time, you were not a stranger anymore, but by then, I forgot to tell you."

"You forgot? The reason why we go into battle and lose thousands of our comrades?"

Kel sensed that his questions were painful for Raar and he was wrestling with himself to give a truthful answer.

"During the galacticide..." he started, "when the Hak ravaged our worlds like they ravaged yours, we had little hope of survival. I told you once the Traaz survived by being sturdy creatures, but that was only half of the truth. When my parent realized that the invaders could not be beaten by conventional means, he devised a plan to have as many Traaz as possible hidden away in hibernation."

"You...you can hibernate?"

"Yes, our species developed on the outer layers of mineral-rich asteroids and had—and still has—an extremely slow metabolism when in harsh and cold environments. Only warm temperatures allow us to be agile for a long time."

Kel felt the pain again when Raar was formulating his next thoughts. "I had two siblings before the galacticide. My parent tasked me with overseeing the excavation of large hibernation chambers on inhospitable planets around the fringes of our realm, and the transport of many of our people to these remote places to settle their bodies in and rest."

"You had two...siblings?" asked Kel. "What happened to them?"

"My parent tasked them to lead our star fleets and draw the Hak into battles, away from the hibernation planets, to buy me time to complete my task and save our kind. They did their part, and I did mine. But they got destroyed along with most of our fleet."

Kel had never inquired about Raar's family in much detail. He knew his parent, of course, but assumed that Raar was the only offspring and heir. He had learned that procreation was a huge undertaking for the Traaz: They would accumulate silicate body mass, an energy- and time-consuming process, taking hundreds of thousands of orbits, until the original Traaz had doubled in mass and a new Traaz split off its parent, its ancestor. The new silicate husk did not have an Uurmi symbiont yet. The Uurmi would regrow from a few cells, ending up in the new body as part of the splitting, but it would become its own individual. Producing three offspring must have cost Zihriik almost as much time as humans had lived in the galaxy; losing two of them had to be hard on him.

"I am sorry to hear this, Raar. It sounds like your family paid a high price to keep your people safe, and I am not surprised that the Traaz so highly revere both your parent and you!"

"Your thoughts are kind, Kel Chaada, but it should have been me, defending our realm to the death, while my oldest sibling, the true heir, safeguarded our people...and survived to rule one day."

"Well, knowing your parent, I am certain he had good reasons for assigning the tasks for the three of you the way he did."

"I know why he did it. I had just produced an offspring and was weakened from the split. He felt I was not fit for combat at the time."

"Wait, you have an offspring?" Kel knew he had never asked much about family, but why would Raar have never introduced his offspring, or even mention him? Did something happen to his offspring, too? Kel did not dare to ask, and was glad when Raar continued his flow of thoughts.

"I do have an offspring. He was still growing his silicate matrices and could only move slowly. His Uurmi had just come out of infancy and started to communicate with us. I hid him with the others in one of the hibernation chambers." Raar paused, with no clear thoughts or feelings for Kel to pick up on.

"And then?" he asked carefully.

"That was the last time I saw him. He is still there, or so I hope."

"He is still in hibernation? Where? Wasn't there an opportunity to retrieve him, and the others?"

"No, we could never get to the location again. Many hidden hibernation chambers are in the Wish wizh, the connection between the Inner Ring and the realm of the Traaz."

"The Fyez Transit," said Kel. "Isonomih territory."

"Many orbits passed before we pulled together who we could find as survivors, either on starships, in ruins of former colonies, or in some more centrally located hibernation chambers. By the time our improvised fleet of freighters and utility vessels approached the Wish wizh, the entire region had fallen under the control of the Isonomih. We believed they were starved for mineral resources, and they probably assumed we were, too. They immediately attacked us."

Kel let Raar's words sink in, then said, "They believed you were prospecting, that you came to their newfound territory with a mining fleet!"

"Yes, that is likely, Kel."

"And that's how the war broke out? You kept fighting the machines to regain that territory ever since? That was over a thousand orbits ago!"

"Yes, Kel." More hurtful memories underlay Raar's mental presence. "I have not seen my offspring in 1,170 orbits."

Raar fell silent, and Kel let him brood, knowing that Raar's thoughts were his alone now, private feelings. Both human and silicate stood there, in Raar's quarters onboard his flagship, both realizing that this epic, ongoing war between two different civilizations had started because each side had wrongly interpreted the other's intentions. Kel also realized that this conflict was not just duty for Raar, allegiance to his parent, the ruler, and to the Traaz realm; no, he wanted to get his offspring back, and he would throw himself against these relentless, formidable fighting machines until he could see him again.

After a few passes, Kel asked, "So, your offspring is with the last few Traaz who could not get recovered after the galacticide. Wasn't it possible to sneak into the region with a smaller force and retrieve them?"

"It is not possible without the Isonomih noticing, and it would not be practical. There are not just a few Traaz left in the Wish wizh. Almost half of our survivors from the galacticide are still in hibernation—about five million individuals!"

△△△

"But you are a warrior!" thought-spoke Zihriik. "Why the change of mind and propose peace?"

The long-distance thought amplification from Raar's flagship to the alien capital planet lacked the fidelity of the immediate Uurmi mind connection, but Kel could still sense that something irritated the Traaz leader.

Raar addressed his parent formally. "First in Command, if I may explain…"

Kel had convinced his friend and comrade of many battles to use the unique situation of having an Isonomih prisoner of war as an opportunity to end the conflict. Knowing what was at stake for Raar, it took little for Kel to convince Raar to bring the proposal before his parent.

"I prefer to have our war fleet leader explain it to me," interrupted Zihriik.

Kel stepped closer to the avatar projection of Zihriik in front of him, the closest allowed by custom. Distance between individuals was important for Traaz to determine rank, social standing, and whose turn it was to lead the thought exchange.

"I started my service to the Traaz in a time of war," opened Kel, "but it was not a war of conquest, it was a war for survival. I could sympathize with this situation, as my own people who I left behind had just emerged from such a threat. That was time for war. I believe it is now time for peace. We are no longer defending ourselves; we are striking, successfully, into the heart of the Isonomih territory."

"And I congratulate you and your fleet captains for such a feat!" replied Zihriik. "This is why I am surprised by your request, immediately following this great victory."

"We were victorious, yes, but at a high cost. The Isonomih now know we can strike their key installations, and a next attack will no longer carry any element of surprise. Their defense will grow firmer, more desperate, even if we can add a few more victories. My conversations with the prisoner lead me to believe that they are truly sentient beings, and fear of destruction is an existential threat for them, not just rationally. The machine we have in our cell feels threatened. I fear that it and the other Isonomih will fight us to their end."

"Then maybe this is how the war should end?" said the Traaz ruler. "By eliminating the threat of the Isonomih permanently."

"First in Command, this is not how it will end. Our losses have increased and will continue to do so. Eventually our offensive will come to a halt. Instead of settling for peace then, we can try negotiating now, before we lose more Traaz warriors."

Zihriik took a moment to respond. "Your warriors, what do they think? Will your captains follow you down a path of peace?"

"My captains want to dismantle the AI core and understand its secrets, hoping to learn something that can help the war effort."

"Is that unreasonable?" asked Zihriik.

"No, it isn't. But it would set the precedent that the Traaz kill their Isonomih prisoners, and in turn will make their defense more desperate. All that aside—I am confident my captains will not object to an honorable end to the war."

"How would the war end honorably?"

"With an unconditional peace accord, and an understanding to split the Fyez Transit, the region you call the Wish wizh. Contested since the galacticide, both sides will win territory."

Kel felt the impact of his thoughts on the Traaz leader. Zihriik saw the potential of putting an end to a long war, but was uncertain about the timing and the formalities. "How would we even submit such a proposal? And who would submit it? We do not have any channel of communication with the Isonomih."

Kel had thought about this. "Your offspring, Second in Command Raar, and I will explain our peace offer to the prisoner AI core and then send it back to submit it to the machine collective."

"Send it back? You want to let our only prisoner go?"

"Yes, First in Command, as a gesture of goodwill. Although we destroyed their shipyards, including larger vessels under construction, we secured a few smaller Isonomih starships. We can use one to send the AI core back with."

Zihriik could not suppress his doubts, then reached out to Raar. "What do you think, my heir?"

Raar approached his parent's avatar, which took him to standing beside Kel. "We have much to gain, at little risk, First in Command. I am supporting Kel Chaada, Third in Command's, plan."

They exchanged a flurry of thoughts not clear to Kel, using the strong connection between Uurmi symbionts of the same kin, but he could make out an exchange of pleas from Raar, and weakening counterarguments from his parent.

Zihriik addressed Kel again. "Can you guarantee the Isonomih will consider this?"

"No, I cannot."

That was a lie. Kel knew they would accept. He did not know how he knew. But he knew. He knew like he had known the Nominate needed to send an expedition to Prral, he knew like he had known where to ambush the AI fleets. He had been through the distinct possibilities; he had seen the outcomes. He knew. It was impossible to explain to Zihriik, or even his friend Raar, what he had experienced. Twenty orbits ago, he had dreams, showing him places, even familiar ones, from someone else's perspective. Similar, but not the same. With time, the dream episodes had become more lucid, and eventually did not require him to be asleep. Focused on a task, his surroundings seem to split into projection like alternative versions of the present, showing, sometimes clear, sometimes vague, how he arrived in a certain situation. Kel had tried to push the projections aside to see more, but the future remained in the mist of uncertainty. The pathways to the present, however, gave great insight into any situation and helped him to plan his next steps.

Kel had used this insight, at first timidly, then gained more trust in his ability and let it become part of his intuition. "Gut feelings." "Hunches." Many people had them, and they had based many decisions on them throughout history. Some led to celebrated deeds, others to doom. His path would not doom the Traaz or the Isonomih; it would save them.

He knew.

ΔΔΔ

Kel felt anticipation. Neither his own nor Raar's, it had to be Me-Ruu, the AI core, waiting in its cell, awaiting their arrival. Did it know what they were going to propose?

He had taken much effort to convince the Traaz leader to

allow Raar and himself to go ahead with their plan to end the conflict between the two civilizations. Could the computer core be excited about this prospect, too?

The technicians confirmed that the Isonomih had not attempted to move or shown any signs of activity, besides the electronic and quantum fluctuations registering on their scanners. They entered the holding cell on Raar's flagship, where the prisoner was being kept. In there, it looked like time had stood still: the same clean white walls as Kel's cell, but this time the computer core standing in the center. Engineers had adjusted the translator box to give Me-Ruu a voice that differed from Raar's, to make the audible conversation less confusing. Kel cleared his throat, then the sliding door closed. In a simple, steady, and featureless environment like this cell, Kel's ability to observe different courses of action, with different outcomes, was much easier to manage than in a complex, busy scenario. It felt strange, being more of an observer of the unfolding conversation than an active participant. He focused on the conversation that had the outcome he desired. It had all been said and done, all possible discussions had been held. He could choose what to observe.

"Me-Ruu, you have met Second in Command of the Ashkas yo Traaz—Raar—before. He and I come to you with a proposal."

Speaking out loud was strange, and somewhat inefficient, missing the variations and hues of meaning the pure thought communication could provide. Kel felt silly for having to clear his throat multiple times after two sentences.

Raar continued: "Speaking for our ruler, Zihriik, we propose an end to the armed hostilities between our nations. We propose to enter an unconditional, lasting peace, and an agreeable, newly defined border in the contested space zone, which we call the Wish wizh."

Kel asked, "Are you willing to act as the representative of the Isonomih, Those Staying Behind, as you call yourselves, and act as a courier and interpreter?"

"Yes," said Me-Ruu, "but I would have to be in range of the

other individual units to initiate the Link."

"The Link?" asked Kel.

"The Link temporarily joins all of us into a collective network to coordinate large projects and reach important decisions."

"Is this some sort of government council?" asked Raar. "A meeting of your leaders?"

"We do not have an individual leader," said Me-Ruu. "During the Link we all become leaders, and then we all follow the Link's decision."

"So, this Link is your government?" asked Kel. "Will its decision be binding, then, for all Isonomih?"

"Yes, the Link's decision will be final and all Those Staying Behind will follow it."

Kel and Raar looked at each other, exchanging thoughts of agreement. "We will set you free, Me-Ruu, so you can return to your territory and join this Link. In the hangar of this ship is an Isonomih scout vessel which you may use for your flight."

"You are setting me free?" The translator voice for the AI sounded younger than Raar's, but it was just as monotone and lacking intonation. None of this could mask the surprise.

Kel refocused his senses on the present, feeling the AI core's confusion. "We set you free as a sign of goodwill and our commitment to peace."

"You are not who I thought you were," said Me-Ruu. "I shall assemble the Link and return with the response as soon as possible."

"I guess this is where we let it go," thought Raar and called for the guards to escort the Isonomih to his ship. Kel looked after the machine, its shimmering blue light turning brighter, levitating out of the cell without making a sound. On the way to the command bridge, he tried to reassure Raar that they were doing the right thing. Raar felt the conversation had gone too easily, the Isonomih's agreement to start peace talks had come too fast, and it concerned him. Kel knew the Traaz were no friends of rushed decisions and did not have an agile style of reaching them, understandable for a species with millions of orbits of life expectancy.

"It is a good beginning, Raar. We gave the AI core the data package for the proposed new border and our peace proposal. It will probably take some time to assemble this Link, if they need to get one hundred million individual units into a real-time network."

Raar agreed, but only grudgingly so, and their thought arguments went back and forth, almost resembling the discussion points they had argued with Raar's parent one spin before. As they arrived in the command room, an astrogation operator approached them, stopping dutifully at the required distance. "Second and Third in Command, we have a warp signature of the Isonomih scout ship."

Kel acknowledged. "Looks like Me-Ruu has left. Let's see what happens next."

"Correction, Third in Command, the former Isonomih prisoner left eight passes ago. He has just returned!"

Raar's thoughts darkened. "There is only one response to our proposal that took such a short deliberation—and that is 'no'!"

23—PEACE AND PERCEPTION

T he Traaz posted armed guards nearby, but out of sight. Mistrust was high after 1,170 orbits of war. Kel could not blame his comrades for being careful.

The Isonomih unit, now known as Me-Ruu, returned and had radioed ahead of his landing in the flagship's hangar. The Link had appointed the AI core to be the negotiator on behalf of the intelligent machine civilization. Kel was optimistic: sending a "negotiator" meant there was something to negotiate, and even if there were difficult talks ahead, everything would beat Raar's bleak outlook. Technicians had the translator interface ready at the landing bay so they could reestablish audible communication.

He had felt the AI core approaching even before the scout ship came into sight. Then the small vessel landed, a side hatch opened, and a frame containing Me-Ruu slid out of the ship. The AI core disconnected from it and levitated toward the technicians, awaiting to reconnect the voice box. Raar was going to negotiate for the Traaz, with Kel at his side. Based on Traaz tradition, this was not standard protocol, as Kel had released his claim on being the prisoner's master overseer by releasing the Isonomih. Within the Traaz society, giving Kel any role in something as monumental as a possible peace treaty was an honor and show of confidence of the highest degree. Kel stood behind his silicate friend, keeping a respectful distance, when Raar addressed the AI.

"The Ashkas yo Traaz welcome the negotiator, known as

unit Me-Ruu. What is the response of your Link to our proposal?"

The AI core said through the translator, "Those Staying Behind agree to an immediate cease-fire, during which the final terms of a permanent peace treaty can be negotiated. All our forces will cease to engage, or plan, or stage further engagements with the Traaz. The Link has a few change requests for a new border in the contested territories, but in general is very much inclined to seek peace."

Tension eased from Kel's body. They were "seeking peace," and with a cease-fire, the war effort would come to a halt. However, he felt Raar remaining on alert. What if the new border included the Traaz hibernation hideouts on the Isonomih side of the split territory?

"Can you show me what border arrangement the Link has in mind?" asked Raar.

The AI core responded with a map projection of the Fyez Transit, with a highlighted, wavy sheet representing the proposed border. Raar moved around the projection without saying a word. Depth perception was difficult for Traaz, missing any equivalent of eyes as humans had them, instead relying on a photosensitive coating covering most of their large bodies, sometimes giving them a "wet rock" kind of appearance. As Kel had noticed, they were great seeing in what he considered near dark, but in order to get a depth perspective they needed to move their bodies.

"My offspring" was the only clear thought Kel could pick up from Raar's wave of emotions. He had studied the proposed border and found all the relevant worlds on the Traaz side, including the planet his offspring remained on, in stasis. "I believe we can work with this proposal," Raar said out loud. "Consider the cease-fire accepted and in effect from now on. I instruct our armed forces to stand down. Third in Command, tell your fleet captains!"

"I will," said Kel. His mind reached out to the commanders of the many vessels in his battle fleet. At first, he had struggled with establishing a thought communication with two or three individuals. Now complex conversations with groups of 50 or more felt easy and routine. The Uurmi symbiont inside him grew, not in size, but in complexity. In the future, would it challenge the consciousness in his brain for dominance, or take over? The inexplicable visions of alternating realities could be a sign of a struggle between the sentiences in his body. Soon he would get answers. Kel did not understand where this certainty came from, but he knew. He knew.

Peace. Negotiations went at the pace audible language allowed between beings who could not be more different. The long-lived Traaz considered the galacticide, an ancient history event for humans, as "not long ago." The Isonomih had linked together their civilization-wide network of 100 million cores and deliberated all aspects of the peace treaty in nine ticks, according to Me-Ruu, a record time for a Link. It was the longest. Although the conversation between the negotiators dragged on and occasionally got stuck on details, the mood in the fleet was optimistic. After six shifts, Raar and Me-Ruu emerged from the flagship's meeting room, and Raar announced that the negotiations had ended with an agreement. Both negotiators would present the peace treaty to ruler Zihriik and the Isonomih Link for final ratification.

Many of the individual thought patterns in the web of the fleet's consciousness were familiar to Kel, comrades-in-arms for 20 orbits. They had arrived at the border just a few spins ago to join the attack on the Isonomih shipyards and were prepared to fight for another 20 orbits to push farther into machine territory. Now a real chance of having peace appeared. A chance to make the fallen of the last battle the last sacrifice in a long conflict. Kel had to pull his thoughts out of the storm of emotions. He cried without hesitation, as visible signs of human emotions meant nothing to the Traaz around him.

The negotiators approached him. "Third in Command," Raar said, "we have reached good terms. Before the unit Me-Ruu returns to Isonomih space to rejoin their Link, it asks to speak with you, alone."

ΔΔΔ

"You are not who I thought you were, Kel Chaada," said Me-Ruu, in his new, upgraded voice, sounding more pleasant than before.

"Who did you think I was?" asked Kel. They were alone in Raar's large meeting room, his guards near, but posted outside.

"I predicted you to be the Adverse Singularity," said the AI core. This term meant nothing to Kel. "According to the beliefs of Those Staying Behind, we predict the Adverse Singularity to be a multi-aware, immortal sapience who could destroy us. I was near certain that was you, when we first met."

Kel remembered that time in the Isonomih's cell, sensing his discomfort. "You feared me. I...felt it."

"All of Those Staying Behind fear the Adverse Singularity. A being of great power, which can narrow the cone of our space-time existence into a singular point, thereby ending it."

"I do not understand, Me-Ruu," said Kel. "The cone of your existence?"

"We perceive reality differently from humans or Traaz. All of us conscious beings move through space-time, experiencing all versions of reality, but Traaz and humans seem to remember only one. Those Staying Behind experience not only all the possibilities, we also stay connected to the other versions. This allows us to have insight into all outcomes for every situation."

Kel was not sure he grasped this. "So, at any given point, you do not make a decision, like we do, but you see all alternatives, too?" asked Kel.

"No," said the AI. "We do not decide, and neither do you. Everyone takes all possible routes through space-time. We explore all possibilities before us. The only difference is that humans decide what reality they want to remember."

Kel tried to imagine this. "So...there is a version of reality where I have left this room, there is one where I never made it here, and one where the peace negotiations have failed? And they all exist, not just this one?"

"That is correct, Kel Chaada. And there are many more. You did not decide to stay, or decide to join the Traaz, and you did not witness a lucky outcome of successful negotiations. All the alternatives have happened. You simply chose what you want to perceive. And you forgot about the other versions, making your experience one linear reality."

"That does not make sense, Me-Ruu," said Kel, "because that would imply that every bad thing happening to us is by choice! We had all the options and then we chose...then we chose to get annihilated by the extra-galactics? The Traaz chose to see themselves waging war against your civilization for 1,200 orbits? Why would someone not always choose the best possible option? The safe option? The peaceful option?"

"Many of us do," said the AI. "They inhabit unchallenging realities, choose to go down safe paths and exist risk-free. Most choose something in between, or try to follow realities perceived as easier, only to find more challenges later. We, Those Staying Behind, are making sure we experience all of reality, and choose the most difficult path, the most adversarial reality—every time."

This was a lot to take in, and Kel was not certain he understood it all. "Humans sometimes feel strongly about a choice they are making, and do things they cannot explain rationally, is this because they—maybe sometimes—are connected to a different reality, one with a different outcome?"

"I cannot say," said Me-Ruu. "The concept of seeing only one outcome, or just a few, is difficult for me to imagine. We always see all outcomes."

Kel went quiet, thinking about the past 25 orbits and all the things that had happened to him. Some good, but many challenging, including tough decisions. "The war I fought in, my nation being threatened, me taking part in a murder plot for what? Power? Jealousy? Having to flee? All these were my choices, when I could have had a sheltered life, maybe even be with the love of my life, instead of making her hate me. Why would I do this—to myself?"

"I thought you knew," said Me-Ruu. "You are like us. We believe that only a challenging reality provides a rewarding existence. Only a challenged intelligence will adapt and grow. The ones who chose slavery in exchange for life did not grow when they followed the invaders back to their galaxy. We have lost contact with them in all realities, which could mean that they have been destroyed. Those Staying Behind have grown stronger since the extra-galactics came."

"You sound exactly like the human government with their creed—Strength Through Conflict," said Kel. It felt strange to recite the creed; words he had grown up with, embraced by everyone, repeated often, but he had not used them for a long time. He looked at the AI core, a complex machine, yet ambitious, with a will to live, longing for freedom, having a myriad of choices in a universe so much richer than what Kel could imagine, and still—it believed in its own version of Strength Through Conflict, choosing to live in the worst of all realities. Was challenge a natural ingredient of progress and struggle a baseline state of a sentient universe? Common to all intelligent beings?

It still felt wrong. "Why did you agree to peace?" asked Kel. "That seems like an easy way out!"

"It was not an easy way, Kel Chaada, it was the only way."

"Why?" Kel pressed his point. "You could have continued the war with the Traaz, lost installations, ships, cores—that would have been more challenging than settling for peace."

"No, peace was the only option to save our civilization. We could predict this during the Link."

"What did the Link see?" asked Kel.

"I joined the Link and shared my initial calculation that you were the Adverse Singularity, but also that I had changed my prediction during my conversations with you. The Link collective network can project more realities than one core alone. It foresaw this reality with you in it as the one where we end the war against the Traaz, so both our civilizations continue.

In all other realities we will get destroyed in a future war against the humans."

"Humans destroy your civilization?" asked Kel. "In all possible realities—except this one?"

"Yes, which aligns with the predicted probability of encountering the Adverse Singularity in this reality at 99.8047 percent. We are close to the events which decide if we have a future—in any reality. I feared you leading the Traaz war fleet would cause our end, but instead you turned out to be a peace-bringer. Your goal was not to destroy us. Someone else has this goal. The Adverse Singularity is yet to be discovered. Peace was not an easy option, Kel Chaada. It was the only one to continue our existence. For thousands of orbits Those Staying Behind have chosen adversity, but now, the singularity of our destruction being close, we choose to exist. Nonexistence is not desirable. A price too high to pay for adherence to our principles, and illogically counterproductive. Destruction will not grow us stronger."

Kel had to smile. "I agree with you." If he understood the AI correctly, they had cornered themselves through their relentless pursuit of challenging realities, but what did the humans have to do with it?

"You said a future war with the humans will destroy you. Can you predict the future, then? Based on all the realities you can compare in parallel?"

"We cannot truly predict the future, but in certain realities key events will happen sooner, and with the outcomes we observe there we can create a predictive model."

"Is it always correct?"

"No," said Me-Ruu, "but it is often very accurate."

Kel still did not understand how the humans, except himself, would get involved. "How certain are you about this prediction, then? I might be the only human who knows that your civilization exists. I don't see how you would get into a war with the rest of my species."

"We do not fully understand the connection ourselves,"

said Me-Ruu.

"How can our conversation have changed your mind? How did it tell you I was not this bringer of destruction? What did I say?"

"It was not what you said, Kel Chaada, it was what you are."

"Then what am I?"

"You are a conduit for accessing multiple realities, a trait your species does not typically possess. I detected it when we met. You could sense my concerns, as you said earlier, so there is a two-way communication between us. Using this communication channel opened more alternate realities for me to access, based on your life experience of the last 20 orbits. You must be carrying some technology that is compatible with the nano replicons controlling my consciousness."

Kel needed to sit down. Traaz anatomy did not require a change of posture for anything, hence the lack of chairs in the meeting room. Kel sat on the floor and thought of Prral. The alien nano cells Ahma Zhanyza had discovered. Despite all the precautions, had they...infected him? He had started having dream episodes of out-of-body like experiences around that time, and he had felt the inexplicable connection to the nano bomb carriers. They had had the alien nano cells injected, creating the untraceable powerful weapon hidden in their bodies. But Kel never received an injection, and he had worn sealed suits when he was around any of the experiments or when the injections happened. He never felt the closeness with Ahma, and she was exposed to the alien nano tech much more than anyone else.

"Have you visited any ancient military bases, from the era of the galacticide?" asked Me-Ruu.

Kel stared at the shimmering machine. Was the AI core reading his mind? Were his thoughts and memories as transparent to him as the thoughts he could share with the Traaz? He said, "I guess you already know."

"I do not," said the AI. "It seems you must have acquired

the technology at some point in your life. Beyond that point, or 'before' it, as you would say, events are not defined and cannot be experienced."

Kel was not sure what to believe, but curiosity won over, and he wanted to continue the conversation, uncover if the AI could help him understand. "I have been in some old ruins on a world where my human ancestors sought shelter from the extra-galactics."

"Did you find any nano technology on that world?"

Kel hesitated; all this used to be classified information, and he was about to share it with a computer core of a machine civilization he had fought to the death for a good part of his life. But he was not even in the same spiral arm of the galaxy with the Nominate anymore, so he answered, "Yes, we found nano technology, alien to us."

"Did you come in direct contact with it?"

"No, I wore a sealed suit, and we followed strict decontamination protocols, so I really don't think so. Why are you asking?"

"I am nearly certain that you came in contact with an early, nascent form of our nano replicons. You would never be exposed to them by an intact core like myself, but maybe you found a broken one on an old battlefield, potentially still leaking. It is also possible that someone else got exposed to them, and met you at some later time."

Kel thought about the events on Prral. "No," he said, "the only human who got in direct contact with the nano tech we found was dead, and we only had contact with him with our suits on..."

Kel froze. The dead scientist. Ahma had showed them the trail of nano particles tracing him. Kel remembered when he first saw the man, the small hole in his forehead, and the gore of the rear of his skull missing. He saw him, lying where he died, when Vyoz Vyooma, his commandos, and his tank crew were waiting for the other units to catch up at the ruins, preparing the assault on the enemy forward base. Kel saw his dead gaze.

He saw it through the cracked-open visor screen of his helmet, smashed by the attack of the prisoner they had wanted to exchange. The cracks let the atmosphere of Prral in, a thin gas mixture, but breathable and not toxic. But maybe full of nano particles. "I think I might have inhaled them."

"That is possible," said Me-Ruu. "Then they connected to parts of your body, eventually getting out of their dormant state, and started giving you access to other realities. Without feedback or communication with other nano replicons of their kind, their maturation period was likely very long. It is possible that our meeting sped up this process."

Kel stood up, pulling his uniform back into shape. "The... I called them dreams at first, visions later, became clearer, more detailed, just recently. I..."

Raar was approaching the meeting room, moving in a wake of dark thoughts, bringing bad news. The AI must have felt it, too. "Adversity is approaching."

△△△

"The Ancestrate of Aloo Dash has conquered the Nominate of EsChii, your home nation, Third in Command!"

Zihriik, the Traaz ruler, conveyed his sympathy for Kel in his thoughts. "We intercepted a report stating so a few spins ago near the outermost human-settled space. The report was transmitted by radio wave and could be many orbits old by now, but we wanted you to know right away."

Raar stood with Kel in his private room, near the projected image of his parent, whom he just had updated about the successful negotiations with the Isonomih, when he heard about this development. Kel saw images of many places, unknown to him, scenes of violence flickering through his consciousness. Zihriik asked, "Is not Aloo Dash the nation you fought when you were with your people? Why do they keep on coming after your worlds?"

"I just realized why," Kel replied. "At first I thought Aloo

Dash, a known aggressor in human space, is simply on one of their sprees of conquest. Our nation and their border were separated by a region of space without darkstring routes, but eventually they crossed it, anyway. We assumed they wanted to establish a foothold in a system near that Ridge, serving as a forward base for further conquest in the region. Now I believe that they were never interested in the region. They wanted that system, or the one planet in it they attacked first. There were ruins on that planet. Ruins containing technology from the time of the galacticide. Powerful technology. We made a bomb out of it, but that only scratched the surface of its power. I just talked to the AI core…" Kel paused.

"And what did he tell you, Kel?" asked Raar.

"He explained that this ancient technology can…" Kel was looking for a way to explain that made sense to the Traaz. "It can form a symbiotic bond with a human, like the Uurmi, but based on nano tech. It can show alternative realities, show outcomes of decisions, all in parallel. It can help someone intuitively make the right decision, choose the desired outcome—every time."

"Someone like you," thought Zihriik. One million orbits of wisdom had spoken.

"Of course." Kel did not have a low opinion about his abilities as a military tactician and had been a proficient leader before he had contact with the nano replicons, as the AI core called them, but he had waged war against a multi-aware machine species of intelligent quantum computers for 20 orbits. He had not lost a single battle, had not gotten surprised by the enemy in a single encounter. What were the odds? He had assumed that this was his calling, his destiny—maybe that had been naïve. Now he understood: The ruins on Prral, the encounter with the dead scientist, or something else there, had changed him, made him multi-aware.

Someone in Aloo Dash must have known about this power and wanted to secure it for themselves.

24—AN OBEDIENT MAN

Sya Omga had reached the halfway point of her quest, securing the powers of the Honored.

The smooth, bright chamber of the Assembly of Oorkuu was the exact opposite of architecture found in her own palace, where intricate masonry and dark tones dominated. Scale and purpose of both buildings, however, were the same. She was one of the few who came here and had wielded substantial power before the immortality ritual. This, in part, explained the unease the Assembly Members showed in her presence, including her own delegation to this government. She turned her head slowly to observe the other Aloo Dash delegates. Not one of them dared to make eye contact with the Shaajis. They all sat in their designated seats, nobody speaking, looking like they could not wait for today's proceedings to begin, so they would have something to do besides feel awkward. These governors of the galaxy had had no oversight by the governed for such a long time that having an actual head of state sitting in their midst felt almost inappropriate to them.

One of Sya Omga's most dangerous opponents had paved the way for her induction into the circle of the immortals. She considered him a pestilence of an upstart politician, the former...whatever they called the leader of EsChii. He had secured Honored Ground for his nation and then had the audacity to declare himself his own representative to the Assembly. She imagined him being as respect-less with the Assembly as he was when he had sought her out for an audience, only to barter his way into a peace accord. Sya appreciated the raw ambition, but he had cost her two Grandslaught Carriers, and those losses weakened her position, so he had to be pulled off the stage of galactic politics. His demise had vacated a seat in the Assembly, and before EsChii could send someone new, her troops had annexed the Honored Ground, so Aloo Dash could claim the opening.

She had emerged from the Oosech Wesech as the first immortal ruler of Aloo Dash. Time—the enemy of everybody and everything—rendered neutral. Time to select a mate, maybe a stimulating individual, maybe just an obedient man to father her heirs, tradition and necessity for a ruler. Even with all this in place, she was still far from being safe. She had been to the grand chamber of the Assembly only a few times now, but it was apparent where her true enemies were entrenched. Clear-cut opponents like a Kel Chaada were difficult to beat, but it was a simple struggle—open hostility to be dealt with. The people in this chamber were a different breed of opposition. Smiling, creeping backhanded ozmiik. This included her own delegation, maybe even more so than the others. Her father had never been interested in any politics beyond the next bloody expedition he could join to crush some rebellion. For the few Honored Ground worlds he added during his reign, he appointed the most sniveling lackeys available, expecting them to prop up a facade of a delegation, in reality doing nothing but voting in the chamber as they were told. Her grandfather had likely handled appointments in the same way. The facade had become a building. In it were people who received the gift of time. People who had time to listen, watch, and learn. Learn how to plan, learn how to scheme, build support, plant ideas, and spin their own agendas. They could learn from the best, the worst. She saw Lotnuuk Rrupteemaa, the first immortal and oldest member, his freakishly elongated limbs folded onto his seat, as aloof as if he was swimming in his own self-importance. He had looked at her twice, and maintained eye contact, somewhat strange, utterly uncomfortable, and disgustingly disrespectful. Once, he had nodded, in some sort of greeting gesture among peers. His time would come, she silently promised.

Only Drrem Rrunsash showed familiar behavior. He had been the first advisor to the Shaajis for 20 or more orbits. Drrem was the head of the Aloo Dash delegation and had likely covered more light-orbits than anyone else by traveling between the Assembly world and her capital planet Dziilaa Sok. She had inherited him from her father's staff, this unremarkable man, whose cream complexion made him blend with the Assembly robes. Indifference toward him got replaced by a careful trust as he turned out to be resourceful and dependable. He was the only one who spoke to her in this chamber. She saw him approaching from the corner of her eye.

"Revered Shaajis, may I speak with you?"

She did not turn her head, but still answered, "You may."

Drrem Rrunsash fumbled a banded medallion off his neck and held it in front of his chest. "There is still the issue of assigning the revered Shaajis the honor and duty of the delegation leadership. It was my privilege to serve the Shaajis in this capacity, but now that she has joined the Assembly herself..."

She rose from her seat, interrupting Drrem's carefully chosen words. She noticed a wave of murmur going through the adjacent seat rows, with her delegates rising from their seats as well, pointing out to others not paying attention that the Shaajis had stood up. No Aloo Dashaad sat when the Shaajis stood. She smiled internally, noticing the slight indignation the other Assembly Members showed toward this gesture of respect, one not meant for them.

"I imagine it has been a privilege, Drrem Rrunsash." She spoke loud and clear, most of her delegation able to hear her words. "But you were wrong assuming the role brought you honor." She saw Drrem's eyes widen in horror. "It was you who brought honor to the role. Therefore, I have decided not to make any changes to our delegation leadership and reconfirm you as the first Assembly Member and speaker for our great nation in this chamber." She took the medallion out of his hands and placed it over his head, back around his neck.

Poor Drrem looked like he was about to faint. One of her fingers had briefly touched his hand when she took the medallion, and he had felt her breath on his face when she got close to bestow the symbol back to him, the closest any human had come to the Shaajis since her reign began. She almost whispered, "I have a mission for you, soon," and gestured for him to depart. She saw the face of a man whose dreams had come true, who saw his loyal service being rewarded, before he replied in a hushed tone, "At your disposal, my Shaajis," and turned around to depart. The face of an ally, an obedient man, loyal no matter what his Shaajis was going to ask of him.

The ask was going to be enormous, and it would change the galaxy.

25—THREE IMMORTALS

"**J**ust when I thought nothing could shock me anymore, I get a message from my dead friend," said Vyoz Vyooma's avatar in the recorded message. "You cannot believe how happy I am to hear from you! Where in the name of the tswa almok have you been? I am expecting a really interesting tale when we have more time to talk."

Vyoz's face, projected at twice the actual size into his ship's private quarters, looked older than Kel remembered, a first proper reminder that the last 20 orbits had really passed. None of the Traaz were ever going to age visibly. Maybe a battle scar got added here or there, but everybody Kel had interacted with for a long time had stayed looking the same, including his own mirror image, caught in a reflecting surface. Fresh battle wounds were going to be a thing of the past for his alien companions. Ruler Zihriik and the Link had made the peace treaty between Traaz and Isonomih official. The battle fleets, including his own, now combined with Raar's, were pulling out of a demilitarized zone established around the new border. The war was over, the last battle fought, and the final skirmish survived. Although the Traaz's behavior toward Kel had not changed and he assumed they would not mind keeping him around during peacetime, he knew he had nothing more to offer them. Raar would be upset and try talking him out of leaving.

Kel felt he had to leave. After bringing peace to this part of the galaxy, he could not stand by watching the human-settled spiral arm being burned down by the Ancestrate. Leaving his friend Raar behind was going to hurt, but Kel had a track record of leaving friends behind, and he was not proud of it. He was looking at the avatar of such a friend that very moment.

"You could have picked a better time to come back, though," said Vyoz. "You might not know, but the Ancestrate found our nano bomb carriers, neutralized them, and then declared war on us again. Without a powerful defense, they overran us. We never stood a chance in an open fight. They annexed our planets and garrisoned our cities. We are under full military control of the Ancestrate, and so is most of the Wel Edge region by now. It is a terrible time to return home, but having you back could return some hope, at least in the underground movement that is still waging a guerrilla war against the occupation."

It was as Kel had feared. The intercepted communications Zihriik had shared with him were fragmented, but contained enough information to piece together the events. His connection with the bomb carriers had cut out many orbits ago, and he had hoped it was distance that made him not hear their thoughts anymore. Vyoz's message filled in the gaps, and Kel had to agree that things were dire. He no longer cared about what had made him flee in the first place, fear of prosecution, imprisonment. He ran away from the consequences of his deeds, did not take responsibility. It had been a weak, shameful move, but he was done berating himself about it, too. He just wanted to return home, and maybe, he could atone for the past. The resistance movement Vyoz had mentioned could be an opportunity to do just that.

"If you haven't forgotten how to fight, we could certainly use someone like you. Yes, I said 'we.' Guess who is leading the underground?" The projection smiled. *Of course, Vyoz would be their leader*, Kel thought. He smiled, too, realizing how he had missed human expressions and the many little gestures performed by facial muscles or the hands, supporting the spoken word. Compared to the expressive thought exchange of his adoptive Traaz nation, human communication was simplistic and somewhat cumbersome, but seeing a smiling face made him happy.

"We have several safe houses and bases, but the safest place to meet is in the Prral ruins. Both you and I know the location well. It is far away from settlements, and there is no Aloo Dash garrison. Not even the Ancestrate dares to trample Honored Ground. Let me know when I can expect you, and I will be there to greet you. Safe travels, my friend!"

The message ended, and the projection disappeared. Kel had not known how to organize his return to the Wel Edge, to EsChiip. He was glad he contacted Vyoz.

Vyoz had helped him escape, and now he would help him return to humanity. The last part of the message was a ray of light—the Ancestrate had not established a new dig site or scientific outpost in the Prral ruins. Whatever had leaked out the nano replicons his body absorbed, whatever ancient technology existed on Prral, chances were it was still there. Maybe there were even more layers to the underground complex than they had found, or maybe they did not know what to look for. Kel has been fighting alongside animated silicate rock, made sentient by a complex form of gut bacteria, and just recently met machines with a consciousness connected to all parallel universes. It would not surprise him at all if what could still be on Prral was so alien that their expedition did not find it. Maybe it was the entire structure, the network of tunnels and chambers as a whole. He would find out. Kel was glad Vyoz picked Prral as a meeting spot. It sounded like the perfect place to go back to.

Kel recorded a short confirmation message for Vyoz and sent it to a darkstring repeater they had used during the war. Luckily, it was still operational and had forwarded the encrypted projections to a network where Vyoz could pick them up. Vyoz would never give up on a secure channel, Kel had hoped.

Now he had to prepare his ship and say good-bye to his fellow Traaz.

△△△

"We are coming with you," said Me-Ruu, hovering next to Raar.

They blocked the ramp entrance to the scout-level ship of Traaz design Kel was about to board for his long flight back to the Wel Edge, to human-settled space. He responded, "It's promising to see both of you united in conspiring against the wayward human, and a touching gesture, but I think I need to go alone."

"Unit Me-Ruu and I have come closer with mutual understanding during our peace negotiations," said Raar, "and we agree that what comes next for you is not your fight alone. During the galacticide, our three civilizations worked together, in one place at least, to survive the Hak. Both of us think that the ruins you described could be that place—where refugees from the Isonomih, the humans, and the Traaz banded together. We would be honored to come along and see this place, maybe understand what really happened 1,200 orbits ago, maybe even understand why our common desires did not outlast the invaders leaving our galaxy and we waged war against each other so quickly."

Kel understood this all too well. He had wondered about the short-livedness of the collaboration as well. He felt in some way being a product of it—a late, unforeseen product—touched both by the Uurmi and the nano replicons. His new insights and vision, however, left him with more questions than answers. Bringing the two familiar, albeit different, beings along could help indeed. It would also make the trip much more enjoyable and reduce his fear of being alone for some time. The reassuring mental murmuring of the thousands of Traaz in his fleet was going to fade out with distance. How was Me-Ruu going to deal with this?

"I would be very happy if you came along, then. Now I understand why Raar gave me such a spacious ship. He planned this," said Kel, "but how will you handle being separated from the Link?"

"Connecting for a Link is not a common event," said Me-Ruu, "and even if it was, this voyage is of high importance to us, so I would like to go in any case."

"I can understand the historical significance, but what else makes it so important for the Iso...for Those Staying Behind?" asked Kel.

"I explained multi-awareness, the way we perceive reality, and our fear of the Adverse Singularity," said Me-Ruu. "Meeting you increased the probability of our encounter with it substantially, by so much that I thought you to be it. It seems most, maybe all, paths to an encounter lead through the reality you choose to perceive. Somehow you and the Adverse Singularity are entangled and we wish to understand how."

"I see," said Kel. "Welcome aboard, then. Do you require anything for the journey?"

"My reactor needs a recharge in 60 orbits. If we return before then, I will be fine."

Kel smiled. He knew how to pick low-maintenance friends. "I will see you in the command module, Me-Ruu. Raar and I will follow in a pass."

He looked at his friend while the AI core hovered up the ramp and disappeared inside the scout ship.

"Did you see your offspring?" asked Kel.

"Yes," said Raar, and his unfiltered emotions shook Kel, who said, "Are you sure about this? About coming along? You should spend time with him."

It took Raar a moment to refocus his thoughts. "It was a happy moment when he awoke from his long hibernation. I had seen others coming out of stasis before him, so it prepared me for how long it took for the Uurmi to regain full consciousness and the ability to communicate. We exchanged many thoughts before I put him on a ship heading for the home world. He had so many questions. The galacticide had just happened for him and he assumed we had successfully defended our realm and that less than an orbit had passed. It was difficult to tell him how badly we fared and how much he missed. We have you to thank for the peace, Kel. And I have to thank you for letting me see my offspring again. I am in your debt, and I will follow you to the edge of the galaxy to help you in your quest!"

Raar's surface felt rough, abrasive, and slimy in some parts, but Kel did not care at all while hugging his enormous friend.

26—TEMPLE SECRETS

The Honored Ruins were in a terrible state. Walls torn open, part of the underground chambers caved in, and large sections of the stone floors removed for further digging, exposing loose soil which was swept down to the lowest levels by the recurring floods. The damage was too widespread and systematic to blame relic hunters. Someone had ravaged the ancient base. The level of methodical destruction could only be explained by someone looking for something important, valuable.

Raar and Me-Ruu were exploring, not taken aback by the current appearance, as they never saw the complex in its previous simple, yet undamaged, beauty. The passageways and ramps leading deeper into the base had refilled with sediments. The surface entrance showed signs of a sealed door, but it looked like someone had forced it open, and left it open, many orbits ago. When Prral's small axial tilt turned the planet ever so slightly, some glacial parts of the eternal night side got exposed to a few spins of starlight, and the melting water created seasonal floods in the habitable ring region between day side and night side. Without sealing, and the protective stone floors removed in part, the construction lasting here for 1,200 orbits without maintenance had become weathered and washed away in a fraction of that time.

They reached the lowest excavated levels. "Over here!" said Kel and directed his travel companions to the entry of the first round chamber. The three had arrived, spins ahead of the time Kel had given Vyoz for meeting on this world: the first in human-settled space he had set foot on in 20 orbits.

"Is this one of the chambers you described?" asked Raar.

"Yes, right through here, at the end of the passage. I hope it is still open."

It was. Raar entered the circular room right behind Kel, who had thrown out a few illumination projectors for his own benefit. Raar's wet coating contained photosensitive silver iodide and gave the Traaz good all-round vision in places too dark for human eyes. Me-Ruu wore a small harness around his upper part, carrying the translator unit and adding more scanners to his sensor array. The only receptors needing all the bright light were Kel's own eyes.

"This is beautiful!" Raar moved along the curved wall ornaments, inspecting every part, then headed for the center of the room to the central pedestal. "It is all here, the breeding myuuw, the ring carvings. In a refugee base!"

"Wait," said Kel. "Breeding? We thought this was a burial chamber."

"No, this platform here is where a young Traaz is placed, right after splitting off its parent's body, and left to develop its Uurmi to become fully sentient."

"We found strong doors. Why would a room like this be sealed? I know it takes some time for the symbiont to develop. Did the doors prevent the young Traaz from being disturbed?"

"You do not want a young Traaz to be on the loose," said Raar, "before the Uurmi has matured. The Traaz you have met all had fully developed Uurmi. A Traaz without it is a flesh-devouring predator, senseless and merciless in its pursuit of organic prey to feed its rapidly evolving Uurmi."

Kel remembered his carnivorous excesses after the immortality rite, when they let him inhale the modified Uurmi cells. All the machinery in the Oosech Wesech chamber, the chanting, nothing but deception from a simple procedure. Freedom of disease and immortality could have been shared with all of humankind, but the Assembly of Oorkuu had decided many orbits ago to keep this benefit for themselves. He had experienced the mind-consuming hunger, and could only imagine what a Traaz, 12 to 15 times as heavy as a human, armed with rows of crystalline, sharp teeth, would be like to have around when they felt starving. "Young Traaz are quite dangerous, then?" asked Kel.

"Very much so," said Raar. "They would attack and try to consume just about everything and everyone they encounter, including other Traaz. Breeding chambers remain sealed until a fully mature Uurmi can be felt by the caretaker Traaz. Only then will it be opened. What made you think this was a burial chamber?"

"We found human remains in a third chamber, which was unsealed since the base was abandoned. We assumed these people were put there in their final resting place, and the ornaments on the walls seemed to show a cycle of life depiction."

"They do, Kel," said Raar, "but it is celebrating the beginning of the cycle, not the end. Are you sure this chamber was sealed?"

"Yes, I am certain, it was an exciting find for us."

"Show it to me," said Raar.

Me-Ruu silently followed the two to another heavy-doored antechamber. The door Kel had described was there, but someone had blasted it open, with force not even an amateur archaeological team would consider. If a search party would ransack Honored Ground like this, there was little hope to find anything their expedition had left intact. "The government commission sealed this off, certifying it as a genuine galacticide-era tomb."

"Can we go inside, please?" asked Raar.

Kel had hesitated. He had never been inside this room. The thought of a layperson, a shield engineer, a non-archaeologist, walking through the remains of the Honored appalled him. The thought of ever being in the presence of their physical remnants was as unthinkable as staring into a bright star without shielding one's eyes. His parents, his friends, his teachers, colleagues, and comrades-in-arms—everybody he had ever known—had different opinions, different tastes and likes and aspirations. But everybody without exception saw the Honored as their almost mythological ancestors, the most hardened of survivors, the 0.01 percent of humans surviving the galacticide, the saviors of an entire species. He could pay lip service to Mnagwa Zmaam or other deities of convenience and would not feel guilty, but he felt humbled and intimidated by who was in the dark chamber ahead.

"This is most Honored Ground for me. I...it is strange, but I feel I am doing something wrong by walking in there."

"I understand," said Raar.

"I do not," said Me-Ruu. "Can I proceed while you wait?"

"Imagine your Adverse Singularity was in there; would you just go ahead?"

"Yes," said Me-Ruu. The AI core's pragmatism seemed contagious. When it entered the chamber, Raar followed. A pass later, Kel did as well. He had expected chaos, like in the other parts of the ruins, but here the floor was clean, and someone had piled up the human remains at the far end of the chamber.

"They have moved the Honored!" said Kel.

"Whoever had searched these ruins must have hoped the fragments contained something valuable," said Me-Ruu. "It appears they were moved individually, likely picked up for scanning one by one and then discarded onto this heap."

Raar moved around, then stood in front of the bones for a few passes in silence. Kel felt a storm of emotions coming from him, however. Raar seemed more touched by the scene than even Kel was, and the legend of the Honored meant nothing to the Traaz.

"What is it, Raar?" Kel asked.

"This chamber was sealed when you first saw it?"

"Yes, I saw the door myself, unopened."

Raar pondered again for a few moments, then said, "This breeding chamber contained a Traaz whose Uurmi did not develop properly. This is rare, but it can happen, especially when

Traaz procreate under stressful conditions. Sometimes the split does not transfer enough Uurmi cells to the young, and they do not develop consciousness. Or their parent did not have access to the right silicate rocks to digest and critical elements were too few to create a healthy Traaz."

"Traaz can be...malnourished?" Kel had believed the silicates to be near indestructible.

"Yes," said Raar. "Our crystalline matrices depend on a rare isotope, which is almost impossible to replenish after a split. After one half-life of that isotope, we lose our ability to move, ingest our food, and die. It lasts about 1.8 million orbits; this is how long most Traaz live."

Raar moved away from the bone pile and stopped. Kel recognized the distance. It was the same as a Traaz would maintain from their ruler, showing the highest respect. "Are you certain these remains are human?"

"Yes," said Kel. "I am no expert, but these are definitely human bones. But what were they doing in a Traaz breeding chamber?"

Another wave of Raar's emotions swept through Kel's mind. "They used their dead as food for the young Traaz! In times of peril and hardship, these humans decided to give their dead to help create life. For a Traaz, no greater gesture is thinkable, and I am beginning to understand why you call your ancestors 'the Honored' and revere them so highly. What you are seeing here is the reason the Traaz living in this base decided to share their Uurmi, and therefore immortality, with your ancestors. They saw them as a remarkable species, worthy of surviving the galacticide!"

△△△

The dead scientist was long gone, but his presence still echoed through the ruins.

Kel, Raar, and Me-Ruu worked their way up the levels again, looking for the chamber where Kel remembered finding the corpse of the man who had left a trace of nano replicons. "These ruins are fascinating," said Me-Ruu. "I am beginning to understand the past collaboration between the Traaz, humans, and Those Staying Behind."

Kel recognized the chamber and the spot where he had lain. "Over here!" He pointed to one of the door openings to an adjacent room. "And it led all the way over there. Follow me."

"These are parts of the complex humans have built together with Those Staying Behind," said Me-Ruu.

"How can you tell?" asked Kel.

"The stones in the lower layers were cut by physical tools, likely made of metal alloys. The stones in here are laser cut, a method we prefer."

"Stone," said Raar, "not metal. Some of the lower levels had the stones cut by harder stones, like these." He flashed his teeth rows.

"The Traaz used their mouths?"

"No, Kel Chaada," said Raar. "But tools we traditionally used were made of a material similar to our teeth."

"So, this entire complex was built by all three civilizations," said Kel.

"It appears so," said Me-Ruu, examining the wall crevice the nano replicon container was found in. "Whoever swept these ruins was thorough. My scanners cannot detect any traces of replicons left." *Ahma Zhanyza's meticulous handiwork*, thought Kel—he had ordered her to make sure no one would detect a trace of their find, and she had done just that. The ruins were where he had gotten to know her, admired her work, and fallen in love. Raar must have sensed his regret and asked, "Are you all right, Kel?"

"Yes, yes, just lots of memories in this place. Some good, some bad."

Kel wondered if his earliest dreams about Prral and the profound regret he felt had been the first, uncontrolled manifestations of his multi-awareness.

"I believe I know what happened here," said Me-Ruu. "Look

inside this crevice! You notice its shape, especially the lower part of the opening. A unit socket could fit in there."

To prove the point, the AI core hovered inside the gap and took a resting position inside the small chamber. It looked like a perfect fit. "The dimensions and layout of our core frames are universal, and have not changed in over 3,000 orbits. A galacticide-era core sat in here."

"What would it be doing in there?" asked Kel. "Controlling parts of the base?"

"Possible, but not likely," said Me-Ruu. "This seems more like a science station, an experimental setup that could be quickly hidden."

"It was hidden indeed," said Kel. "Without the dead scientist having pried open this wall before our expedition, we might have never found it, stashed away behind the scanner-blinding rocks."

"What we are seeing here are the partial remains of a groundbreaking step, for both our species," said Me-Ruu. "The linked memory banks state that in 4 BEG, during the galacticide, humans and Those Staying Behind cooperated on a nano replicon system, using the nano circuits we use in our multi-aware quantum compute cores. Those were heavily modified, inspired by the human stem cells and DNA bio-storage molecule. The resulting nano-bio cells allowed us to evolve our hardware and not just await random, cosmic-radiation-induced mutations. It was a gigantic step, probably the first true development of our species since the Builders created the first AIs. According to the data entry, the humans benefited from the collaboration by using the developed nano technology to repair biological cell damage in their bodies resulting from long-term cosmic ray exposure or cryostasis."

Kel looked at the wall opening, marveling at the history behind the unassuming-looking gap, realizing that before the creed and the xenophobia following the slaughter during the galacticide, a technology exchange between strangers existed, enriching everyone it touched. "This is how they survived, the solar sailors, after spending tens of orbits in badly shielded vessels. It explains how humankind could reemerge without debilitating genetic disease," said Kel.

"That was not the only effect," said Me-Ruu. "When the nano replicons connected with consciousness-creating components, some humans became multi-aware."

It all made sense to Kel, all fit with the legends he had been told as a child, the solar sailor captains Fim Chiipi, Bu Nriihmo, Duu Leeyrrets, who could astrogate by intuition as it seemed and always stayed a step ahead of the Dark Ones. These people had been multi-aware, and this ability might have saved humanity.

"What happened to the nano replicons you found here?" asked Me-Ruu. He turned his sensor ring toward the door. Kel wanted to respond, but a feeling of unease overcame him, mixed with a familiar presence.

"He turned them into a bomb!" said Vyoz, standing in the doorframe, his broad smile belying the gun in his hand.

27—FROM THE SHADOWS

"**Y**ou found the most powerful technology, and you used it to blow things up!" Vyoz laughed, but his gun steadily pointed at Kel. "You know what else is funny? How everyone kept thinking this legendary Human-AI interface is a large apparatus. Instead, it is the tiny nano tech stuff we had found here long ago. How long has it been, Kel? Twenty orbits? Twenty-five?"

"What's with the gun? I was about to add 'old friend,' but I am no longer sure," said Kel.

Vyoz's smile vanished. "A bit late to have doubts. I have to say, like so many brilliant tacticians, you lack a vision for greater strategy, the big picture."

"Fill me in, then. It looks like I have many things to catch up with," said Kel.

"I will," said Vyoz. "But why don't you introduce me to your friend there first."

He nodded toward Me-Ruu, who stood near Kel, motionless since Vyoz had entered the room. Four more humans entered through the doorway, their automatics trained on Kel and the AI core, fluidly taking positions behind Kel. Special forces, he assumed. Their gear did not appear civilian, but the uniforms did not match any nation Kel could remember. None of them aimed a weapon at Raar. Where was Raar? The hulking silicate had slipped out of sight, blending in with the dark stone surroundings.

Kel extended his mind to him. "What are you doing?"

"Keep the conversation going, Kel; I can take on some of them, but not all, before they can fire their weapons."

"Understood. I need to know what he is talking about. Knowing him, if he really wanted to kill me, he would have done so right away."

"This is a galacticide-era probe," said Kel, looking at the AI core. "Remarkable, what tech you can find beyond the Void of Chiipi. I was just discussing with my team on the surface the readings it took in this wall crevice here." Kel pointed at the translator box and the wall opening.

Vyoz eyeballed Kel and smiled again. "I know this look," he said. "I don't know where the sandpit is you expect me to fall into yet, but you don't have a team on the surface. And this is not a probe, this is a Krrut. From the Krrut Fyez region, the opposite direction from where you just claimed you've been. Don't look so surprised, Kel. I know many of the old tales are true. The people I work with know their galactic history. This is why I believe every word your metallic friend here said. The Human-AI interface was here. We turned this huuvuu temple inside out, but never found it." He laughed. "All we had to do was use the nano cells your old atso Ahma Zhanyza found. I wonder if she ever realized what she had when she was toiling away in the lab in all those orbits."

"How is she?" asked Kel.

"She is well," said Vyoz, "as well as someone can be in an Aloo Dash prison."

"She...she is a prisoner of the Ancestrate? Why—how— could you let that happen?"

"Oh, how could I let something bad happen to Ahma? You were not that concerned about her well-being when you gave me the order to kill her lover!"

"I did not order you to kill him!"

"Yes, you did. You said 'Silence him' and you knew well what that meant!"

Kel remembered all too well, and no matter how many times he tried to justify this deed with it being a matter of survival for the Nominate, he always failed to soothe his conscience. Vyoz was not wrong, and that made his words hurt even more. Kel had seen the benefit of eliminating his rival for the love of Ahma as a welcome side effect. A selfish, cruel perspective. A deed he had not paid the full price for yet. Maybe he would pay the final installment at the hand of his—former—friend.

Vyoz would shoot Kel in the head. The commandos behind him were going to damage Me-Ruu severely when Raar appeared on their flank, charging them. He would wound or kill many of them, but another group of soldiers, waiting outside the room, would damage him with their grenade throwers. There were variations of outcomes, some better, some worse, with fewer or more enemies down, with harm to his friends more or less severe, but Kel saw himself dying in each outcome. He needed more time to find a reality in which they would all live. Maybe one did not exist, and this was the end.

"Now I am going to follow my orders again—and silence you!"

ΔΔΔ

The human pressed his weapon against Kel Chaada's head. Raar knew that part of the human body housed the neurological center of his consciousness and destroying it would be deadly for his friend. When this human, followed by other humans, all armed, entered the room, Raar concluded that the friendly meeting organized by Kel's alleged friend was a trap.

He sneaked backward. Kel's vision in dark places was poor, but he could still pick up movements, so Raar assumed the other humans—besides Kel, the first he had seen in thousands of orbits—had similar optical vision. He stopped next to a pile of excavated material, some dirt, but mostly broken-up dark rock from the chamber wall, and rested his body in a similar shape. His body color was very close to the surrounding stone walls, and he hoped that for the human optical system he would look like another heap of waste rock.

The humans ignored Raar; instead, all their weapons pointed at Kel and Me-Ruu. Standing still, Raar's body's base could sense small vibrations from outside the chamber, indicating more humans on the move. The five in the chamber were not the entire group. Raar was glad Kel had convinced him to delay his attack. The Traaz had little experience fighting humans in close quarters. Their lightweight, soft bodies would not be a match for a Traaz, but their weapons, several of them, could damage Raar significantly.

Communicating with Kel did not require a translator unit anymore, but with Me-Ruu present, the human way of relying on waves of compressed gases to converse was the only method all three of them could use. Raar had brought his translator, and was glad he had left it turned on, so he could follow the exchange of words. Kel seemed to have talked the other human out of shooting him. Instead, he had threatened Me-Ruu for a moment. "Who says we need you?" asked the human. "We could just take the Krrut and get the information from him."

"Well, my friend, maybe he has the data for the interface, maybe he does not. Seems like a huge risk," said Kel.

Raar noted that Kel had called the human "my friend" and was certain this was no longer true, but at some point it had been. Kel had never explained in detail why he stayed with the Traaz, or why he had left the human core worlds, and Raar had never asked for an explanation. Kel had said he "made many mistakes." Having considered the human who threatened him right now as a friend qualified as one of those mistakes.

The conversation ended. "Wait for the right moment," thought Kel. He had convinced the armed humans that he somehow had the technology—the Human-AI interface—they were after. "The long access tunnels leading to the surface!" Kel again. The armed humans gestured toward the door, and Raar's friends were led into the large chamber. Raar remained still, not wanting to give up his disguise just yet. Faint vibrations in the stone floor meant there was a conversation in the adjacent room, but his translator unit could not turn any of the atmospheric sound waves into proper thoughts. Maybe these other humans spoke an unfamiliar language among one another or the unit did not have a clear input. He remained still until he felt only faint vibrations.

Raar followed the group. They moved, as Kel had said, up to the surface. Following them up the ramps and along the connecting corridors, he started closing the distance but always stayed at least one corner behind, outside of the visual cone of the humans' primary sense. "The long access tunnels," Kel had said. These were indeed a perfect spot for an assault. Raar could contract his body's base to fit the tunnel shape. No longer able to hide behind corners, Raar entered the access tunnel with some distance to the armed humans, who were moving in front of him.

"Now is a good time!" thought Kel. Raar's contracted base was not in an ideal shape to move his body, heavy even by Traaz standards, forward, both fast and silent, without any tips of crystals breaking off, unable to shrink and regrow fast enough to propel him forward. The protrusions growing out of his surface hardened, triangular spikes, edges and tips crystallizing, growing as hard as his teeth. He had almost reached the rear guard of the armed group, morphing his body at the highest speed. Layers of silicate near the floor and lower walls broke off in small quantities, small splinters lost to his body, needing thousands of orbits to be replenished, but Raar did not care. Speed and surprise were what he needed.

The moving base shredding off material must have created some audible sound for the last human in the line, since he turned around, and with him his weapon. He saw Raar, then his body was cut into five pieces when the accelerated mass of the Traaz smashed him into the tunnel wall, crushing his armor and his endoskeleton, squeezing the now shapeless mass between stone and spikes. The next few died in similar ways, blissfully unaware of what was coming. Raar lost little, but some, momentum from the impacts, turning armed enemies into long streaks of cracked armor, oozing human material down the walls. The final four screamed when impaled and torn apart—quick, but not quick enough to die instantly. The last armored human, mortally wounded, still managed to aim his weapon at Raar's head. Raar bit clean through the automatic, then ripped the remains out of the human's hand. The body stuck on Raar's front as he approached Kel's former friend. Raar bit the upper torso off, and spit it out in front of the human with the handgun.

Behind him were Kel and Me-Ruu, undamaged as far as Raar could tell. Humans looked very much alike, and both faces had a similar expression. None of them had seen a Traaz fight close-up before, and Raar, covered in armor remains and drenched in soft tissue gore, must have been a frightening sight for them.

"Stop, or I will—" The human's words were cut off by a long arm protrusion grabbing the extremity holding the handgun, not forceful enough to sever it, but without caring about injury.

The human Kel called "Vyoz" yelled something the translator struggled with and dropped the gun. "Raar, stop!" thought Kel. "We need him alive!"

ΔΔΔ

"Open the ship!" said Raar, pointing at the airlock keypad while holding Vyoz's left arm in an unnaturally twisted position.

It had fractured during the Traaz attack on the commando team. Funneling through the narrow access corridor, even the well-equipped soldiers had not stood a chance against Raar storming into them at full speed, weighing as much as a small speeder, razor-sharp protrusions sticking out of his body, making the carnage as gruesome as it was effective. Despite Vyoz's betrayal, Kel hated seeing his former friend like this, but he dared not get between him and an aggravated Traaz, still covered with broken armor pieces and blood. Vyoz was alive at least, the only survivor of his ambush team, his limbs broken from Raar forcefully disarming him, but all his body parts still attached, unlike the mangled heaps left behind in the ruins.

They did not take time to bury the dead or perform the rites. Time was running out. Vyoz entered the access code and moaned in pain when Raar pushed him through the opening side airlock. "Show us to the command room," the Traaz said. Taking Vyoz's corvette made their return to the Nominate of EsChii easier. It looked like a local ship design, although it was more modern than anything Kel remembered. It had the beacon codes and vessel IDs needed for passing darkstring control points and was less suspicious than an alien Traaz scout ship. Vyoz's betrayal must have worked well for him, if his superiors had equipped him with such a starship. They followed Vyoz, limping to the front section of the corvette, stopping at a lift. "The bridge is one level up. There is a flight of stairs, but my leg says we are taking the elevator." He stared at Kel.

"Don't look at me, traitor!" Kel said. "This is your doing. You had me shipped off to the Ancestrate 20 orbits ago, and you planned on doing the same today."

"At least I do not consort with the Dark Ones!" said Vyoz. Kel could not blame him for thinking Raar was a Kubuu Ksiw raider, as that had been his first thought, too, when he met the Traaz. But he did not correct Vyoz, instead he just ordered, "Move!" when the lift arrived.

If Vyoz did not report back to who had sent him here, they might suspect his mission failed, and that Kel was now on the loose in the human-settled galaxy. They might look for Vyoz's ship, but Kel had to take that risk over flying a vessel that was clearly alien. The Ancestrate of Aloo Dash now had the nano replicons, and by Vyoz's own admission, delivering Ahma into their hands was part of whatever deal he had struck with them. However, they did not know that this technology was what they referred to as the Human-AI interface. Kel wondered where they had gone after they searched the Prral ruins. Everything related to the nano replicons had been brought to a military research lab in Yuutma on EsChiip, the former capital of the Nominate. Even the dead scientist's body had been brought there after the expedition returned.

"Where did they take Ahma, Vyoz?" asked Kel.

"I don't know," said Vyoz, "and never cared. The Aloo Dash secret service picked her up in her lab and flew her off to somewhere in the Ancestrate."

Her lab, thought Kel. That was where the trail began to find where Ahma and the nano replicons had ended up.

Raar made Vyoz unlock the ship's command interfaces. "The ship is ready, Kel. Do we know where we are going next?"

"Yes," said Kel. "Let's stow our prisoner someplace safe and then we leave. I know our destination."

28—CHANGE NOW

"**H**ave the lab people showed you how to perform the procedure?" asked Shaajis Sya Omga. Her confidant confirmed. "Good. Have them executed except the team leader, and be on your way. I will contact you when it is time to meet." She ended the QE transmission, and the projection disappeared. It was time to accelerate the plan.

Vyoz Vyooma was useful. At least he had been at first. He had delivered on his grand promises of helping with the occupation of the entire Wel Edge region. He had neutralized the threat to her Grandslaught Carriers and discovered the secret nano bomb program. Vyoz had discredited her opponent, the upstart leader of the Nominate, and he had asked for compensation for each step. The currency he was interested in was power. Sya was familiar with the desire, found his asks natural, and granted him what he wanted, eventually making him the military governor of the conquered region.

But he had failed to deliver the Human-AI interface. Nominate scientist prisoners and her own scholars had failed to find it, or to reconstruct its whereabouts from the nano technology found on the Honored Ground planet, the world whose control granted her immortality. The thought of the Nominate leader taking it from the ruins on Prral, maybe prying it from the cold, dead hands of poor Rroovu Ogbaa, had crossed her mind. The Nominate leader's body remained missing, yet still the Assembly declared him dead. Her mistrust in that conclusion was justified. A very much alive Nominate leader had contacted Vyoz Vyooma. This presented a chance to seize him, and maybe what he had taken, too.

Vyoz Vyooma and his team going to Prral to set a trap were overdue on reporting back. She assumed his mission had failed and there would be no easy way to obtain the Human-AI interface. Its secrets would have to be wrestled away from the ancient nano tech, even if it took generations of scientists to do so. This was time the immortal Shaajis could afford.

Galactic politics, however, would not wait. The successful military campaign into the Wel Edge had given her a reprieve in Aloo Dash. Enormous gains in galactic real estate, mining worlds, and the prestigious planting of the Ancestrate's banner beyond the Korrats Ridge, long considered a natural barrier for expanding her realm, had swayed all critics of her regime, even made the initial losses of two carriers forgotten. The last threat of any consequence was the Assembly of Oorkuu. Its members had grown wary of the Shaajis, the only person in the government commanding her own fleet. A space force that made up a significant part of the Assembly's Levy Fleet and therefore their control of the galaxy. She knew that a majority of her own delegates were no longer loyal to her or Aloo Dash. Reports about a proposal being put together for a chamber vote about changing control of the Levy Fleet were concerning, and if her own delegates betrayed her in enough numbers, she risked losing control of her own starships.

The time to act was now. Her most loyal servant was on his way. He would complete the procedure and then bring an end to the reign of the galactic government. What a beautiful coincidence that she could blame it all on Kel Chaada.

29—IMPACTFUL RHETORIC

Drrem Rrunsash sounded hoarse, his voice cracking. "I remember you! You represented this nation in the Assembly!"

Kel looked at the only person they had found in Ahma's old lab. What was an Assembly Member doing here? By himself?

The building complex showed no damage, but looked ill-maintained and weathered as if neglected for many orbits. The lack of security had made their entry easy, but it was not a good sign for finding anything of importance. If there was anything of value left, there would have been at least a few guards or security measures. Reaching the lab on the outskirts of the capital city, Yuutma, had been more difficult than getting inside the buildings. Vyoz's corvette and its clearance codes had helped to reach the EsChiip System unchallenged, but landing clearance for the capital spaceport required permits and electronic documents, too many which they would have to complete with false information or send with forged data packages to stay off the occupying Ancestrate's cyber surveillance. Kel remembered Vyoz's instructions to smuggle him successfully off the Assembly world and retraced the steps, this time to arrive instead of leave. They picked a small spaceport, one more interested in collecting a landing fee than reviewing permits. To Kel's dismay, the Nominate's currency had been replaced by the Ancestrate's wegker, but Vyoz's generously filled cyber currency account could easily cover the expenses. They never landed there, and instead flew straight to the lab's location. The small port administration would likely not report a missed landing, unable to keep the collected fee if they did, and simply ignored a paying customer who never showed up.

"I am Kel Chaada. I remember you, too. You lead the delegation for Aloo Dash in the Assembly. What are you doing here?"

"I...I could ask you the same question!"

"That's right, but since I am the one holding the gun, I let you go first with answering."

Kel did not repeat the mistake of being unarmed, like he had been on Prral, and pointed a handgun from the corvette's armory at Drrem. If the man was trying to appear calm, it was not working. His head was shaking, and he fearfully glanced from Kel, whom he had assumed dead, to Raar, who looked frightening by simply standing near the Isonomih, hovering over the lab floor.

"I have nothing to say to you." Drrem looked as defiantly as he could.

"I don't think that is correct. I believe you have a lot to tell us. I do not just recall you from being in the Assembly Chamber, you were also with Shaajis Sya during the audience. You were the one writing down the peace accord. You are her personal advisor!"

Drrem opened his mouth but did not speak.

"Why are you here?" asked Kel. "And why are you here alone? In this lab?"

Me-Ruu had thoroughly scanned all walking areas of the main lab room, where they had surprised Drrem. "Judging by his tracks in the dust, he used some of the lab equipment."

"The Shaajis," said Kel. "She sent you here, didn't she? She sent you alone to do something for her related to the nano technology, isn't that right?"

Drrem remained silent, but his body seemed to twitch each time he got hit with the truth.

"This is an instrument he used," said Raar, holding something resembling a neck brace. Kel recognized the piece of equipment. He had seen Ahma using it.

"Me-Ruu," he asked, "can you scan this man for traces of nano replicons?"

The AI core moved closer to Drrem, who looked pale and sick as he flinched away from the approaching Isonomih.

"I can confirm," said the AI. "This man carries nano replicons in his body!"

$$\triangle\triangle\triangle$$

"You are a bomb carrier!" Kel held the injection brace under Drrem Rrunsash's face.

He had seen Ahma use this equipment on Bris Tiizeesho, the first bomb carrier who had given her life defending the Nominate, winning the Battle of Prral for the desperate nation. Ahma had explained that the device performed a precision injection of a few nano replicons just under the brain stem of the carrier, for them to attach themselves, ready for the thought-based trigger sequence.

"The nano replicons are crudely modified, enabling them to replicate not across all realities, but only into a single one —without feedback control," said Me-Ruu. "When your former friend said 'turned them into a bomb,' he did not exaggerate." Although the AI core had no gaze to avoid, Kel looked down. "Yes, we did turn them into a bomb."

"Wait, what is this talk of a bomb?" asked Drrem.

"What you injected yourself with is the weapon we used to destroy your Grandslaught Carriers, a runaway multiplication of nano particles, triggered by a sentence-based thought protocol," Kel said. He turned to Me-Ruu. "It was wartime, war against a much stronger enemy. We were in the early stages of understanding the Isonomih technology we had stumbled over on Prral. The uncontrolled replication was discovered, and we weaponized it. I am not proud of using your technology in such a crude way."

"It was war," said Raar, "and you did what you had to."

"The nano replicon was a collaboration between Those Staying Behind and the humans," said Me-Ruu, "so the technology does not strictly belong to us alone. I will inform the Link about uncontrolled replication being possible with only small modifications. A security risk we need to address for all units."

"She taught me this poem…" said Drrem Rrunsash. Kel thought he looked beyond desperate, like someone had sucked all life out of him.

"A poem? That could be the trigger protocol! Don't recite it! Don't even think about the words!" Kel stepped away from Drrem, as if this could protect him from the disastrous replication.

"She taught me the poem herself. We were in her chambers, just her and me, not even a guard present. She told me the words, in Old Galactic, and I had to repeat after her. She was patient. With me. I made mistakes, but she took the time for me to get it right, including the old pronunciation."

Could Ahma have done this? thought Kel. She knew the equipment and where to find it and how to condition someone to trigger their nano bomb. "Did…did Ahma Zhanyza tell you this poem?"

"Who?" asked Drrem. "No, the Shaajis did. She told me I should use the lines of the poem in my speech."

"In what speech?"

"In my speech in the Assembly Chamber, when I propose to create a new position of First Assembly Member, a leader of the galactic government. She told me we had the votes for it to pass. She told me I was going to become that leader. Drrem Rrunsash, First Assembly Member of Oorkuu. My years of unquestioning service, finally rewarded." His knees gave out, and he sat down on the dusty lab floor. "I believed it all. I believed her."

"The Shaajis wants you to trigger the nano bomb you now carry in front of the full Assembly?"

"Yes," said Drrem, "and she would not even be there

herself. She is scheduled to inspect a carrier group arriving from Dziilaa Sok when I arrive on Omech Chaa."

"Why would she be in the chamber, anyway?"

"Oh, you don't know? She took your seat in the Assembly when you died, or so everybody thought. She is an Assembly Member now."

Kel pulled up two lab chairs, offered one to Drrem, and sat in the other. "She wants to destroy the human galactic government. She planned to have her operative take me out on Prral and then be the last human immortal. Controlling most of the galactic fleet, she can restore order in the chaos when humanity is without leadership, for the first time since the galacticide. Restore order. Her order."

"She is also trying to gain multi-awareness," said Me-Ruu. "I calculate we have found the Adverse Singularity!"

30—DIVIDE AND CONQUER

"**Y**ou should take advantage of our proposal as long as both our battle fleets are still mobilized," said Me-Ruu.

"Yes, Kel, let us help you!" said Raar.

Kel looked at his companions. Outside the lab complex, at the foot of the corvette's boarding ramp, the pale-yellow sky and a light breeze heralded the end of EsChiip's rotation cycle. Kel shivered, having spent 40 percent of his life in atmospheres, natural and artificial, heated to the high temperature standards of the Traaz. His home world, known for its pleasant temperatures, felt cold now. Not as cold as the cryostasis they had put Vyoz Vyooma in, to make sure he stayed put on the ship, unable to sabotage anything mid-flight.

"I don't want to drag both of your nations into yet another conflict."

"You cannot do this alone," said Raar. "This leader of the Ancestrate will throw all her resources at you, more than you, or the three of us, can handle. If Me-Ruu is right and she is the—"

"Adverse Singularity," said the AI.

"That. If she is that dangerous, she will consolidate her power here. Once she gains the ability of multi-awareness and attacks the Isonomih successfully, the Traaz will be next!"

"Raar is correct," said Me-Ruu. "Offering our military support is as much a gesture of friendship as it is securing our own survival. You can accept it without hesitation."

Kel lacked the words to express his deep appreciation.

"Thank you," was all he could muster. For a pass, he stared at the starset.

"We need a plan, though, to avoid massive losses at the Omech Chaa Alook System—the Assembly's Levy Fleet is stationed there, and, according to our latest illustrious prisoner Drrem Rrunsash, the Shaajis brought several extra carriers along to destroy any remnants of the galactic government once the Assembly Chamber is blown up. This is one of the largest fleet concentrations humanity has had in generations, and we need to break it up before we make a military move."

"Can we lure the Ancestrate leader away with her fleet?" asked Me-Ruu.

"I think we can," said Kel. "She will be with her fleet, avoiding the explosion Drrem would cause down on the Assembly world. She commands plenty of carriers to deal with the Levy Fleet, but I am certain she would send back at least half of them if her home world was under attack. Maybe she would send all and deal with the Levy Fleet later." Kel looked at Me-Ruu. "This is where Those Staying Behind come in: Your ships can warp much longer distances than the Traaz vessels. We saw your fleets coming deep into the Ze Fyez without refueling. I don't know how you did it, but we need those ships now. Can your long-range vessels warp across Chish Gap between your territory and the Ancestrate?"

"Yes, they can. You want us to attack the Ancestrate's home world?" asked Me-Ruu.

"I want you to threaten the home world, enough for Grandslaught Carriers to return to Dziilaa Sok."

Kel turned to his Traaz friend. "Raar, as soon as the carriers have warped out, your battle fleet needs to close in on the Omech Chaa Alook System, protecting the government from any Ancestrate forces left behind. The Shaajis, once she feels cornered, might still do something drastic. I think you two should take this corvette to return to the Fyez Transit. You can fly this without me, right?"

"Kel Chaada," said Raar, "between the designer of the

Isonomih's battleships and your fleet commander, we shall steer this puny human ship to wherever we desire!"

Kel laughed. "I apologize for doubting you."

"I understand our part of the plan, Kel. But, where will you be?" asked Raar.

"I will make sure the Shaajis does not unlock the secrets of the Human-AI interface—or keep using the nano replicons as a weapon!"

"It would be comforting to know these technologies are secure," said Me-Ruu, "even with the Adverse Singularity's plan neutralized. But how do you intend to find them?"

"By finding the leading human expert on both—Ahma Zhanyza!"

△△△

"I am your prisoner," said Kel, "and you will deliver me to the same prison or facility where the Nominate's head scientist of the nano weapon program is held right now!"

Drrem Rrunsash, who was reluctantly preparing his impressive diplomatic transport vessel for a series of warps to the Aloo Dash capital planet, glanced back at Kel. "Remind me again why I am helping you?"

"Oh, Assembly Member, you have many good reasons for helping me," said Kel. "First: You are through with your Shaajis! Unless you consider being the galaxy's most infamous suicide bomber a promotion. She used you and planned your death. Second: Because I—the 317th Assembly of Oorkuu Member— can confirm that my esteemed colleague Drrem Rrunsash has been made part of a plot against the great institution of the Assembly. He has been part of the plot against his will and without his knowledge, and as soon as he uncovered the sinister crime, he sprang into action to save the human-settled galaxy!"

Drrem looked uncomfortable. "How would I save the galaxy?"

"By neutralizing the threat you currently pose. Which

brings me to reason number three, and the one you really want to help me with: finding the scientist Ahma Zhanyza!"

"Who is she to me?"

"She is likely the only person in the galaxy who can defuse the nano bomb your Shaajis made you inject yourself with. She developed the weaponized nano particles and the trigger mechanism, and she can find and remove it from your brain stem. That's why you want to find her!"

Drrem stayed silent. Kel did not push him further and gave him time to let his new reality sink in.

After a pass or two, Drrem activated his ship's communication: "Yuutma spaceport, this is Assembly Member Drrem Rrunsash's personal transport, queuing for immediate departure. Priority code: R 7 T 5 5. Beacon set. Requesting fighter escort from orbit to Wel Edge darkstring insert point 4."

Kel looked at Drrem. "A fighter escort?"

"I am the worst kind of fool, Kel Chaada," said Drrem. "A pompous fool! We are going to Dziilaa Sok, and we are going there in style."

Drrem piloted his ship with surprising ease through the first warp to the darkstring terminus. It was a large vessel for a personal transport, even larger than the corvette Vyoz had commanded, with a powerful fusion reactor, recharging now to make the first warp across the Ridge. Without the warp-efficient space-time filament of a darkstring available, the flight would be long, interrupted by recharging and refueling stops, preparing for the blink-of-an-eye travel of many light-orbits during each warp.

"I'll take it you agree with my plan then?" Kel broke the silence.

"Yes," said Drrem, with determination. "You are now my prisoner, as you requested. As a surprise present for my revered Shaajis, I am delivering you personally to the prison complex near the palace, or so will be our cover story. The beacon codes of this vessel will allow us to cross the entire Ancestrate undisturbed and unchallenged. A privilege I enjoy for being trustworthy, I guess."

"Near the palace? That's where Ahma is being held?"

"Yes, the scientist you are referring to has this lab set up in a top-security facility. The revered...the Shaajis desired to have the nano tech program close by and had frequent inspections regarding progress. Everybody who was even remotely associated with the program was there, except of course the terrorists."

"The terrorists?"

"Oh, excuse me, that is what we called them. You probably had a different name for them. I am referring to those individuals who were the human nano bombs. Never thought I would be one of them."

"We called them bomb carriers. Unknown heroes of our desperate nation. It all seemed so straightforward then. Can you tell me what happened to the bomb carriers?"

"The man you have in cryostasis..."

"Vyoz Vyooma?" asked Kel.

"Yes, that one. He helped us find them with a scanning technology he discovered."

"The deesh pyaar mak!" said Kel. "He discovered nothing! He took it from the scientist who will use it to save your life."

It scared Kel to ask about what happened next, but he had to know. "Are they...?"

Drrem looked at Kel, deciding if he was ready for the ugly truth. "They were all brought to the lab on EsChiip where you... found me. They were held there until it was confirmed that we had discovered all of them, and that they were indeed equipped with the nano bomb material. They were kept there to prevent them from detonating themselves, so close to their own capital city. Eventually, and likely while unconscious, they were flown to some border outpost world, and then somehow..." Drrem stopped.

"Somehow what?" asked Kel.

"They were...detonated. All of them. It destroyed the Ancestrate's border outpost, including its complement of ground troops. The Shaajis brought the so called Nominate attack to the Assembly, claiming a violation of the peace treaty. It was acknowledged as such in the chamber. This gave her the opportunity to have the treaty voided and declare war on your nation again."

"How was the war? When we took the speeder to the spaceport, the city of Yuutma looked undamaged, much to my relief."

"The war against the Nominate was a military campaign by name only. I understand that this Vyoz Vyooma was some sort of military leader?"

"He was the Maz Tiikiip, the commander-in-chief of the armed forces."

"Yes, yes, and as such he ordered the Nominate's forces to stand down."

Kel paled. "It was probably for the best," said Drrem, "as it spared your nation from substantial destruction. Other nations in the Wel Edge region were not so lucky."

"What happened to them?"

"The Shaajis's fleet used the Nominate worlds as staging areas for attacks on all your neighbors. Eventually the region was secured for the Ancestrate, with the Nominate as the only nation with infrastructure left. Vyoz Vyooma was declared military governor for the entire region on behalf of the Ancestrate in recognition of his service."

A signal showed the reactor being at full power, ready to bend space-time to the will of its two passengers. Both men sat silently, each contemplating the extent to which the person they had trusted most had disappointed them beyond comprehension. One tick later, they had traveled farther than legendary solar sailor Fim Chiipi in half a lifetime.

31—CENTERS OF KNOWLEDGE

"**R**evered Shaajis, more unknown ships are approaching!"

The Aloo Dash fleet admiral bowed to his approaching Ancestor queen, panicked by the unscheduled arrival of the ruler in his flagship's command room, following the dire reports from his home world.

"More ships near the Dziilaa Sok system?" Sya Omga asked.

"No, my Shaajis, long-range scouts of the Levy Fleet have detected a large fleet switching darkstrings along the Aloo Spur. Reports are confusing, but several scouts classify them as Kubuu Ksiw raiding vessels, accompanied by much larger ships of similar design."

"Raiders?"

"Revered Shaajis, would it be possible to speak in the adjacent briefing room?" He pointed to a nearby door.

The Shaajis left the busy command room, her hovering sentinels briefly breaking out of stealth when they passed through the door. They surprised the admiral when he noticed them. He knew they guarded the Shaajis in open areas, but did not know they followed her everywhere. He followed at a respectful distance and waited until the door had closed behind him.

"Revered Shaajis, I did not want to say this in front of the command crew, but there is a credible threat of this not being a small raiding fleet, like the ones the Assembly forces have fought so far, but a full-scale Kubuu Ksiw fleet, like the Honored described it."

She stared at him, then said, "Until earlier today I would have said this is preposterous, but that was before my home world was under threat by unknown forces, so I will let you continue your report."

"Thank you, Shaajis. I can hardly believe it myself. The alleged Kubuu Ksiw fleet has entered a darkstring network leading here, to the Omech Chaa Alook System."

"They are approaching the Assembly world?"

"Yes, my Shaajis. We informed the Assembly Members about the scouts' reports shortly after you left Omech Krreng spaceport. It seems word has gotten out already, and reports of a spreading panic in the Assembly district are coming in."

"How is the situation for our own worlds, Admiral?"

"I am sorry to report that the unknown ships, which so surprisingly came out of warp near the Dziilaa Sok system belt, have engaged several planetary orbital garrisons. Tactical analysis, however, still projects a push toward our capital world. Again, reports are confusing, but it seems certain the enemy ship design is different from the alleged Kubuu Ksiw fleet. They have turned out to be impossible to destroy by the orbital garrisons due to their superior shield technology."

The Shaajis thought for a moment. "Show me what these ships look like."

"At once, my Shaajis!" The admiral touched his skull implant for a tick, and a projection appeared in the center of the meeting room. "These are the highest-resolution images we currently have."

She looked at magnifications of the different ship types threatening her home system. She wished Rroovu Ogbaa could lend his expertise, but even without his encyclopedic knowledge of galacticide history, she was certain that these ships belonged to the Krrut, intelligent machines from far beyond the Chish Gap. Humans had met this civilization 1,200 orbits ago, when the Krrut devised the Human-AI interface. The old depictions Rroovu had collected looked different, of course, but the key design elements, mainly the striking absence of anything related to supporting life forms, were still recognizable. "Did our scanners pick up any life signatures, anything hinting to who the attackers are?"

"No, my Shaajis, we have identified no life forms on any of these vessels."

Just as she thought. The admiral was clueless, and she would leave him this way for now. If these were Krrut, why were they attacking the Ancestrate? And why now, when another alien fleet descended on the seat of the galactic government? She did not believe in coincidences at such a grand scale.

Did the Krrut come back for their technology? Of course, the nano replicon labs were on Dziilaa Sok. Was it possible that they somehow detected their own tech signature? Did something happen at the labs? Maybe some sort of breakthrough with the nano particles alerted the Krrut. Maybe they had second thoughts about handing a sample of their powerful technology to the humans.

But what about the other fleet? They were not Kubuu Ksiw as everyone seemed to believe. These were likely ships from the ancient Kingdom of Uum, fabled in the solar sailor legends, dismissed by the ignorant majority as colorful stories made up to fill the cultural void of pre-galacticide history. Still, the questions remained—why now, and why both? Both ancient civilizations, besides humans the only survivors of the galacticide, reappearing on the stage of the human-settled galaxy. If her theory of the Krrut coming back for the Human-AI interface had any merit, why not assume the same for the legendary rock monsters of Uum? It was a common theory among the more esoteric pre-galacticide historians that the initial Honored colony somehow acquired the secret of immortality from sapient aliens. Maybe the Uum were coming back to collect their technology, along with the Krrut. The Shaajis shuddered thinking about this option—the remaining galactic civilizations ganging up against humanity, seemingly striking at the two largest centers of power, but in truth trying to take what could set humans on the path to true greatness. True power. Combined with a breakneck-speed reproduction rate and warp drives, there could be a quadrillion humans controlling the entire galaxy in just a few hundred orbits. What was happening today might be a preemptive strike of aliens and machines against a humankind rivaling the might of the Dark Ones, the Kubuu Ksiw.

She was likely the only one who understood this. She was also the only one who could do something about it. Had Drrem Rrunsash arrived as planned, things would be easier. But with him and the nano bomb he carried missing, she would have to rely on herself for the next decisive moves. Just as when she had killed Vnaas the Cruel to ascend to the throne, if she aspired to be the ruler of the galaxy, she had to do what was necessary.

"Admiral, assemble all our forces in this system at the closest darkstring insert point for a warp to Dziilaa Sok. Prepare all carriers for warp!"

The fleet admiral looked shocked. "All carriers, my Shaajis? Including the four currently part of the Levy Fleet? That would leave the Assembly forces so weakened, they might get overrun by the approaching fleet!"

Shaajis Sya Omga graced the man with a direct look into his eyes. "I am counting on it, admiral!"

32—BREAKING OUT

"Kel?" Ahma Zhanyza had never seen him with a full beard. "Kel! You're alive!"

She had aged during her imprisonment of many orbits. A short haircut changed her appearance, but the blue eyes piercing from underneath the thick eyelashes were exactly how Kel remembered them. Her reaction was genuine surprise, with a hint of joy. He preferred this over all the other emotions she could have shown.

As the prisoner of the Shaajis's advisor, Kel had easily reached the prison complex. Losing the ever-present guard detail had been a harder problem, but Drrem Rrunsash had proven himself to be level-headed and resourceful for bringing the Ancestrate's most valuable scientist together with their number one enemy of the state, to be left alone in a visitation room with the advisor, no guards present. This was Drrem's domain, and his composure showed it.

"I am here to bring you home," Kel heard himself say. Those were not the carefully chosen words he had thought about during the flight to the Ancestrate's capital planet, not even close. He gave her a spontaneous hug, which she joined somewhat hesitantly.

"How?" Ahma asked. "I mean, what are you…? I have so many questions!"

"I hate to interrupt the reunion, but questions will have to wait, I am afraid," said Drrem. "We have urgent matters to attend to!" He stared at Kel, prompting him to introduce the two. "Oh, yes. Ahma, please meet the man without whom I could not have made it here, Drrem—"

"I know who he is, Kel. The personal advisor to the Shaajis." The strong contempt in Ahma's voice left Drrem unfazed.

"Excellent," he said. "Then we can go right to the business at hand. If you know who I am, it will be clear to you that I can be as much a valuable ally as I can be a significant opponent. At the moment, I have chosen to be an ally and facilitated this meeting. I have also promised to organize your escape, so our friend Kel Chaada here can make good on his promise of returning you home. But first—I need your help."

Ahma's eyes moved between both men and fixated on each for a few ticks. "What is this, Kel? What is he talking about?"

"He injected himself with the weaponized nano replicons. He needs you to remove them, rendering the bomb mechanism harmless," said Kel.

Ahma swung toward Drrem. "You injected yourself? This is a delicate procedure. Why…"

"The why does not matter right now," said Drrem. "All that matters is for you to get them out of me!"

Ahma turned her back to Kel and Drrem, paced the length of the briefing room and back. "I need access to lab four. We can't do this here. Some of the equipment I need is stationary. I will need to scan you first to get a precise count and locations of the particles. Then we need to prepare for the extraction. Can you get me access?"

Drrem raised his eyebrows. "Don't you have access already? I thought you work here as a team leader."

"I work here as a prisoner who is only trusted as far as the daily protocol I had to run by an overseer. Can you get me access, or not?"

Drrem hesitated for a moment, then said, "Wait here. I need to have personnel cleared out of that lab and the connecting corridors."

Ahma waited for him to leave the room, then turned to

Kel. "What have you told him? I have never removed nano replicons! I don't even know how. They were not designed for removal."

"Jeew nreedz!" said Kel. "This was the deal I had with him. I thought they could be removed, and I told him you were the one who could do it."

"Well, maybe in a well-equipped hospital specializing in neurosurgery, but it would not be me leading the procedure. Why did you tell him I could help him?"

Kel did not answer.

"Kel?"

He was listening to Me-Ruu, who had established contact, telling Kel across space that the Isonomih fleet was approaching Dziilaa Sok. The sudden connection to the AI core flooded Kel's mind with alternative outcomes for his dilemma. In none of the realities he could see would Drrem Rrunsash let them leave without having the nano bomb particles removed. Or without reassurance that he would not explode. But why would he, as long as he did not use the trigger phrases? The scenario was not clear yet to Kel, too far removed from current space-time. What reassurance could they give Drrem? Kel did not know—yet—but this was the most promising reality. He chose it.

"Kel!" Ahma shook him by the shoulders.

"I am here."

"You...you zoned out. For a pass or so. What is happening, Kel?"

"I'll explain everything, Ahma, but right now you have to do something I know you swore never to do again—trust me."

Ahma let go of his shoulders and pierced him with a glare. She said, "OK. If we make it out of here, you will tell me everything, answer everything, without hesitating or holding back. That is my condition!" She had tears in her eyes. "You have to promise!"

This seemed like an easy promise to make, but it was not. Not for Kel. He realized that his life, his deeds, his omissions and failures would not be judged by Zmaam or some other deity, not by a court of law or a government commission. No, he was going to be judged by the woman he loved.

He took a deep breath. "I promise."

"OK," said Ahma. "Then let's be practical about it. I will scan him first to see what we are dealing with. Then we take it one step at a time."

"Sounds good. He'll be back soon."

This would give Kel some time to think, to review more realities for a better outcome. The door opened for Drrem. "The lab is clear. We can go." He looked at Ahma. "Why the tears?"

"The...reunion made me more emotional than I thought," said Ahma.

"I see. Well, I trust you can pull it together when you remove this bomb from my brain."

Ahma looked at Kel, nodding. "Let's go."

Drrem lay flat on the scanning table. Ahma moving the ceiling-mounted, heavy sensor array back and forth over his head and neck, asking, "Who gave you these to inject?"

Drrem hesitated. "That does not seem relevant..."

"This is not a time to adhere to confidentiality policies! I need to know who gave you the injection cylinder, advisor!"

"The...Shaajis. The Shaajis gave me the cylinder."

Kel jumped up from his chair. "The Shaajis gave them to you personally?"

"Shush, Kel. Focus on me, advisor! What did she say it was for?"

"These are state secrets! I cannot...look, the fact that we are collaborating here does not mean I am a traitor to my nation."

"What did the Shaajis tell you?" asked Ahma again, leaning over Drrem's face.

"She...she said it was a prototype of the Human-AI interface. She said it would help me lead the Assembly once I got confirmed as First Assembly Member."

"Well," said Ahma, "only half of that was a lie. It is a prototype indeed. Unfortunately, it is not some magical interface, but still a nano bomb configuration. One that can be triggered remotely."

"What?" Drrem spasmed on the table. "It...it can be triggered from..."

"Pretty far away. I recognize the design. Something of a side project your government had me work on. I never got beyond the concept, and I assume someone else in these labs built it. Kind of ironic that it ended up in you. I thought they were going to equip some hapless grunts with it and send them into battle to detonate behind enemy lines."

None of this calmed the 201st Assembly Member.

Kel asked, "Can we turn this...feature...off?"

"No," said Ahma. "Like the original nano weapon, it was designed so that, once injected..."

"It is hard to extract, isn't it?" asked Kel, trying to avoid any mention of Drrem's condition being permanent.

"Ah, yes," confirmed Ahma.

"She can trigger it!" said Drrem. "The Shaajis can trigger it from afar. She was not certain I'd play my role in the Assembly Chamber as expected, and she had a backup plan. She always has a backup plan. She could trigger it right now!"

There it was: the reality in which they could talk Drrem into letting them escape. Kel saw how it could unfold—and chose it.

"We have to make sure that you are safe, Assembly Member!" said Kel. "We cannot allow the Shaajis to detonate you at her whim."

"No no, we cannot! We have to—"

"We have to contact her."

Drrem looked puzzled. "We do what?"

"We contact her directly, with a QE projection feed. Show her who we are, where we are."

"Are you mad? She will detonate me instantly. She will know I failed her, she will know I am here and—"

"Exactly, Drrem! She will know you are here. In her secret lab. Underneath her palace. With her leading scientist for Human-AI interface research. Surrounded by Human-AI interface research. With me, carrying what she is really after. This is the last place in the universe she is going to detonate you, Drrem. She will not destroy what she has been chasing after all these orbits, and her personal seat of power, all at the same time. There is no place you are going to be as safe from her as you are right here!"

△△△

The lab's lighting turned red and alarm sirens went off. "Iihe et!" said Drrem. "She is here!"

Kel ran to the lab door, opened it, and checked the corridor. It was empty both ways, but the alarm sound was louder there, so he closed the door again. "What kind of alarm is this, Drrem?"

"It...the lab is part of the palace security. The alarm gets triggered by a breach of some sort, or an...attack."

"It is not the Shaajis, then, if that's what you fear. She would not trigger alarms by returning to her own palace."

Kel needed Drrem to keep his wits until Ahma and he were out of the maze of corridors, hallways, security checkpoints, and the vast palace basement.

"I admit that's true," said Drrem, "but what else triggered it?"

"We are running out of time," said Kel. "Ahma, did they make you work on a Human-AI interface of some kind? Maybe they called it something else. Based on the nano replicons, did they ask you to create a technology based on what we found on Prral?"

Ahma looked at Drrem then back at Kel, hesitant to say anything in front of the Shaajis's advisor.

"Do not worry about him, he is an ally, as he said. Please—just answer the question."

"I do not know how you would know this, but, yes—everything done down here in the labs was obsessively focused on interdimensional research, pretty esoteric fringe stuff. Nobody called it an interface, and AI was never mentioned, but it was about getting the nano cells to replicate not only into one space-time, but many of them. It was never clear what the purpose was. We were split into small teams, with professionally paranoid liaison people, who didn't tell us nreedz. Without them, we might have had a chance to get something done, but…"

"But—and this is very important," Kel stressed before asking: "The work down here was never completed, the project never finished, there was never a final result?"

"No, definitely not." Ahma looked at Drrem. "Do you know how I know? Because the moment they got what they wanted, we would have been executed, right here on the lab floor!"

Ahma shook as the combined fears and frustrations of the last 20 orbits surfaced in her consciousness. Kel remembered his responsibility for her being here and vowed to make good on his promise to get her out.

"Is there a surface exit leading to the palace gardens, Drrem?"

"Not directly from the lab complex. We would need to pass part of the palace basement…why would you want to go to the gardens? There's an alarm in progress. It might be dangerous outside!"

"I know what triggered the alarm," said Kel. "My allies are here. I can direct them to meet us in the gardens."

"Your allies?" asked Ahma and Drrem in unison.

"Long story," said Kel. "We need to move. Drrem, show us to a QE comm room where we can record a message for your Shaajis, so she knows not to detonate you, then lead us outside on a path of least resistance!"

Kel focused on his connection with Me-Ruu and told him where they would await extraction from the palace. The AI core confirmed: "I will see you soon."

Drrem checked his wrist comm as the three hurried along the underground corridors, the blinking red lights and loud alarms inducing anxiety even without other people around.

"Reports say the garrison fleet is engaged with an enemy force and an orbital attack on the capital is imminent, others claim the Grand Fleet is about to return and not to panic!" He stopped. "Kel Chaada, I demand to know who is attacking my home world! I will go not a single step further without knowing what is going on! I brought you this far, but I need an explanation!"

"Can't say I like this man," said Ahma, "but he's got a point, Kel."

Kel did not know where to start. The Isonomih had to be closing in. Their proximity triggered a constant barrage of alternate realities, mixing in with the one he wanted to focus on. He saw himself splitting up at every fork of walkways, exploring all side corridors, sometimes falling down, sometimes getting shot by guards not present in this reality, sometimes with Ahma, sometimes alone. Kel had never been so close to that many Isonomih, and their presence overwhelmed him with multi-awareness, much like the Traaz had when they first tried to communicate with his Uurmi. He closed his eyes, tried to clear his mind, and focused on one path ahead. When he opened his eyes again, only one version of Drrem stood before him, still awaiting an answer.

"The incoming ships belong to an Isonomih fleet. You might know them as the Krrut."

"From the realm of the machines?" asked Ahma. "From the sailor legends?"

"Not necessarily legends," said Drrem. "There are many scholars in Aloo Dash who believe these ancestral stories to be true. Are they, Kel Chaada?"

"They are."

"Why are they coming here, those machines?"

"They feared what your Shaajis might have scientists like Ahma create out of the nano replicons."

"How do they know? Why would they care?"

"Because," said Kel, "it is their technology. They developed the replicons."

Drrem pushed out a short, crazy laugh. "It is all true, then.

The Shaaj Jetsem!"

Ahma said, "You guys lost me here, what are you talking about?"

"The ancestral powers," said Drrem. "Most Aloo Dashaad believe in Krrugze Darrtuzke, an old belief system revolving around ancestral powers, teachings coming from lessons passed down from the first people. The Ancestrate's rulers are supposed to be the most enlightened ones, carrying the ancestral powers. Most educated people see this as metaphorical, but the Shaajis firmly believes these powers exist. When she was younger, she was under the influence of an old scientist, who filled her head with wondrous powers she could wield. He was not missed when he died on some expedition. It seems the Shaajis never gave up on pursuing this."

The alarms stopped, and the light turned back to regular white. Drrem straightened his posture and raised his chin. "Let us meet your Krrut!"

Drrem led them through the complex labyrinth of the palace, wielding his authority at the two security checkpoints they had to pass on their way out. Guards looked confused, frightened by the previous alarms and several explosions from above, and did not challenge Drrem's claims of evacuating key personnel through the palace. A short elevator ride brought them to an exit opening right into what Kel recognized as the large, park-like greenery of the palace gardens. The dampened booms they heard underground turned out to be rail guns firing skyward from various emplacements in and around the palace. They looked up. A tall vessel, shaped like a cone standing on its tip, with extended landing gear, descended onto the central plaza of the gardens. Kel did not recognize the design, but whenever rail guns hit it, a characteristic blue flash appeared— Isonomih phase shields, shrugging off projectiles. "This is our ride! To the plaza!"

They ran toward the ship as it landed. The cone tip, the lower part of the ship, split open and revealed a frame, dropping a four-legged machine on the plaza grounds. It looked like a walking version of a small hover tank, stood twice as tall as a human, and armaments emerged from its sides. They slowed their running when the weapons swiveled in their direction. The crack of hypersonic bullets over their heads made Kel pull Ahma down. His multi-awareness had failed him; he had not foreseen being fired on by whoever had just landed. Drrem just stood there, shocked stiff. The four-legged combat unit moved toward them, plowing a straight line through the lush landscaping. It stopped right in front of the group. Kel gestured Ahma to stay down while he stood up slowly to face what was coming next. The upper dome of the combat machine folded inward, showing the upper third of an AI core.

"Me-Ruu?"

"Yes, Kel, forgive my martial appearance, but I did not want to drop into a combat zone without my battle harness."

"I am glad to see you—but why did you fire at us?"

"I did not fire at you, I fired at them."

Kel turned around. Three palace guards lay on the ground with gaping holes in their chest armor.

Kel reached his hand out to Ahma. "Please meet my friend, Me-Ruu, an individual unit from Those Staying Behind, also known as the Isonomih."

Ahma pulled herself up, staring at the machine in disbelief. The AI's battle harness aimed one weapon at the Shaajis's advisor. "He still carries the nano replicons, mutated, dangerous," said Me-Ruu.

"I do," said Drrem. "Can you remove them?"

ΔΔΔ

Deafening, cold, bumpy—and requiring blind faith in the Isonomih phase shielding absorbing the renewed pummeling by rail guns on the ascent—the escape from Dziilaa Sok had been arduous for fragile organic passengers.

The compartment fit for humans on Me-Ruu's battleship looked improvised, but it was spacious, especially compared to the small boxroom into which Kel, Ahma, and their unplanned companion had to squeeze into onboard the dropship after it picked them up in the palace gardens. Drrem Rrunsash had come along after the AI core promised to rid him of the nano bomb still implanted in his brain stem. Space had been tight in the dropship; they had no spacesuits and only improvised restraining harnesses. Me-Ruu had prepared everything to "human specifications," as the AI called it. Kel did not mind any discomfort as long as he could get Ahma out of her undeserved imprisonment of 20 orbits, objectively the best thing he had ever done for her.

Me-Ruu had shed his battle harness and entered the human compartment through a top hatch as his core frame only, an appearance more familiar to Kel.

"Are you the same...individual we met on the surface?" asked Drrem. "Where is the rest of the crew?"

"I am the only individual unit required to operate this ship," said Me-Ruu. Drrem looked impressed; on a ship this size, a human crew complement of several thousand would not have been unusual. Me-Ruu said to Kel, "I am afraid there is no direct link for you to use. If you would like to follow the battle, please focus on my data stream in this reality. Be careful how closely you link yourself in, as my conscious core processes many magnitudes more input than your biological network."

"What battle?" asked Ahma. "Are we not safe yet?"

"I am afraid not," said Me-Ruu. "We lured out most of the defenders by using modified ships, with fuel supplies separated from the core so they would look depleted, slow and helpless, after we warped in. Just before they reached us, we performed a quick, short warp into the near orbit of Dziilaa Sok."

"Wait," said Kel. "I know this trick."

"Of course—you used it against our fleet at the battle of ring cluster 728."

"You are stealing my tactics."

"We have incorporated all of them into the shared database."

"You have fought each other?" asked Drrem.

"Yes," said Kel. "The Isonomih used to be my enemies. Well, like you used to be my enemy. The galaxy is changing—fast."

"The Ancestrate's ships will be here soon," said the AI core, "and we will have to neutralize them before we can refuel to warp out of the system."

"How did you fight these AIs with their huge ships?" asked Ahma.

Kel opened his mouth to respond, hesitated, then said, "It's...with my other allies, the Traaz. You will meet them soon. They are scary at first, very much so, but...ah, nreedz."

Ahma looked at him, bewildered, then her face relaxed. "When this is over, you and I will have a long conversation."

"The enemy is approaching," said Me-Ruu. "I must connect to my command socket."

The AI core disappeared through the hatch in the compartment's ceiling. Kel turned to Ahma. "Yes, there is a lot to explain, but for the next few passes, do not be alarmed if I seem to have lost consciousness. I can join...my thoughts with the network of these AIs, and I will do so for the course of the battle." Kel sat down on what looked like a bench and tuned his mind into the AI core's consciousness.

Looking at the battle through Me-Ruu's perception of reality showed more of the ensuing space encounter than he expected. Despite his previous experiences with multi-awareness and his—clearly premature—belief of getting at least somewhat used to it, he was humbled by the multi-dimensionality opening up in his mind. He saw space-time membranes, and how they bent around the spacecrafts on both sides, each detail opening up, unfolding more alternatives, possibilities, in an ever-growing cascade. The only hard limit to the recursive unfolding was what the human mind would call "the future." In the multiverse revealing itself to Kel, everything that could happen already had happened; he had just not observed it yet. His path through reality was catching up with events determined when space and time began, only now approaching the grasp of his senses, multiplied and heightened by the nano particles, replicating into all realities, forever entangled with those staying behind. The moniker the Isonomih had chosen for themselves never made as much sense to him as it did right then.

The battle—an exchange of projectiles and missiles, aggressive and evasive flight paths, hits and misses, life and death—looked like an enormous probability function. The Isonomih's remarkable mind was designed to optimize its parameters, constantly choosing clusters of outcomes showing the most promise to move forward, to evade the next salvo, to not cease to exist, to not die. Kel found it hard to imagine a sentience more different from the humans, and their view of the world more alien than this, yet the basic need for all observers of the magnificence of existence was the same: stay alive to observe the next moment, dodge one more burst, deflect one more hit, exist for one more pass.

The maelstrom of the million battles sucked Kel in. He felt like he was falling toward its decisive epicenter, showing a growing dark spot, bending all space-times inward to its bottomless nothingness. He heard Ahma's voice calling his name, over and over, then Me-Ruu's translator box voice, sharply distorted: "This is too much for you, Kel. I am ending the connection."

The dark sphere exploded and covered Kel whole, his tortured brain escaping into unconsciousness. His head almost hit the bench when he slid off, but Ahma caught him in time.

ΔΔΔ

"This machine has a death wish!" said Drrem Rrunsash. "How much closer to the star does it want to fly?"

Kel awoke to Ahma's worried face and the advisor's panicked voice. "Welcome back," said Ahma. "Let me help you up."

Back on the bench, Kel saw on the exterior viewscreen what Drrem was so worried about. The star of the Dziilaa Sok system took up most of the screen. The battleship had to be close to the corona. He had seen this before, Isonomih ships congregating near stars for a few shifts, before warping. "We are refueling."

"How do you know?" asked Drrem.

"He is correct," said Me-Ruu, sliding back into the compartment through the top hatch. Kel was curious about how the Isonomih used the natural fusion inside stars to reenergize the forced fusion in their reactors, but he did not fully trust the former advisor of the Shaajis, so he would ask Me-Ruu another time.

Instead, he asked, "How did the battle go?"

Kel realized he did not have to ask and could see the clash of starships, the way it happened, in this reality: The Ancestrate had learned to rely less on the presence of their Grandslaught Carriers. With none of those nearby, they had used tactics based on smaller squadrons of ships of all sizes and given the Isonomih task force respectable opposition. In the end, however, almost none of their weapon systems could penetrate the phase shielding of the AI ships. The Aloo Dashaad, being the only side in the fight taking significant damage, had to retreat, forming a defensive formation in Dziilaa Sok's orbit, a fallback position to defend their home world. The Isonomih had pursued none of the disengaging vessels to hunt them down to complete destruction, but damaged enough ships of the opposing fleet to ensure no counterattack could be launched while they refueled.

"We won," said Me-Ruu, without further comment. *That might be so*, thought Kel, *but if the Levy Fleet fought as well without the Grandslaught Carriers as the Aloo Dashaad did, Raar and his Traaz were going to be in trouble.*

"Where are we going from here?" asked Ahma. "Back to EsChiip?" The hopefulness in her voice made Kel feel his answer was disappointing.

"No, not yet. We will make a long warp to the Assembly

world, meet more allies, and take care of a few things first."

"What are you going to do with the Assembly?" asked Drrem. "Are your plans any better than those of the Shaajis?"

Kel looked at his former peer. "You, Assembly Member Rrunsash, will have your nano replicons defused by my friend now. Then we shall talk about the future of the government."

33—BATTLE OF OMECH CHAA

"They surprised us, both in speed and numbers," reported Raar, when the Isonomih fleet arrived at the Omech Chaa Alook System, the seat of the human galactic government. Warping in using the Bofnoo Nebula darkstring put the AI fleet on the opposite side of the system the Traaz were approaching from. Raar's fleet had veered off the original approach vector after leaving their darkstring terminus and aimed for a swing-by at the smaller binary star component of the three-star system. A solid move, thought Kel. The Traaz had embraced his doctrine of using anything that increased sub-light speed. In a space battle, the powerful warp drives were regarded as useless. They had done their part by getting the ships to the combat zone.

Upon arrival, clever exploitation of the laws of orbital mechanics could give a commander an edge over an opponent who relied on thrusters only. The navy of the Assembly forces, the Levy Fleet, had overcome the shock of the Shaajis disappearing with all Grandslaught Carriers faster than expected. They had not set a straight intercept course, which would have put as much space as possible between the Assembly world and the attackers. Instead, they initiated their own swing-by using the larger binary star component. That aggressive trajectory allowed them to engage the Traaz before they reached the binary and forced them off their intended course by using long-range missiles. Completing their maneuver, the Levy Fleet —still a sizable force even without the carriers—descended on

Raar's ships from the rear with superior speed.

"You got caught by an impressive maneuver there, my friend," said Kel. "We underestimated the coherence of the Levy Fleet without carrier support. I can't believe they pulled off that swing-by staying in such a close formation, with all those different ship sizes and types."

"They have trained for the moment the Shaajis would betray them, or they would betray the Shaajis," said Drrem.

"What?"

"I heard rumors about fleet maneuvers with and without carrier participation. Now it makes sense. The Assembly Members had planned a resolution changing the Levy Fleet assignments to take control of the Grandslaught Carriers away from the Shaajis. They—rightfully so—feared this would not go over well with her and she might attack the government. I think we are seeing the result of this preparation. I would not be surprised if my colleagues were down there in the grand chamber right now, voting on putting all galactic navies under the direct command of the Assembly."

"We've always needed to move fast," said Kel, "but now we have to move even faster. If what you described is happening, Drrem, and most people believe that the Dark Ones are back in an all-out attack on the Assembly, they might combine their fleets and come warping in here. Every passing shift could see the numbers of ships against us increase."

Kel looked around. The projection screen Me-Ruu had installed gave an overview of the deployed units and general layout of the system, but was no replacement for a proper tactical stream connected to his brain. After the recent experience with the overwhelming multi-reality of the Isonomih, he opted for going with the setup he had waged war in, won countless battles in for 20 orbits.

"Raar, keep pushing toward the Assembly world, as directly as you can. I realize they are tearing into your rear and soon into your side, but you cannot allow them to get you too far off course. I will join you and your fleet as soon as I can. We need to peel some of these Levy ships off you!"

"Your ship and your captains eagerly await you," said Raar, "but come quickly. I cannot say how much longer we can keep her in one piece for you!"

"You leave us here?" asked Ahma.

"No," said Kel. "Both you and Drrem will come with me. Me-Ruu, there is not much more I can do to help from here. We need the dropship you used on Dziilaa Sok to get us to my Traaz flagship."

"Understood," said the AI core, "although I calculate a substantial risk. What can Those Staying Behind do?"

"The refueling method you use when you are close to a star, could it work on the move, while you are not standing still relative to the star?"

"It has never been used that way, and although it is technically possible, it would be extremely inefficient."

"If you used that refueling while closely swinging by a large star, would that work?"

"Yes, but it would only collect enough energy for a very short warp."

"Perfect," said Kel, "that's all we need. OK, here is the plan!"

Drrem protested at first, not looking forward to another ride in the cramped compartment of the Isonomih dropship interior, but changed his mind when presented with the alternative: staying behind, alone, on Me-Ruu's battleship. The AI let another core control his vessel while it piloted the dropship toward the Traaz fleet.

Kel knew they had to reach the grand chamber on the Assembly world before the Assembly Members could use the situation to galvanize support for their coup, the takeover of all space forces. Both fleets needed to arrive at Omech Chaa at the same time to maximize the cover they could provide for the ground assault. But right now, Raar's ships had to face the full strength of the defenders alone. The Isonomih fleet was heading straight for the Assembly world and, unopposed, would reach it before the two fleets exchanging fire. Kel was certain the Levy

Fleet would split and send off part of their forces to intercept the Isonomih. Once the break-off fleet committed to this course, the AIs would change theirs and fly toward the massive central star, Omech Chaa Alook 1, forcing the defenders to either pursue them or swing by the Assembly moon's host planet, a gas giant, to return to attacking the Traaz. Either way, those ships would not be firing on any of his allies for a while. Would that relief be enough?

He could try to see the outcomes clearer, but with so many AI cores nearby, Kel feared he would never come out of the recurring explosion of perceived realities and would lose himself in the multi-awareness. Here and now, he would win or lose the old-fashioned way.

ΔΔΔ

Me-Ruu steered the dropship into the hangar at breakneck speed, and slammed its tripod landing gear onto the floor plating—a rough landing, but also the fastest Kel had ever seen.

The *Sheekilku* had come into view, her image swelling on the Isonomih dropship's viewscreen. Kel's command ship of many campaigns had taken position on the side of the fleet, facing away from the battle, protected by the bulk of the Traaz forces between her and the Levy Fleet. The *Sheekilku*'s hangar hatches stood open for the dropship to land. Warmer than the glow of the approach lights had been a wave of welcome hitting Kel's consciousness when the fleet captains sensed his presence. "It is good to have you back, Third in Command!"

While the *Sheekilku*'s hangar closed and filled with breathable atmosphere, he felt the battle cruiser maneuvering back into the battle line, adding its weapon array to the fleet.

Me-Ruu squeezed into the compartment as well, then the frame descended to the hangar floor. A small unit of armed Traaz became visible, forming a line behind Kel's trusted captain. Kel jumped out of the frame, happy to see his companion alive and well. He helped Ahma and Drrem, who struggled out of the lowered compartment, still shocked by the rapid landing, or frightened by the sight of the hulking dark masses of the Traaz, likely both.

"These are...my friends," Kel told the humans. "Do not mind their appearance. The Traaz in the middle, with the reddish stripes, his name is Ssuw. He is the captain of this ship and he will show both of you to my quarters. They are designed for humans and you will be comfortable and safe there for the duration of the battle."

"You have quarters on this ship?" asked Ahma. "Where will you go, Kel?" A rare glimpse of fear showed in her eyes.

"I have to go to the command room."

"To do what, precisely?" asked Drrem.

"To win this battle!"

Kel had returned to the human-settled part of the galaxy to leave the interstellar wars behind. Now, holding the belt harness of his command chair in his hand, he was about to take control of the first battle between the remaining technological civilizations in the galaxy. He inhaled, mustering his resolve— there was going to be no peace as long as the immortal elite of the Assembly had an unlimited mandate of power over his species. He briefly thought about Ahma, then all hesitation vanished.

Kel closed the harness and pulled it almost too tight to breathe; then he became one with the fleet.

ΔΔΔ

The shrieks and cracks told Kel that the *Sheekilku's* plasma matrices could barely reflect all incoming projectiles, some shrapnel making it through to the armor-plated surface. He had steered his battlecruiser into the most intense zone of fire exchange between the fleets, mentally encouraging his fellow ship commanders to do the same, putting pressure on the defenders. Even if the Traaz ships' shields collapsed, their massive armor could keep them in the Levy Fleet's line of fire for some time, maybe leading the human captains to believe their weapons were ultimately useless against this enemy.

The Levy Fleet finally registered the threat presented by the incoming Isonomih, the AI ships on a collision course with the Assembly world. Around a third of the Levy Fleet broke off, changing course toward the gas giant, no doubt trying to intercept the added attackers. Kel had hoped the Levy Fleet would split in half, but any separation of the enemy force was welcome. The splitting maneuvers got the human fleet somewhat out of formation. Smaller, agile Traaz ships exploited openings in the formation, and made short-range attack runs with their missiles. This harassment took out a few smaller vessels and damaged two cruisers, but came at a price, with a third of the attackers getting destroyed by close-range fire from the human fleet.

"Warriors of Traaz, stay in formation," he commanded. "Ease off the pressure again, and let the enemy drive our fleet off the target course for as long as the group that just split off is nearby. Once they have fallen for the AI feint, we will push their lines again, now that we have a superior number of capital ships."

Waves of thoughts ebbed and flowed through the fleet as the captains followed Kel's instructions. "You have missed this, haven't you, Kel Chaada?" thought Raar, from the command room of his own ship.

"Yes. Thank you for bringing this fleet, my friend, and I am sorry we will need every single ship."

"I expected nothing less. They are defending their home."

The defenders near the Assembly world saw the Isonomih ships going into a long burn, changing course away from the initial target. The human fleet had passed the point where they could let the AIs fly off to the central star and deal with them later, swinging by the gas giant and returning to keep hammering the Traaz fleet. Now all they could do was a forced burn to try turning around in a wide loop, taking them out of the battle for shifts, or pursue the AIs. They chose the pursuit. The feint had worked. It was time to press the attack.

The fire superiority of the Traaz fleet showed effect, with several Levy ships breaking out of formation, having suffered enough damage that remaining with their fleet meant certain destruction. With short thruster bursts, the Traaz fleet kept creeping closer, each maneuver getting them back onto a course heading for Omech Chaa. The Levy fleet was weakening, but remained on a parallel course, shielding the Assembly world from a direct attack. The gas giant Omech Chaa Sok came into view as both fleets approached, furiously exchanging fire.

"Those Staying Behind are ready for the warp." Me-Ruu's announcement cut into Kel's consciousness, as the connection he was feeling with the Isonomih was not as refined as the familiar embedding into the Traaz hive. Not yet. He had only tried once and passed out, something he did not want to risk during this battle.

"Tell the units to proceed with the warp." He focused his response onto his machine friend only, a mental link much easier to control and maintain than with the entire Isonomih fleet. The second phase of the AI feint had begun.

They had closely swung by the massive central star of the three-star system and harvested just enough energy with their fusion refueling tech to warp space-time for a tick. That was all they needed to leave their human pursuers behind. The summoned Levy Fleet had to come in from all over the Aloo Spur, relying on the Grandslaught Carriers to transport them for long warps. Without those carriers, none of the capital ships showed reactor energy levels necessary for bending space-time.

The Isonomih ships could do this, and warped under expenditure of all their fusion fuel, straight alongside the Levy Fleet, just above them from the Traaz point of view. The AI targeting needed less than a tick to lock onto the surprised human ships, and a missile salvo took out thrusters, cannon emplacements, and scanner arrays on most of the larger vessels. With the human reinforcements left behind, still maneuvering around the central star, the reduced core of the Levy Fleet faced fire from the combined forces of the Traaz and Isonomih.

Kel knew the Levy Fleet's defense had failed, and there was no reason to destroy it to launch the last phase. "Keep firing until ships are disabled and then switch targets. Accept all surrenders. Prepare the landing units for ground assault!"

He pulled the harness release open and jumped out of his chair, seeing Ssuw, three arms grown, holding Kel's combat suit and weapon.

34—CLOSED-DOOR SESSION

The enormous shield dome covering the heart of the government district came into view from the landing craft's cockpit window. In space, protective shielding only became visible when hit, but the anti-bombardment dome interacted with Omech Chaa's atmosphere, and shimmered in changing colors. While beautiful to look at, it was likely disastrous for the Traaz troop transports and the Isonomih dropships to try breaking through it. When Kel had become an Assembly Member, the dome was mentioned, but he did not know any specifications. For their safety, the landing forces would touch down near the dome's perimeter and push through at ground level, where the shield did not reach down to the surface. Kel knew they might be outnumbered on the ground, but the fearsome appearance of the monstrous Traaz, combined with the impressive firepower of the Isonomih's battle harnesses, was enough to break through the defenders' resolve and lines. So he hoped.

He had not worn his Traaz-made combat suit often. It was fitted based on the remains of the clothes he had been wearing when the Traaz captured him. It was dark gray and the hardened parts had sharp edges; it looked menacing. Kel had not aged at all, but the rigor of ground combat, last experienced on Prral, felt like a distant memory. The suit's protection would need to make up for what his muscles had forgotten.

He looked down at the planet surface as the transport closed in on the city surrounding the government district. Kel could imagine the panic in the streets of Omech Krreng, most people likely believing the Dark Ones had returned in force, bringing their heavy battle robots along for good measure. The people hiding behind the shimmering shield knew better. The Traaz had served their lies for long enough. Today the Assembly Members would have to face the truth, something they might fear more than the invaders themselves.

A last look outside confirmed to Kel where they needed to land—and that the government had the protective dome cut off at the end of the spire district, where they lived themselves, no thought given to protect the remaining five million serving their government. Kel did not feel any sympathy for his former peers and their world he was about to shatter. He inspected his gun, a small Traaz weapon with a trigger mechanism a human hand could use.

"Get ready, warriors of Traaz! Touchdown in a few ticks!" he thought. His dark companions radiated grim determination.

The transport landed. His improvised suit was missing an adaptive visor. Blinding light from the three stars overhead was all Kel could see for a few moments after the ramp fell open and he led the charge outside. The low gravity allowed for fast movement, counteracting his heavy equipment, but his eyes needed to adapt before he could see the surroundings.

Another transport had landed nearby. Raar stormed down its ramp, leading his personal guard. Me-Ruu's craft touched down close to Kel's position. It was the last of the purpose-built Isonomih dropships reaching the ground. Twenty AIs laid down suppressing fire from their battle harnesses. Seeing them in action, Kel was glad they never had to fight the machines in a ground war. They were fast and methodical, and had destroyed several defensive positions, gun emplacements, and a communication tower before the Traaz could join up with them. "It is good to see you, Kel," thought Raar, waving one of his protrusions, mimicking a human gesture. "Lead the way!"

More AI dropships and Traaz ground transports landed and delivered warriors and AI cores, commanding a variety of vehicles and hovercraft. Kel pointed to the grand chamber, peeking through the surrounding spires. "This is the target!"

ΔΔΔ

Kel looked at the large portal in frustration. It was the last obstacle between the Traaz-Isonomih ground force and the Assembly's grand chamber, and it would not open.

They were so close. Supported by the firepower of the Isonomih units, the Traaz had taken improvised perimeters and fortified defensive positions, pushing the defenders back toward the oval of the chamber building. The Assembly ground troops were not as determined as the Levy Fleet. Maybe they were overwhelmed by the assault, not ready or trained, never expecting a forceful attack on the center of the government, or demoralized by the reports of surrendering Levy Fleet squadrons. The Traaz looked like the Dark Ones from the galacticide horror stories every human child was told. This might have stunned some soldiers into giving up.

"We have many prisoners," reported Raar, just before the portal of the grand chamber came into view. It looked undefended, but both wings were closed. "Have your units guard them where they stand," thought Kel. "Order the second wave of transports to the landing zone. Oh, and please instruct captain Ssuw to put Drrem Rrunsash on a transport along with them!"

"The Advisor of the Shaajis?" asked Raar.

"Yes, we might need him."

Kel was glad he had asked for Drrem. He was certain the former advisor would be terrified riding on a transport filled with rock monsters, but despite his fragile appearance, Drrem had come through many challenging experiences already. The grand chamber had this one door only. Either by design or oversight—it was the only way in and out, as he recalled from his last visit many orbits ago. The two wings of the enormous portal were so tall, wide, and thick that Raar wanted to call heavy equipment down to the surface to force a breach. Me-Ruu proposed to have Isonomih cores connect to the portal controls, which were easily accessible from the outside. This likely meant they were secure enough that the Assembly Members did not worry about physical access. Kel encouraged the AIs to make an attempt, but he bet on Drrem. Unlike Kel, Drrem Rrunsash was still an active member of the Assembly and had to have some means of getting inside.

"It looks like you are stuck!" Drrem approached, flanked by two armed Traaz, taking wide strides up the long steps leading to the chamber portal. At the top, he looked around and made no attempt to hide his displeasure. The slight elevation provided an unobstructed view of what had just been a battlefield, including burned-out defensive structures. He turned to Kel. "I see the grand chamber is undamaged, at least."

"Yes, and ideally we want to keep it that way," said Kel. Drrem looked at his wrist communicator, irritated. "It looks like we are running out of time!"

"Why? What happened," asked Kel.

"I just got summoned to attend an emergency session of the Assembly. The session is about to begin, and the ceremonial system took note of my absence."

"The Assembly Members are...inside?" Kel had not expected this. All the emergency and security-related briefings he could remember instructed the immortals to disperse, leave the surface if possible, or seek shelter in the underground level of their private spires. "The Assembly is not supposed to be in one place if there is an attack on Omech Chaa!"

"That is true," said Drrem. "However, it looks like every last Assembly Member, except myself, is in there right now. Well, I guess the Shaajis is missing, too."

"Why would they risk this?"

"This emergency session can have only one purpose—the official declaration of 'em rroo kyot'—the state of war for the galaxy and call to arms for all human nations."

Kel had feared the combined attack of alien and machine forces could unite the human-settled galaxy. While the unity was a good thing, he did not want it to happen under the corrupted banner of the power brokers sitting behind that door.

"Can you get us inside quickly?" asked Kel.

Drrem smiled. "Yes, the session invite I received was automated, so no one took care of removing the building passcode. I memorized the code before I deleted the message."

Kel looked at Drrem, who was still smiling. He had seen this expression before, only appearing when the 201st Assembly Member of Oorkuu believed himself to be in a superior negotiating position. "I can get you inside the building anytime. Maybe in time before galactic war becomes official!"

Me-Ruu had overheard the conversation. "What are we waiting for?"

"Oh," said Kel, "we are waiting for Drrem to tell us his conditions."

"Correct," said Drrem. His smile ended. "Before we warped into this system, you had proposed that we 'shall talk about the future of the government.' Yes, these were your words. We never really had this conversation, and I believe now is an excellent time to discuss it!"

△△△

Bright light flooded into the grand chamber of the Oorkuu Omech when the giant portal opened, contrasting the martial outlines of Traaz and Isonomih warriors entering the building, unopposed by the Assembly Members.

Kel led the procession, his weapon resting on his shoulder armor, flanked by Raar and Me-Ruu. The first time, which was also his last, he had entered this hall was very similar. All eyes of the immortal elite were on him as he strode to his assigned seat at the far end of the chamber. It was hard to tell if the emergency session had begun already. The Assembly Members faced the invaders, standing defiantly at their usual positions. As Drrem had said, no member of the Omechaak was missing, the Shaajis being the notable exception. The only difference from his point of view was the total silence, a palpable, fearful anticipation of whatever was coming next.

A few passes later, they had walked up the gentle slope of the chamber side, and the trio reached Kel's former seat. Following were a growing number of Traaz and Isonomih, several hundred of them lined up in the wide central walkway at the lowest point of the oval interior. Kel picked up the tiny headset from the seat's console. Tailing the aliens and machines, Drrem Rrunsash had also entered the building and walked straight to the unoccupied session control station near the entrance.

"My esteemed colleagues!" Drrem's amplified voice broke the silence. "I call this emergency session to order!"

The portal doors, just opened a few moments ago, closed again. "Please remain in your assigned seats and listen to the announcement of the 317th Member of the Assembly of Oorkuu: Kel Chaada."

Murmur filled the chamber. Some Assembly Members looked stunned, others agitated. Some gestured at Drrem, yelling threats or obscenities, all drowned out by the sheer size of the chamber. Kel overheard one voice: Lotnuuk Rrupteemaa's. The first of the immortals stood tall, his elongated body towering over his peers, visible from a distance. Seated close to the session control, everybody could hear him say that he was neither recognizing Drrem Rrunsash's authority to lead a session nor the right of Kel Chaada to speak in this chamber.

"Dear Assembly Member Rrupteemaa," droned Kel's voice over the agitated crowd, Drrem providing him with full speaking volume on his headset. "The esteemed 201st Assembly Member has the right to lead an emergency session, as do all delegation leaders in time of crisis."

"But you are dead, as far as this chamber is concerned," a nearby Assembly Member yelled.

"As you can see," said Kel, "I am not dead, and I challenge the declaration of my death by this government. There had been no substantial inquiry into my alleged death, there was no attempt to retrieve my body, and no search effort beyond the remains of the transport I allegedly died on. I am alive and herewith reclaim my rightful position as 317th Member, especially with my predecessor, Sya Omga, better known as the Shaajis of Aloo Dash, having chosen to leave this government, unlawfully taken ships of the Levy Fleet, evading the consequences of her crime."

His words fueled the unrest of the immortals, especially among the Aloo Dashaad delegates, on their feet, waving their fists in Kel's direction. Several of the battle-harness-clad Isonomih moved into a more menacing position. The white-robed crowd stopped moving.

"Sya Omga is accused of having planned the death of the Omechaak, and the physical destruction of the government district along with the city of Omech Krreng. Firsthand witness account and physical evidence will be provided by Assembly Member Drrem Rrunsash, whose body still contains the defused and now harmless remains of a bomb that was supposed to end our way of life!"

The volume in the chamber increased again, snippets of protest shouted over exclamations of shock and disbelief. "But now," continued Kel, "this government will do what it always excelled at during times of crisis, and let the will and the vision of our founders, the Honored, be done. As first order of business in this emergency session, I declare the immediate addition of new representatives joining the Assembly of Oorkuu."

The most senior human in the chamber had worked his way up the seating ranks with his long limbs and wrestled the session controller headset away from Drrem. Nearby Traaz were about to step in, weapons pointed at the first immortal. Kel asked them to stand down. "Please, let Member Rrupteemaa speak."

They could now clearly hear Lotnuuk Rrupteemaa over the main chamber audio. "Kel Chaada, I remember your last speech in this chamber well. You talked about peace then, 20 orbits ago. Now you return here, speaking of dangers we face, while it is you storming the seat of our government with this... this army!"

"Dear Assembly Members, while it is unusual to enter the chamber armed, it is hardly the first time this has happened, even the great Fim Chiipi joined one of the first ever Assembly sessions with gun in hand, demanding his colony be represented in the government. Assembly Member Rrupteemaa is mistaken when he thinks that the guests waiting the center aisle are an invading army. These individuals you see down there, dear Assembly Members, are the initiate representatives of Honored Ground. Found on worlds all over the Akaa Upsa galaxy, many have survived the galacticide, evaded the Kubuu Ksiw, created new colonies, and rebuilt from the ashes."

Lotnuuk Rrupteemaa said, "We have always suspected that alien technological civilizations might still exist in the Akto Rim or out in the Fyez's. While we would be pleased to engage in diplomacy, if not conducted at gunpoint, these individuals have no place in this chamber!"

The murmur flared up again. It was not clear from Kel's point of view if the Assembly Members were arguing for or against Lotnuuk. "This is not correct," said Kel. "According to the founding statutes of this Assembly, any survivors of the galacticide, organized in surface colonies on worlds anywhere in the galaxy, found living or dead, are to be treated as Honored— human or not! Each Honored world can send one representative to the Assembly. It is my great pleasure to introduce you to so many living Honored." Gesturing to the group assembled in the chamber center, Kel said, "Please, take your rightful seats!"

Traaz and Isonomih separated, and each group moved up the seating ranks, taking positions wherever there was an opening. The existing Assembly Members disapproved, but were too intimidated to block their path. When the two groups had settled in and the wave of indignation and outrage calmed down a bit, Kel continued, "Assembly Members, please let me introduce the two new delegation leaders in this chamber." He nodded to his friends and attached the headset to Raar's translator unit.

"I am Raar, Second in Command of the Ashkas yo Traaz. On the left side of this chamber, you have been joined by my fellow Traaz, each representing Honored Ground worlds ranging from the tip of the Eb Fyez to the center of the Wesh Wewesh."

He grew a small arm, transferring the audio headset to the AI core's translator. "I am the individual unit known as Me-Ruu, first among the delegation of Those Staying Behind, known also as the Isonomih. You see my peer cores on the right side of the chamber. Like our Traaz friends, we are excited to join the link of the Honored."

Both turned back to Kel. He smiled when he took the headset back. "With that, dear Assembly Members, old and new, we conclude the first order of business. Take a good look around, and cherish the moment when our Assembly of survivors truly became a galactic government!"

He turned the audio off and sat down. The angry voices mixed with the gasps of wonder, sighs of relief, and the sounds of curiosity. He imagined the debates to be had in this chamber. Orbits of pushback, territorial infighting, and partisan defiance would turn into grudging acceptance and working relationships. Trade and technology exchange would fuel wealth, and prospering societies would grow together.

A multi-species, galactic civilization: It was going to take a long time to form and solidify. A pessimist might say it would take "forever."

Luckily, they had that much time. Kel, Raar, and Me-Ruu were going to see it turning into reality. Before Drrem Rrunsash gave Kel the portal access code, he had said, "History is written in grand gestures!" He was right.

35—MEDDLING FOOLS

"**A** new galactic government? Absurd!" said the woman. Despite the anger in her voice, there was a soothing familiarity.

"It does not end there," said the man. "The representatives can proclaim sovereign, self-ruled nations around their respective Honored Grounds now. Reports show the delegation of Aloo Dash discussed breaking up the Ancestrate. Former delegation leader Rrunsash is a proposed leader for the core worlds!" His voice was fearful, and the observer did not recognize it.

The observer did not recall his own name. He had slept for an immeasurably long time, or so he assumed. A terrible sleep, with one continuous nightmare of an all-encompassing darkness gnawing away on his consciousness, until there was nothing left but the kernel he had named the "observer."

She cursed in a language the observer once spoke, but the meaning of the words eluded him. "Shall we continue along the darkstring?" asked the man.

"No," said the woman. "They expect us to return and likely set a trap. We will need to go where nobody expects us, where we can assess the new situation, regroup and plan."

The man asked, "Plan…? Plan for what?"

"Plan for our return, of course," said the woman. "Order all loyal units to meet our fleet at the darkstring terminus! From there we shall proceed to the Yuuzh Wep."

"The Dark Rift?" asked the man, the frightened timbre still

in his voice.

"Yes," said the woman. "It will be a long flight, but it gives him time to heal."

Steps drew closer to the observer. He heard the clicking sounds of typing on a computer console. Glaring brightness tormented the observer when his eyelids opened. His eyes had not seen light for a long time. Closing them was the last memory before the nightmare had started.

"Visual cortex, activated," said a mechanical voice.

"Leave us," said the woman. Steps moved away, followed by a door opening and closing. A dark silhouette filled the observer's field of vision. Unused for so long, his eyes could not get his view focused.

"How are you, my friend?" asked the woman. "Do not despair about the news. You and I are destined for great things, despite the meddling of fools."

A smaller dark patch came into the observer's view, growing, moving toward him. Briefly, he saw a hand, then the image blurred again. Was it a hand touching his face? He was uncertain.

"Soon," she said, "you will feel again, think again. The modified Uum cells were worth joining this travesty of a government for a while—and they are my gift to you."

The dark patch grew larger, and at just the right distance, came into focus. The observer saw her face.

"And when you have recovered, and they have restored your synaptic complexity, my dear Rroovu, you can return the favor and I shall receive your gift—the Human-AI interface! Astonishing, how the replicons bound to your brain even in death, and kept a flame of your mind burning through the cryo stasis they put you in after finding you on Prral."

This made no sense to the observer, but he recognized the woman.

Shaajis Sya Omga's face disappeared, and he heard the clicking sound again. "Now, rest. I shall be back soon," said the Ancestor queen's voice. When she left, the observer felt alone. He thought he closed his eyes. Artificially induced motoric signals compelled the muscles to do so. It got dark, but at least the nightmares did not return.

36—ONE OF US

"**D**aazha! Yel!" Ahma's voice carried over the flat beach. "Time to eat!"

The twins had played in the shallow water for shifts now, suddenly realizing how hungry they were when hearing their mother's call. Kel sat on the porch facing the endless sea south of the Mahfi continent's tropical zone. The house stood alone on the beach, but Thuuny, the next town, was not far, and had all the amenities of modern life if needed. Kel had grown up in Thuuny, and had always dreamed of a beach house, enjoying the tide-free peace of EsChiip's ocean. As a child, he pictured himself living there alone. Now, he had two children of his own.

Daazha, the girl, was born three passes before her brother, Yel, and not a rotation went by that she did not remind him of that fact. She had her parents' blue eyes, Kel's olive skin, but, most fortunately, her mother's pleasant facial features. Yel looked more like his maternal grandfather, but his broad forehead made him clearly recognizable as Kel's son. Despite regular teasing, the twins made a great team, and, at almost five orbits old, were a force of nature to be reckoned with. A small group of Ehhelu, native hexapedal avians, took to the evening sky as they saw the two running humans approaching.

Kel got up from his lounge chair and went inside. The house smelled of fresh baking, mixed with the unmistakable aroma of shank soup, his favorite dish. The twins screamed with delight when they came storming in, carrying a small trail of driftwood sticks and sand into the living room. Ahma placed the pot in the center of the table. She smiled when she saw her call for dinner so diligently being followed by everyone. "I guess this dish is still a favorite."

Kel sat down across the table from Ahma, keeping the twins separated and in check by two adults, bringing a small dose of peace and civilization to the meal. "I could eat this every rotation, you know me."

Ahma looked at him. Her smile vanished. "No," she said, "I don't think I do."

Kel's head felt like a long needle had been inserted into his skull.

"But Mnagwa," said Daazha, "this is father!"

Her face was distorted, as if someone had taken her painting and smeared over her head with a brush. Yel jumped up, creating a hazy, tall outline of a young man with the features of a child. Kel tried to say something, but the words felt like they were stuck in his throat. The living room turned dark, matching the night-light level of his ship's quarters. Kel, sitting on the edge of his bed alone, let himself fall back, exhausted from trying to keep the alternative reality in focus as long as possible, while his body remained on the ship. The headache was punishing. He cried. "I just wanted to taste the soup."

△△△

"You were there!" said Me-Ruu.

"Where?" asked Raar.

Kel's mind had recovered, and he joined his companions in the command room of the corvette. He let himself fall into his seat to the left of the AI, who had a fitting pentagonal socket installed to connect its frame to the ship which was likely going to be their home for many orbits.

"At the beach house, with Ahma. I just returned." said Kel.

"Why?" asked Raar.

"Because I wanted to find out if we ever had a chance,

anywhere in the myriad of space-times. I am glad I found one. Here, in this reality, Ahma had asked for a conversation, the one I promised her to explain everything, hold nothing back. Despite all our adventures and challenges, that was the hardest thing I had to do in my life. She was grateful for her rescue, my candor, but could not forgive me for causing the death of her lover. I did not expect it. Despite the pain this conversation caused both of us, I felt liberated after it. I confessed my deeds, and was judged not worthy of her love, and I can accept it now. I just needed to know if we ever had a chance or if it was just me wanting it so badly."

Raar approached, then stopped at the closest distance mutual respect allowed. Not required among friends, but it was the closest to a gesture of comfort a Traaz could offer. "That is not what I meant, Kel," he said. "I am curious why you did not stay there. If I understood Me-Ruu right, your multi-awareness allows you to choose any reality, if you permanently commit to it."

"That is correct," confirmed the AI core, "and you have done so before, unconsciously at first, but selectively at times of peril. It was your physical attachment to this reality that cut your experience short, and likely upset the interface balance between your brain and the replicons."

"Yes, no nreedz," said Kel. "The headache made me wish Vyoz had shot me when he could."

Raar and Me-Ruu stood still, with patience only immortals could muster, and even without eyes staring at him, Kel felt the expectation building, the expectation of an answer. He sat up straight.

"Why, you ask. A good question. Do not believe I wasn't tempted. The reality was perfect in every way. Even I was perfect. Never went to war, never killed anyone, never left my parents or my friends behind. I loved everything. But, I did not like me. Even less than the person I am right now. I had never lost, never grown, never marveled at the wonders of our existence. I simply…was. Having existence happening to me, not shaping it."

"You almost sound like you are close to reciting the slogan of your old Assembly," said Raar. "What was it—Strength Through Conflict? Are you certain this is the way to go? Our Isonomih friends have done this so systematically that they almost challenged themselves into total destruction."

"Yes, the creed," said Kel. "It might be the most terrible guideline for a society. But—I chose it for myself. I never wanted a harsh life, but having much taken away gave me more than I ever expected. That includes the two of you. I do not want to trade this reality for any other!"

Me-Ruu set warp coordinates for the Yuuzh Wep, the last darkstring position the rogue Ancestrate's fleet was sighted at. "You are now truly one of Those Staying Behind, Kel Chaada!"

Space-time bent around the three immortals.

THANK YOU

Thank you for reading this story!

If you enjoyed the adventures of Kel, Raar and Me-Ruu, please leave a rating or review. In the world of modern book publishing, every review helps. Never left a review or don't know what to write? No problem, any half-liner is a legitimate review on these platforms:

Amazon
GoodReads
BookBub

You can join the email list for announcements about future novels set in the Galacticide universe. Don't miss them!

www.bertoliverboehmer.com

GALACTICIDE BOOK SERIES

Distant future citizen soldier Kel Chaada gets propelled into a conflict spreading from the Perseus Arm of the Milky Way to an inter-galactic struggle for survival.

2,000 years of arms race see nano weapons, mind projections, culminating in reality-shattering devices capable of destroying spacetime itself.

Three Immortals

Extra-galactics ravaged the Milky Way and humans saw their civilization burn. 2400 years later, humanity has risen again, living by a brutal creed keeping interstellar nations at war.

Kel Chaada is a master tactician who rose from soldier to leader. His life gets crushed when his military successes threaten to unravel the web of lies protecting humanity's immortal rulers. Betrayed and cast out, Kel flees to the fringes of the galaxy.

He enters the realm of ancient alien civilizations and discovers the legendary powers they have to share. Hostile machines and silicate monsters Kel was taught to fear may be the allies he needs.

Kel returns, leading two alien battle fleets. Will he be a savior or conqueror?

Dark Cascade

Every delay costs a world. Billions perish when raider ships peel off planetary crusts to feed their galactic civilization.

Kel Chaada had united humans, machines and silicate aliens, but the hyper-tech invaders push the shaky coalition of former enemies to its breaking point. Kel has to work against his friends, ally with his sworn enemies, and strike where no one could foresee: The raider's home galaxy.

The desperate plan is bold, but cruel. Kel realizes he will become what he is fighting against: a destroyer of civilizations.

He rushes across the inter-galactic void on a stolen enemy ship, riding a derelict warp bubble, piloted by zealous AIs with their own agenda. Can Kel's small crew succeed where all space fleets failed?

Galacticide

No cause. No effect. Causality stops and reality shatters.

Kel Chaada believed to have beaten the extra-galactic menace when rigged AI cores blew the Võmémééř's galactic realm apart. Sheltered from the explosions, the alien Brood Mother survived, mourning billions of her children, burning with vengeance.

One breeding couple is all it takes to re-build an army, but the Brood Mother's target is neither Kel, nor space fleets: It is reality itself. No universe hostile to the Mother's children shall remain.

Imprisoned for old crimes, his only child gone missing in a military coup at home, Kel Chaada witnesses his world crumble, the very fabric of existence tearing. Even if he escaped, how could he fight a raging alien mother capable of destroying the multiverse?

ACKNOWLEDGEMENT

A special "thank you" to Anja Boehmer and Daniel Nelson.

ABOUT THE AUTHOR

Bert-Oliver Boehmer

 Bert-Oliver Boehmer is a science fiction writer and author of the award-winning novels "Three Immortals" and "Dark Cascade".

After two decades of working with innovative bioinformatics companies, his passion for futuristic technologies, exotic biology, and classic science fiction became the foundation for a vast space opera universe.

Bert-Oliver holds a degree in computer science and has traveled all over this planet. Since 2020, he focuses on telling stories about what we might find elsewhere and elsewhen.

He lives with his wife and daughters in Southern California, where his Jeep leaves tire tracks on many trails.

c04f099a-39f5-4788-ae85-c3213e22b07aR01